NO GOOD
ASKING

NO GOOD ASKING

FRAN KIMMEL

Published by ECW Press
665 Gerrard Street East, Toronto, ON M4M 1Y2
416-694-3348 / ecwpress.com

Editor for the press: Jen Knoch
Cover design: Michel Vrana
Cover artwork: © Catherine MacBride / Stocksy
Author photo: Monique de St. Croix
Printed and bound in Canada by
Friesens   1   2   3   4   5

Purchase the print edition
and receive the eBook free!
For details, go to ecwpress.com/eBook.

Library and Archives Canada
Cataloguing in Publication

Kimmel, Fran, 1955–, author
No good asking / Fran Kimmel.

Issued in print and electronic formats.
ISBN 978-1-77041-438-9 (softcover);
ISBN 978-1-77305-262-5 (epub);
ISBN 978-1-77305-263-2 (PDF)

I. Title.

PS8621.I5449N64 2018   C813'.6   C2018-902555-7
C2018-902556-5

The publication of *No Good Asking* has been generously supported by the Canada Council for the Arts,
which last year invested $153 million to bring the arts to Canadians throughout the country, and by the
Government of Canada. *Nous remercions le Conseil des arts du Canada de son soutien. L'an dernier, le Conseil a
investi 153 millions de dollars pour mettre de l'art dans la vie des Canadiennes et des Canadiens de tout le pays. Ce
livre est financé en partie par le gouvernement du Canada.* We also acknowledge the support of the Ontario Arts
Council (OAC), an agency of the Government of Ontario, which last year funded 1,737 individual artists
and 1,095 organizations in 223 communities across Ontario for a total of $52.1 million, and the contribution
of the Government of Ontario through the Ontario Book Publishing Tax Credit and the Ontario Media
Development Corporation.

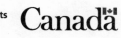

To Jim

PART ONE

THEY ALL COME FROM SOMEWHERE

Friday, December 20

one

From a distance, it looked like a small smear of blood on a white blanket. Perhaps a wounded coyote, staggering along the road in the relentless wind. Eric drove on, a flurry of white surrounding his car, keeping to the faint tracks he'd made the day before. As he drew nearer, the speck transformed into a withered old man, startling him with legs, arms, torso bent into the gale. But it was worse yet. He finally recognized the shape as a young girl. People didn't walk along his road, not out here in the middle of nowhere. Not a girl, certainly not in this weather.

He slowly pulled the car alongside her, creating new tire tracks in the snow. The girl ignored him and kept walking. A red scarf tied under her chin covered her ears; long hair fell in damp strands down her back. She looked twelve, thirteen at most. Her coat was a grubby grey felt, too small, thrift-shop variety, the kind that let the cold howl through the gaps between buttons. Her jeans were dirty and frayed at the bottom. She wore runners, not boots.

Eric opened the passenger window, letting in a blast of cold that made his bones creak. "Hey," he shouted, to be heard over the wind.

Plodding forward, she kept her head pressed down, hands in pockets. He stopped the car along the side of the road and jumped out.

She didn't stop moving as he caught up and walked beside her. His eyes watered from the wind. "I live down the road a ways." He sucked air through his teeth, swallowing the sting. "You're not dressed for this weather. It's freezing out here. I can drive you to wherever you're going."

He stepped in front of her, blocking her path. She stamped her runners and peered around him with exhausted eyes, as if there was something to look at and he was obstructing her view.

"I'm going to give you a ride. You can decide where to." For a brief second, he wished he was still in uniform. "Look, I know you're not supposed to get into a stranger's vehicle, but it's your—"

"You're not a stranger." She sounded dazed, croaking. "You live across the road from me."

Wilson's place? There was no other house along this road. "You've walked all that way?" It was a good five kilometres back to where their houses stood facing each other on either side of the road. Who was this girl?

Her nose ran and she lifted a bare hand from her pocket and took a feeble swipe. Jesus. She didn't even have mittens. He could give her no choice in the matter. He held out his arm, pointing to his idling car, stepping closer, forcing her to back up. Finally, she turned, trudged back to the car, pulled on the frozen latch of his back door with her bare fingers, and fell inside.

Eric hurried to his side of the vehicle, got in, and cranked the heater as high as it would go. He would have preferred her in the front beside the vent.

He turned to look at her, passing her the box of Kleenex they kept under the console. "My name is Eric Nyland."

"I know," she said, wiping her nose, her running eyes.

Nigel Wilson must have told her his name. What else had he told her?

"What's your name?"

"Hannah Finch."

Eric couldn't fathom what Wilson was doing with a girl named Finch. Couldn't fathom what the girl was doing in the bitter cold, so entirely unprepared, as if she were out for an afternoon stroll in September.

"Okay, Hannah. Where to?"

After an ungodly long pause—where had she been going?—she said, "I have to go home. Can you drive me back?"

There was something in the way she said *home*. Her shoulders slumped as she fought with her seat belt. Her fingers looked brittle, like they might snap off in pieces.

"You sure?" he said. "Because I can take you to town. Or to a friend's."

She shook her head. "I left Mandy with him."

"Mandy?"

"My cat."

"Never did own a cat," he told her as he turned the car around. He'd seen his share of runaways during his twenty years with the force. If he'd spotted this girl at the shopping mall, he would have thought her a go-to-church, finish-your-homework, listen-to-your-mother type.

He kept on talking to help put her at ease. "Dog people, our family. Down to one mutt at the moment. My father's dog, Thorn. That's the dog's name. He's a big, fat black lab mostly. Poops all over the house. Guess he can't help it because he's so old and doesn't know what he's doing anymore. Falls down if he barks too loud. It's sort of sad. Woof, woof, and down he goes."

She shifted slightly in the back seat. "I've seen him. Sometimes he comes down to the road."

So why had he never seen her? He'd brought his family back here nearly a year ago. "Thorn wolfed down a whole bag of dog food one time. One of those giant twenty-pound sacks you get at Costco. That dumb dog found it while he was sniffing around the shed. Tipped it over somehow, chewed through the corner of the packaging, got his head inside, and gobbled it all up. He waddled out of that shed looking mighty sorry about what he'd done, his stomach stretched so low it swept the ground. Took three full days to work all those nuggets through. Stunk so bad we made him sleep on the porch."

They dipped into the valley, forcing his eyes to the road and keeping them there. During the warm months—all two of them—the view was of mustard-yellow canola fields, farms dotting the distance. Today, Eric saw nothing but blowing snow.

"I hear house cats are pretty smart," he said.

Hannah sat perfectly still, her hands folded over a button on her flimsy coat.

"They know how to pace themselves. You can fill their bowl and they'll nibble a bit here, a bit there, dainty-like, all day long. Not a black lab. No sir. Put down a bowl and they make it their job to suck up every morsel like a vacuum. Sometimes they forget to chew, they're in such a hurry, and end up choking it back out again."

He adjusted the vents, raising his voice to compensate for the added noise. "Tell me about Mandy," he said, delaying his real questions until he could catch her eye.

"She's a dainty eater."

"Like I thought," he said. "Have you had her a long time?"

"Since I got my tonsils out. Mom brought me home from the hospital and told me to look on my bed. Mandy was in a shoebox with just her pink nose sticking out of the towel. She was crying, so I picked her up and she stopped."

"How old were you when you got your tonsils out?"

Her eyes shone right at him in the mirror. "Five. Now I'm eleven. Almost twelve."

She sat taller and pressed herself against her seat belt. They crawled along, still a ways off.

"So where were you headed, Hannah?" She'd walked all that way without turning back. "Your mom will be worried, don't you think?"

She looked at the mirror and caught his stare. "My mom's dead." She gave a little shiver.

"I'm sorry, Hannah. That must be tough."

She shrugged.

"So Nigel Wilson is your dad?" Stepdad, whatever.

"No. He was with my mom, so he got me."

"Nigel and I used to go to school together."

"I know."

"You don't think he'd hurt Mandy, do you?"

She looked down at her hands on her lap.

"Because you know there are laws against hurting a cat. Or a kid." Nigel Wilson was a snivelling excuse for a human being. "If there's anything like that going on at your house, we can make it stop. I mean the police can make it stop. But you have to tell them so they can help."

The girl was done talking. She kept her head down and said nothing more as they inched along the empty road.

"Almost there." Eric looked in the mirror; her cheeks were the greyish colour of week-old mushrooms. "You okay back there?"

She nodded, though she was clearly not. She seemed to be panting a little. He flipped on his turn signal out of habit, although there was no one in the barrenness to see it.

He took the last corner slowly. Barely clearing the deep snow, two weathered mailboxes, one of them Wilson's, were nailed high on posts beside a dead-end sign. The narrow tunnel of a road felt closed in and too dark. Giant aspens loomed on either side, frozen branches hanging low and so overwhelmed with snow they nearly scraped the car top. Old snow was piled in man-sized shelves along the road's edge.

"Please," she said. "Stop the car."

Eric turned his head, attentive to the panic in her voice. She'd already unbuckled her seat belt and had her fingers wrapped around the door handle. Their houses were not yet in view, just snow being lifted by the wind and swirling about the car's windows.

"Whoa. Slow down, Hannah." She couldn't be planning to go out there again, not with him sitting three feet in front of her, not with that wind screaming through the tiny cracks in the glass.

"Please." She jerked on the handle. "Hurry. I have to get out."

"It's all right, Hannah. Just give me a minute until the road opens up a bit and I can pull over."

"I'm going to be sick. I'm gonna throw up in your car."

Vomit had been a frequent back-seat occurrence in his former line of business. Eric braked more firmly than he'd intended, all four tires skidding out of the earlier tracks and into deep, wet snow, the car crunching to a halt, angled across the road.

"Hang on, hang on. I'll get your door." Eric stepped into a gust of icy cold. He scrambled around the car, intending to help her to the bank, but she was already out and falling forward into snow up to her knees.

Eric came up behind her.

He grabbed the back of her coat as she bent low, her retching so noisy and violent he worried she'd crack a rib. "That's right." There was nothing to do except stand behind her heaving body and hold a fistful of coat.

It kept coming and coming, a trail of the steaming stuff running down the white slope toward her snow-buried calves. Nigel Wilson needed to get her checked by a doctor.

"All done then?" He cupped her shoulder with his other hand, trying to hold her steady. The wind shot under his coat collar, under his cuffs. She brought her arm up and wiped her face with her sleeve. Her breath came out in short, choppy puffs that caught on the wind.

"Come on, Hannah."

She'd started to shake so badly she nearly fell sideways. She turned her head toward him, blowing snow clinging to her lips and lashes. She was a frozen sparrow cemented in winter.

Eric wanted to place his hands on her waist and lift her out of the snow, but not even ex-cops were to touch kids that way, especially young girls. So he held his arms out to her instead, and she twisted and grabbed on, and as he stepped backward, she fell into him.

He pulled her toward the dirtier, more packed snow of the road, where she stamped her feet feebly, one at a time, and then he led her to the car and helped her get settled into the front seat, close to the heat. She said thank you as he closed her door. His ears stung, and his right thumb, the arthritic one from his football days, throbbed as he trudged through the snow to his side of the car.

As he buckled in beside her, Hannah ran her palms up and down her thighs. She wouldn't look at him. He thought she might be embarrassed, so he played with the heater and revved the engine a few times. If a truck came along, there would be no way to pass with his car parked sideways across the road. But no vehicle came along. Winter was a lonely, desolate place along their road.

They couldn't idle there indefinitely. The kid was traumatized and smelled like puke. She needed a hot bath and bed. He maneuvered the car back and forth into the snow, tires grabbing, until they were centred again in the tracks laid down earlier, facing toward Hannah's place.

"Hannah, are you okay? Put your hands close to the heat."

She spread her fingers wide in front of the vent, tipped her head back, and closed her eyes. Eric studied her mottled, thawing face. Her skin purpled around her closed eyes, making it look like she'd been smacked.

"Do you feel better now?"

"Yes. Thank you." She kept her eyes closed.

"I hate throwing up," he said, easing the car forward at a steady crawl.

"Me too." Her nose started to run again but she sniffed it back.

"I do anything to avoid it."

"Me too."

They were out of the trees and into the open again. Eric could see smoke coming from Wilson's chimney. He couldn't see his own place on the other side of the road; their house was tucked far back on the cleared driveway.

He could have thrown a stone and easily hit Hannah's front door. He'd always wondered why the Wilsons had rooted themselves right there. Why they had hunted for property in the middle of nowhere and then built so close to the road they could hand lemonade to pass-ersby through their kitchen window. There was nothing but the small two-storey house and a half-buried Ford station wagon. No garage, no barn, no motor home or boat. Not a tree or a fence. Nothing to show where Wilson's property ended and the next began. Just bil-lowing heaps of snow, whipped to a frenzy in the driving wind.

Eric parked the car next to Wilson's Ford. He kept the engine run-ning and aimed the warm air at the windshield. He couldn't get her any closer. Wilson had shovelled a path no bigger than a deer trail.

The house was the original, pre-1940s. A war house as the townsfolk liked to call them, shutters over the upper-floor windows, a glassed-in porch that could double as a freezer in winter and sauna in summer.

"Here we are, Hannah. Ready?"

She turned her head and looked at him, eyes wide, as if he'd managed to surprise her by getting them this far.

"I have something for you." He wished he could give her one of his old RCMP cards with the horse and rider in his scarlet jacket, but those days were behind him. He reached into his inside pocket for one of his flimsy security guard cards and a pen, printed his cell number across the top, and handed it to her.

"I want you to call if you need anything. Anytime. Or stop by our place. A few of us are usually home. We're your neighbours. I mean it, Hannah." And he did. He wondered if Wilson had food in the fridge, or if he'd plugged in that Ford.

They sat beside each other, not talking. Eric kept his eye on the house, thinking it strange that Wilson didn't come to the door. He had to know she was out there. Eric's idling car made a hell of a racket.

"I have to go now," she said.

"Okay," Eric said.

"Okay," she echoed, stepping into the biting wind. Eric trudged along behind her on the skinny path.

They crowded into the empty porch, so cold inside the useless room Eric could see Hannah's breath curl around her dry mauve lips. She pointed her finger at the doorbell beside the bevelled glass door and pushed twice before she stepped through. Eric thought about why she might have to ring her own bell. Why hers was the kind of house you couldn't walk into without announcing yourself first.

Nigel Wilson came down the stairs and stood before them, arms crossed. It had been decades since they'd spoken to each other, since Eric had stepped inside this house. The small living room was still filled with the furniture of their childhoods: velveteen chairs, stuffed couches, floor lamps with tasseled lampshades. Eric had been in this room often as a little kid, he and Nigel swapping Star Wars figurines and cold germs. When school started and Eric had a choice, he looked elsewhere, preferring the company of the rowdy kids over the brooding boy from across the road. Now Wilson just stood there. His pose irritated Eric, who thought Wilson ought to have been worried about Hannah, or alarmed at least to find Eric with her. Nigel was a big guy, bigger than Eric remembered, his muddy eyes still spaced too closely together. He wore a white pressed shirt tucked inside a pair of dark pressed trousers, hair combed back respectably behind his oversized ears. This too irritated Eric, who thought he could have spent less energy dressing and more tackling the driveway, watching out for this girl.

"Eric," Wilson said, stepping forward and taking Eric's hand firmly. "It's been a long time. Thought we might have bumped into each other before now."

Eric had waved a few times as their vehicles passed on the road, but Wilson had not acknowledged him.

They stood eye to eye. Wilson smelled faintly of cheap aftershave, like rubbing alcohol. Christmas hadn't yet entered this room. No stockings hung by the chimney with care. No tree garnished with the decorations Hannah had made at school over the years. There was a sour smell leaking from the kitchen at the back of the house. He could have taken out the garbage, Eric thought, adding another strike against him.

"I see you've given Hannah a lift. Getting into a stranger's car. Not the best decision, Hannah."

Hannah was hunched over, off to the side of the floor mat, busying herself with her runners, one of which was missing its shoelace. Wilson still hadn't looked at the girl.

"I'm not a stranger," Eric said, feeling the heat rise up through his throat. "I live right across the road." Why wasn't he concerned about what she was doing out there in the first place?

"Who'd have thought we would both end up back here," Wilson said.

Eric glanced over at Hannah, who wasn't making a sound. "Hannah's had a time of it. She'll need to crawl under the covers."

"Yes, well, of course."

"And Child and Family Services will be stopping by."

"Oh?" Wilson raised his eyebrows and crossed his arms again. "For taking a walk? Overkill, don't you think?"

"It's what we do," Eric lied.

"We? What's this to do with you, exactly?"

Wilson was right. Eric had no business poking his nose in police business. But he wanted his friend Betty Holt to meet this girl, to sit near her, maybe up in Hannah's room, maybe beside her on the bed.

"Where's Mandy?" Eric said. "I'd like to meet her."

Hannah looked up and their eyes locked and she almost smiled. Then she stood, slow-motion slow, more an unfolding, crimson blotches spreading over her cheeks and neck. She looked even scrawnier now that she'd taken off her coat.

"Ah," Wilson said. "The cat."

Wilson turned to Hannah then, mouth smiling, eyes cold and hard. She stared back, matching steel with steel. Good for you, Eric thought.

"Probably under the bed," Wilson said. "Or in the closet. Right, Hannah? I doubt she'll show herself."

"Maybe next time then," Eric said.

Wilson's eyes flickered. If he understood Eric's warning, he didn't flinch.

———

After Sergeant Nyland left her with him, Nigel stood in the living room and glared at her.

"Where did you think you could go?" he asked. When she didn't answer, he snorted. "Perhaps you could try harder next time."

He turned for the kitchen, leaving her shivering in the hallway. She'd brought the frozen world into the house with her, the cold a burning sensation, flames licking her fingers and toes. She jumped when she heard Nigel slam the cupboard door and again when his bottle clanged on the table.

Hannah ran up to her room. Mandy was in her usual hiding spot, a mound of long black fur wedged behind the empty boxes in Hannah's bedroom closet. Besides the boxes and a few empty hangers strung on a rusty pole, her closet was bare. She hadn't been allowed to bring much of her stuff when Nigel moved her down from Bear Creek.

She stripped out of her frozen jeans and sweater and folded them neatly on the chair beside her bed. Then she put on her thin pajamas and wrapped herself in a blanket and lay down on the floor in front of the closet. She whispered Mandy's name and made her favourite bird sounds—*twee twee twee*—but Mandy wouldn't budge. It was as if she knew that Hannah had planned to never come back.

It would have been easy to pull the boxes aside and unhide her cat. An empty box weighs less than snow. But Hannah wanted Mandy to come to her. So she lay on crossed arms until they were blotchy blue against the frigid floor and told her cat everything that had happened. Hannah talked haltingly at first, scarcely above a whisper. Soon the words tumbled out, one on top of the other, until she could hardly catch a breath between. She'd never been that close to the sergeant before. That's what Nigel called him, "the sergeant." Nigel had told her he'd been booted off the police force and had crawled back to his mommy's house with his tail between his legs. He'd told her the sergeant was a sick, twisted bastard who thought he was God. But

Hannah didn't believe him; Nigel lied all the time. When she got in her neighbour's car, the sergeant was kind and didn't press her with questions or call her stupid for walking down the road in a storm or for puking in the snow. She wanted to tell him that bad things were happening in this house, but Nigel's words came bubbling up from her stomach. They'd drag her off to a foster home full of brats or a school for troubled girls that had locked doors and bars on the windows. She didn't tell Mandy about her other attempts to get away, because she didn't want to think about them.

She told Mandy the things she knew about Nigel. About him standing in the backyard looking up at the darkening sky, clouds sewn like flowers on an apron. This was at their first house, the three of them starting out together, and she hadn't yet learned that she didn't belong. Nigel stepped onto the back porch and Hannah turned to him and announced, "Rain's heading our way," mimicking what she'd heard the adults around her say. A look of disdain passed across his face, a fast-moving storm, barely discernible before he buried it behind a smile and told her she'd better come inside.

She told Mandy how much space that look on his face came to take up in her head. Her throat was a dry creek bed, words rasping in the still air. She wanted to tell Mandy how sorry she was too, but sorries meant nothing to a cat.

When Mandy rolled over and scratched her paws along the width of the box, Hannah raised herself to her knees and then stood on legs achy from her long walk. She tiptoed on bare feet to her dresser and pulled her spelling bee medal, with its red ribbon, from her drawer. Then she came back to the closet and dangled the medal, pulling the ribbon so it bobbed up and down. Mandy poked her head from around the box, and as Hannah backed up, she followed. After they played with the medal, Hannah sat on her bed, cross-legged, and Mandy hopped up and kneaded a spot on the blanket, cocooned between her legs.

She focused on a spot on the wall and waited until her eyes saw somewhere else. She'd done this trick a lot lately. Now she was at the lake. Seven years old. She was on that beach with her mother, just the two of them, the waves so loud they had to shout to be heard. The trip was her reward for getting her latest swimming badge. It was a hot, windy day and their wide-brimmed sunhats kept lifting off their foreheads and they kept clamping them down again with sandy palms. They dug deep with their plastic shovels, filling their pails with wet, heavy sand, flipping them over for castle walls. They built moats and tunnels and bridges with seaweed-wrapped sticks covered with lady bugs. They found white feather flags with tips sharp as thistles.

But it was the whale that was the real prize. A gift her mother had to save for weeks for. After they finished their cheese and cucumber sandwiches, her mother told Hannah to reach down into her huge woven bag. When she pulled out the plastic package with the picture of a girl on a black-and-white whale, Hannah jumped up and down and ran in circles around the castle. She could be a whale rider, just like Pai in the movie. She could climb onto the whale's back and coax it back to the sea and ride faster than all whale riders before her.

It took a long time for her mother to get enough air inside the whale to make its fins stand straight. When it was finally full grown, Hannah pulled her whale by its tail through the foaming suds at the shoreline and into the shallow, choppy water and swung her leg over its wide back. She fit snugly, her arms easily reaching the small handles above each fin. She stayed close to shore, as she'd been told, while her mother stood on the beach and clapped and cheered like the people in Pai's village. Her mother was afraid to go into the water herself. Hannah loved her for this. For bringing her to the edge of the place she feared most.

Hannah leaned forward, hugging her whale to keep from tipping in the waves. It was as if she had been born in the water, as if she and her whale could skim across the surface of the whole beautiful world.

A ferocious gust whipped Hannah's sun hat up into the air and carried it like a leaf across the water. Hannah didn't know how to maneuver her whale toward her hat, so she hopped off its back and pushed through the knee-deep waves in order to fetch it. Her hat had been carried along the shore a great distance by the wind, and when she finally got to it, she scooped it up and rung it out, then waved to her mother. But it was the whale her mother was looking at. Hannah's precious whale, riding the waves without her, swimming farther and farther away.

Hannah cried out, ready to chase after it, but it was her mother who crashed through the waves, running through shallow water at first, then getting farther from the shoreline, sinking deeper, until she was thrashing arms, a bobbing doll's head, little more than a speck. The whale, a much better swimmer, was too far away to catch.

Come back, come back, Hannah yelled into the wind. Why had she been so stupid? She'd abandoned her whale for a silly hat that meant nothing to her. Now she just wanted her mother.

It took a long, long time, but she eventually staggered out of the water and fell onto the sand. Hannah wrapped her arms around her marble-cold skin and said *I'm sorry, I'm sorry*, over and over, while her mother lay there gasping. Finally she stood, wobbly at first, and dusted the sand from her suit. She bent down and kissed Hannah's forehead, whispering in Hannah's ear, "I should have known better. Today was too windy for hats." Then she stretched tall, raised her arms, and started laughing. Hannah would forever remember her like that, her beautiful mother, laughing to the sky.

———

Eric drove too fast in his hurry to get away. When he neared the place where Hannah's vomit sullied the bank, he pressed hard on the gas, fishtailing in the wet snow. By the time he pulled onto the main road, the plow had been by on the other side, while his lane was still pocked with ruts of ice and drifting snow. Ellie would be white-knuckled if she were out in this. She mapped her route in advance, chose the quietest roads, avoided left turns, and braced herself to make a mistake. He tried to encourage his wife, tell her she was a good driver, but he didn't really believe it. He'd pulled her out of so many snow banks over the years he thought she must aim for them on purpose.

Before his detour back to Wilson's, Eric had been on his way to Gerry's place to get Ellie her spruce tree, something he promised he'd take care of. Ellie was disappointed when he hadn't got over to Gerry's last Saturday as planned, even more so when Sunday came and went and they were treeless still. He'd woken up that morning with one purpose only and that was to get this done for her today. He'd work his last half shift before Christmas, get Ellie the tree, make things right between them. But the morning turned sour before he even got out of the house. And then he couldn't find his keys again, prolonging the unpleasantness. He and Ellie hunted through the usual spots—top of the dresser, beside the phone, coat pockets. She found them in the front closet, inside Walter's boot. "You're such a child, Eric," she'd said, hurling the key ring across the room, hitting him in the chest.

He imagined Ellie back at home. She'd be standing at the kitchen sink, peeling potatoes or pulling the skin off chicken breasts, and she would turn her head and before she could think to change her expression, he'd see the deadness in her eyes. He couldn't remember when she'd started going blank like that. After Sammy stopped letting them hug him? After Daniel started slamming doors over every little thing? After his father quit aiming at the toilet bowl? Ellie was a mess of trying too hard, and Christmas only made it worse.

He parked on the road as he neared Gerry's turnoff. He started to dial Betty's number, planning to fill her in on what he'd seen. He'd tell her he was aware that the timing was terrible, Friday and all, Christmas coming, but this Hannah Finch walking along the road, a wind chill of minus twenty-six for God sakes, dead mother, alone with Nigel Wilson. Could Betty get out there and talk with this kid?

But as he rehearsed the words, his pitch seemed laced with bad history and unsettled grudges. He wedged the phone back into his pocket. He'd drive to Child and Family Services in Neesley and sit across from her instead.

two

After Eric left the house that morning, Ellie stood beside the laundry heap in her cotton nightgown. She'd forgotten slippers, and her bare toes curled on the cold concrete floor. The old washer and dryer leaned against the far wall in the bowels of the dingy basement, freezer on one side, furnace on the other. She'd needed two laundry baskets, thirty-one steps per trip, to haul down Sammy's toothpaste-splattered towels, Walter's soiled sheets, Eric's work shirts, her panties and bras, shapeless and faded. Danny's jeans and t-shirts were off to the side, where he'd chucked them over the course of the week, stray socks unable to catch the pile.

There was a time when she'd dreamed of a main-floor washer and dryer, maybe tucked into a hallway behind white-painted louvered doors or set off to the side in a room of their own. A window with yellow curtains, a chrome light fixture instead of a bulb and ratty string, built-in shelves, a shiny enamel sink with a sprayer faucet.

Now, she just tried to get through each day without doing something foolish, without falling down the stairs and shattering.

Ellie filled the plastic cup with detergent, dumped it into the washer, and stabbed the button for the heavy cycle. She could feel the steely gaze of Eric's dead mother over her shoulder. This had been Myrtle's domain, her plot of land for eternity. Myrtle had stood on this very spot in her solid shoes, scrubbing clean the countless spills and stains that were her family.

Walter's sheets reeked of urine and the old-man smell he left in the bathroom. Ellie stared at the brown stains, as big as hens' eggs. She should scrub away the worst of it, but her fingers reached to her temples instead. The pamphlet had said to use the same firmness as one might drum fingers on a desk, middle three fingers of both hands. Tap tap tap tap tap tap. Not too hard—it shouldn't hurt. She wasn't to worry about hitting the acupuncture points, just draw her mind to her problem using a manageable statement. The statement needed to be specific and focused, according to paragraph three. Not one of those murky thoughts that swim to the surface unnoticed. *I've entered a black lagoon of despair* wouldn't work. The declaration had to be snappier, more immediate. Something like, *Even though Walter loses control of his bowels, I love and approve of myself*. Ellie had tried countless beginnings—*Even though Sammy won't use his words, even though Danny nearly killed himself in his grandfather's truck, even though Eric has been checked out for months*—always finishing with words like *I accept myself anyway*, because the pamphlet said so, not because she did.

She couldn't concentrate enough to come up with anything peppy, especially with the thought of Myrtle, standing right beside her, larger than life—*Pull up your socks, girl, it's Christmas. Oh, for God sakes, put on some socks.*

Ellie knew all about her mother-in-law's idea of Christmas. Before her family moved here last winter, Ellie had escaped to this place for the holidays each year, though in hindsight she wished she hadn't. Eric worked Christmases—every damn one, it seemed—so Ellie searched for bus routes to Neesley from wherever they were stationed. She packed up the boys, mounds of diapers and baby wipes, then Tonka trucks and big boy pants, stuffing everything she could think of into mismatched suitcases. She endured Sammy's tears and strangers' stares at his outbursts, ratty bus seats, and startling snowstorms—whatever it took to get to Myrtle's doorstep.

Myrtle always met them in front of the Esso coffee bar on Main that served as the bus station. She squeezed them into the front seat of the big truck and drove the terrible winter roads home, making no fuss whatsoever over the black ice. Then once inside the front landing, dazed and bedraggled, Ellie breathed deeply while Myrtle scooped up the boys with her strong farmer's arms and stripped snowsuits and mittens, carried suitcases to bedrooms.

Ellie had liked the way Myrtle arranged the garland over the mantel and scattered the tiny toy soldiers and crocheted snowflakes about the tree's branches. The way Myrtle took over the kitchen, robust and rosy cheeked, mashing potatoes in the old copper pot, stirring vats of perfect, lump-free gravy, checking the doneness of carrots and Brussels sprouts, the brownness of pie crusts. She could as easily pull gizzards from the turkey cavity as fold napkins into dainty flowers. It was incredible to watch.

Every year, Ellie repeatedly offered help. Her mother-in-law repeatedly refused it. She said things like, "You need rest, dear" or

"Why don't you go have a lie down," so Ellie backed away, tamping down feelings of unworthiness and choosing to be grateful for the woman's generosity instead.

Those Christmases might have saved her or they might have been her ruin—she was not sure which. All she knew was that she craved getting to this place, earlier and earlier each year, like it was a drug and she an addict. Certainly now, she could see hairline cracks in her fairy tale. At the time, she barely noticed Walter's sullenness as he sat in his chair, or Myrtle's sideways glances of pity, her tsk-tsking about Sammy's growing number of compulsions—and Eric nowhere to be found.

After Myrtle died in this house, Walter lived alone for a few months, homecare workers coming in and out, failing to keep him satisfied. It had been her idea, not Eric's, to move back to the home he was raised in. The RCMP had had him too long already, stolen too many Christmases, too many weekends and nights away from his family. He could quit the force, get a less formidable job, and start over. They could all start over. Neesley, with all of its fond memories, was the right place to be. And here they'd be able to look after Walter. Wasn't that what families were supposed to do?

She regretted it now, of course. Myrtle seemed less tolerant after her death. Ellie could feel her hot breath on her neck. You should be dressed. The beds made, porridge bubbling on the stove for the boys. What have you been doing with your days? Where was the Christmas pudding? Why were there no boughs on the mantel, no paper snow-flakes in the windows?

She waited for the washer to fill, tapping furiously, reciting some nonsense about accepting herself. There was something not right with the water pressure; the hot water trickled into the spinner like the tail end of a pee stream. Eric had taken a look at the pipes, but he'd been interrupted by a call to the plant for an overly heated union meeting and had never gotten back to it. Outside of their walls, Eric loved a good crisis, loved taking charge. He was called away so often these days; Ellie questioned if he was making up calamity just to escape the house.

Ellie heard the dog bark upstairs and tried to ignore it. She told herself that her thoughts stayed hidden from her husband, that none of what went on in her head had leaked into the air between them. But she knew that wasn't true. Every word she'd said to Eric that morning had been wrong. By the time she'd come out to the kitchen, he was finishing his toast, the *Neesley Advance* open to the Local News page.

"How'd you sleep?" she asked, walking around him when he reached for her.

"Walter had a rough night," he said.

Which meant Eric had a rough night too.

Ellie stared past Eric to Sammy, their five-year-old, who sat on the floor in the corner of the living room, still wearing his Superman pajamas as he sorted his Legos.

Eric waited until Ellie's eyes met his again. Then he called over his shoulder without turning to face his son, "Hey, slugger. Come have some cereal." When he got no response, he whistled and raised his voice. "Hey, bud. Come on."

Sammy kept sorting.

"He's not a dog," Ellie said, reaching for the coffee pot.

"He's not a dog," Sammy repeated from his corner.

Ellie filled Eric's cup before pouring the dregs into her own. Thorn moseyed down the hallway and then collapsed at Eric's feet. Eric rewarded him with a pat on the head.

"So you're only working the half shift? Today's your last day until the new year?" She sat across from her husband at the table, Myrtle's napkin holder and salt and pepper shakers between them.

He passed her the newspaper. "Over one hundred calls for police," the headline read.

"That's not a question, is it?" he said. "Because we've been talking about this for a month. Today's my last day."

"Unless there's an emergency," she said.

"Unless there's an emergency."

She scanned the newspaper column, reading out loud. "December 12. An abandoned blue Neon car towed from Marsh Road. Dog reported stolen from a Harder Road residence returned home an hour later. So many emergencies."

"Not my problem, obviously," he said.

They'd thrown a big party for Eric up in Smoky River on his last day with the force. After they moved back to Neesley, he moped around the house day after day until Ellie thought she would go mad. She was relieved when he took a nine-to-five security contract at the Chitwood Gas Plant, even though she knew he thoroughly hated the job. From sergeant to rent-a-cop—in his mind, he could sink no lower.

"The plant should be quiet over Christmas," she said.

Eric said nothing, just blew into his coffee as though it was still steaming.

"And if they ask for extra hours?" She was unable to stop herself. "Say one of the night guys parties too hard and they call you in?"

He stood quickly, causing Thorn to humph and roll to avoid being stepped on. "I'll be here, Ellie. And I'll get you your tree. I'll do it this afternoon, just like I promised. What more do you want?"

Ellie watched her husband's forehead grow angry-red, like skin under the rim of a baseball cap on a blistering hot day. Thorn licked Eric's sock, the only trick he knew when he sensed a change in mood.

She wasn't trying to badger him. She just wanted this Christmas to be perfect—their house full of laughter. She wanted tender turkey and smooth gravy that tasted better than Myrtle's.

Eric strode to the closet and retrieved his parka. She assumed he'd wanted to make a clean exit, but he'd misplaced his keys again and stood there dumbly, patting his pockets.

"I'll find them," he said, although they both knew he wouldn't. "I put them in my pocket."

"If you put them in your pocket, they would be in your pocket."

He poked around the kitchen and then headed to yesterday's pants in the bedroom, as predictable as snow in winter. She rummaged through the family's pile of boots in the front closet. The key ring lay wedged behind one of Walter's old Sorels. Eric came back down the hallway, empty-handed, and before she could stop herself, she pitched the keys at him, giving him no time to react.

That had been their morning. Ellie dipped her fingers in the washing machine's sudsy water. She must try harder. Thorn let out a series of mournful bursts above her. She could hear the thump of Walter's cane as he shuffled down the hallway. She trudged up the stairs and pushed the dog outside to do his business. By the time she got back down, the washing cycle was spinning merrily minus its soiled load. Sensational.

——

It was a quarter to three by the time Eric walked into the cramped Child and Family Services office. The woman behind the reception counter wiped the sleep from her eyes, yawning.

"I'm here to see Betty Holt," Eric said, leaning against the counter.

The woman stayed blank.

"Could you just tell Betty that Eric Nyland is here? I'll only be a few minutes."

She stifled another yawn, sloppy red mouth twisting, and then shuffled down the hallway. Her brown woolly sweater hung over a turtleneck and multiple t-shirts of different lengths.

Eric sat in one of the chairs in the waiting area. When the woman came back she stood in front of the bulletin board, fiddling with tacks and rearranging postings.

"Have you got any plans for Christmas?" she asked him.

He wondered if she'd forgotten about Betty on her way down the hall. "Just time with the family," he said. "Will Betty be long?"

She stood with her back to him. "Christmas is my favourite next to Easter, what with eggnog and Nanaimo bars and turkey this and that! I haven't put out one snow globe this year, not one, and my romances are going to stay on the bookshelf so I can focus all my attention on chapters six and seven. Financial statements. They make my eyes swim, they really do."

Eric hadn't a clue what she was talking about. He bent to pick up the scattered papers she'd let fall. "You dropped a few."

He passed her the papers as Betty came bustling down the hall, arms outstretched. He and Betty had been friends since grade school.

"Eric Nyland. Well, aren't you a sight," Betty exclaimed. "You've come to wish your dear friend a merry Christmas."

The receptionist stepped back while Eric braced himself for the collision. Betty wrapped around him in a bear hug.

"The office closes at four today," the receptionist said, her back flat against the bulletin board.

Betty laughed, her ample belly jiggling. "Yes, Cindy. I remember."

"You still haven't signed my time-off schedule."

"I'm just going to have a quick chinwag with Eric here. I expect he's come laden with gifts."

"Sorry, no gifts," Eric said as Betty whisked him down the hall and into her crowded office. The room had a window view of the parking lot, Eric's car in one of the visitors' stalls.

"Cindy Simpson," Betty whispered before closing her door. "Our new receptionist. Did she tell you she's studying for her book-keeping exam?"

"She said something about finances." Eric moved stacks of folders off the chair and laid them between the desktop Santa and the bowl stuffed with candy canes.

Betty wheeled a chair out from behind her desk. "She tells everyone who'll listen that she's studying for her bookkeeping exam. She's flunked four times already—she tells everyone that too. She seems to swell in the awe of her own persistence."

Eric's mind flashed to his own stream of recently failed tests. Ellie's look, as she pitched him his lost keys that morning.

Betty maneuvered her chair right across from his, sat down, took a breath, and leaned forward. "This is a lovely surprise, Eric. Merry Christmas. I'd offer you a cup of Cindy's coffee, but it's truly undrinkable."

Eric felt himself relax for the first time all day. Betty put him at ease. She always had.

"How are you doing, Betty?"

"Still fat and happy." She laughed and he did too. Then she shook her head and sighed. "But I'm still ripping children from their parents, sadly. You should read some of my emails. You'd think I was the most hated woman in the county."

Whenever Eric thought of goodness, Betty came to mind. She could unearth chances in the unlikeliest places. She'd once invited their entire school to her grade four birthday party just to make sure the Buckland kids—snot-nosed and shabby and never included in anything—got their fair share of cake and ice cream. When the school bus emptied in front of the Holt farmhouse, her mother nearly had a heart attack.

Betty patted her hand lightly against his knee. "I thought we might see more of each other, now that you're back."

Eric didn't want to think of all he'd not done since moving back to Neesley. "Sorry," he said, clearing his throat. "Still settling in."

Betty raised her eyebrows, not convinced. "I was surprised to hear you'd quit the force. So you're at the plant now. How's security working out?"

"Pretty quiet." The cheap shirt with the Chitwood Plant logo, his rent-a-cop outfit, chafed his neck under his jacket. "I've booked off the week. My first stay-at-home Christmas in over a decade." He said this lightly, although the thought of spending a week with his family, no distractions, made him feel defenceless.

Betty smiled. "Well, there's one advantage right there. Time off at Christmas. Leaving behind all those testy holiday husbands and fathers and boyfriends. All those extra fender-benders. How are Ellie and the boys?"

"Fine," he lied. "Adjusting to life around here. Sammy's in kindergarten. Dan's pumping weights."

"Such good boys. And Walter? How's he doing?"

Eric's string of couch nights was making it harder to be civil to his father. Eric had wanted to install an outside lock on Walter's bedroom door, to stop his shrivelled white feet from wandering into the freezing cold, but Ellie wouldn't have it. You wouldn't lock a child in for getting confused in the night. They didn't lock in Sammy, who sometimes prowled around the house in his sleep, opening and closing bedroom doors. No, their home would be no one's prison, not under Ellie's watch. But it was Eric who lay in wait on the couch, who kept his ear to the floor, who listened for the sound of his father shuffling down the hall. If he let himself think about it, which he tried his best to avoid, he'd been listening for those footsteps his whole damn life.

"The same," Eric said. "Dan cracked up Walter's truck."

"I heard. Thank God he wasn't hurt."

Of course she'd heard. Ex-RCMP's kid out for a joyride. Everybody had heard.

When he continued to sit without speaking, she asked, "Did you come in just to have me grill you about your life?"

Eric leaned forward. "What do you know about Nigel Wilson?"

"Nigel?" she asked, surprised. "I haven't talked to him in years. Not since school days. You're the one living right across the road from him."

"What the hell is he doing back here?"

Betty sat back and studied his face. "The return of the prodigal sons. He might be asking the same about you."

"There's a young girl living with him. Hannah Finch."

"I heard."

"Well, what do you know about her?"

"Nothing, Eric," she said, raising her hands. "She's not one of mine. Nigel brought her with him, without the mother, when he moved back home. Tragic story. He finally finds a woman who will have him, and she dies. He's started up some kind of accounting practice. Farmer's books, that kind of thing. Keeps to himself. The girl is being home-schooled as far as I know. What's this about?"

"I picked her up on the road today in this godawful weather. She was miles out. Not dressed right."

"Oh. Well, that's not good." She sighed, glancing toward the burgeoning cabinets, each filled with familial disasters. "What did the girl tell you?"

"Nothing. She asked me to drive her back home."

"How did she look?"

"Cold. Miserable."

"Aren't we all this winter."

"Something's not right. Wilson's not right."

Betty did not answer at once but stared out her office window. "You're not likely the best judge of Nigel Wilson," she said at last. "Did you talk to him?"

"Briefly."

"How did that go?"

Eric had returned plenty of kids. They all came from somewhere. Some had parents who called the station day and night, voices husky with worry. Some had parents who made no call at all, parents who kept their eyes on the TV when he arrived on their doorstep with their offspring in tow. Nigel Wilson fell more into this second category, but worse. He was not fit to be around children. Not a good person.

"I want you to check on her."

"On what grounds?"

"Something doesn't smell right."

"So I should barge through his front door and do a sniff test?"

"You're defending him?"

"Against what?" She was not the least bit ruffled, despite his accusation. "He's not my favourite person either, Eric, but you haven't given me much to work with here. You know how it works. If she's been hurt, or talked about being hurt, or showed signs . . ."

He hesitated, staring at her. "It's just this feeling—" he said. What was he thinking? He had plenty to worry about this Christmas without dredging up demons from his childhood. He stood, angry with himself. "No, you're right. Let sleeping dogs lie. I should be off. I'm supposed to be getting Ellie her tree." Although he'd clearly missed his window. It would be dark before he got back to their road.

Betty stood and wrapped her arms around him. "I'll see what I can do," she said. "And don't be a stranger. Give Ellie my best."

When he got back to the reception area, Cindy Simpson was down on the floor, coat on, unplugging the Christmas lights from the spindly tree tucked into the corner. She looked up and said, "We're closing early today for Christmas. Shutting down until New Year's. Not that I'll get a break. I'm studying for my bookkeeping exam."

"Stay safe," he said. She turned, mouth open, but he ducked out of the office before she could say more.

———

Hannah wanted to stay on her towel, pinned to the dazzling hot sand, the warm sun pressing down and making her crave sleep. But her stomach hurt. She needed something to eat. When she stepped into the hall, Nigel's office door was closed, so she tiptoed past his room and down the stairs in the dark.

There was little food in the house. She found some tired frozen chicken strips and lined them in rows on a cookie sheet for the oven and boiled water in a pot for peas and carrots, which had been in the freezer so long they were covered with snow. She set out the salt and pepper and knives and forks and poured water into the blue cups with glass thin as paper. When she turned from the sink, a glass for each hand, Nigel had appeared, standing right behind her, his half-empty bottle in one hand, drinking cup in the other. She nearly lost her balance, water sloshing over her fingers.

His eyes were too glassy, his face too red. He just stood there, so she worked around him, dishing food onto their plates, carrying the plates to the table. By the time she sat down, her stomach had filled with rocks.

Nigel wedged into the chair across from her, thumping the bottle on the table as he sat. He pushed his plate to the side and filled his glass.

"You're a supid girl, Hannah. Ungrayful." He took a long drink. "A joyride with Eric Nyland. Supid."

Nigel leaned toward her, his boozy smell all over her. Her whole body twitched, legs jumping under the table, but she didn't look up, forcing herself to shovel down bites as fast as she could.

"Whad I say 'bout him. 'Bout saying away." He leaned back again and took another drink. "Sorry piece a shit. The pair of you."

She needed to finish and get back up to her room and out of sight. She took two more wretched bites of the cardboard chicken.

He tilted sideways in slow motion, like a dead person falling out of a chair. But then his arm shot out, and he managed to right himself again, and when he came back up, he had Mandy in his clasp.

Hannah jumped up. "Put her down!" Mandy hissed and struggled, a flurry of paws, but Nigel held tighter. "I hate you," she screamed, lunging toward him, pounding her fists on his head. Mandy shrieked, a sharp cry she'd never heard before. Nigel pushed Hannah hard in the chest and she staggered backwards, her head thudding on the corner of the table. Her ears filled with a high-pitched buzzing noise, Nigel's shouts echoing from far away. She felt weak, like she was sliding off her whale into dark water. No matter how hard she tried, she couldn't stretch her arms out to brace her fall. The last thing she remembered was a muffled thud as she hit the floor face first.

three

By the time his dad walked through the door, they had already arranged themselves in their usual spots, plates still empty, food laid out in bowls, no steam rising. Daniel slumped at the table. He'd been cooped up all day in this dismal house, grounded.

"You shouldn't have waited," his dad said as he shook the snow off his shoulders and hung his coat in the front closet.

"You might have called." His mom was mad at his dad again. She'd been weird all week. Who knew why?

"No fish and chips?" his grandpa asked for the fourth time. His place was beside Daniel, across from his mom and Sammy. He had his napkin tucked into the buttonhole of his faded shirt like a flag and poked it with his thumb.

"Not tonight, Walter," his mom said again. "Tonight, we're having chicken."

"Not tonight, Walter," Sammy repeated. "Tonight, we're having chicken."

Sammy was an excellent impersonator. His mom used to call him on it—find your own words, Sammy—but she hadn't got after him lately.

"Smells good." His dad stomped across the kitchen in his sock feet and kissed Mom on the top of her head. She didn't let on she noticed, just stared straight ahead.

"Hey, slugger," his dad said as he tousled Sammy's hair. Sammy flinched.

"He hates it when you do that," his mom said.

"Yeah, well, that makes two of us," his dad muttered.

Daniel stared at his brother. Sammy never did talk much, but you knew he was out of sorts when his hands got going, and they seemed to be going all the time these days, like right now, his fork zigzagging at lightning speed between his fingers and his thumb.

"Can I eat downstairs?" Daniel asked.

"You can eat with the rest of us like a civilized person," his dad said, folding into his usual spot in the only chair with arms.

His mom's fingers curled into fists. "Just say grace. Please."

His dad bowed his head, and his mom squeezed her eyes shut and thumped on her forehead. Daniel counted the taps. She'd been pounding on her head a lot, like she was knocking on a door that nobody would answer. Sammy rolled his fists in tight circles.

As soon as his dad said amen, his mom scooped peas and potatoes onto Sammy's plate and then cut his chicken into tiny pieces as bowls were passed around the table.

"Where's the chips," his grandpa said, his finger stuck in his button hole, napkin floating to the floor beside Thorn, who rolled over and lay on it like a pillow.

"We're not having chips tonight," his mom said.

"We're not having chips tonight," Sammy repeated.

"Use your fork, Sammy. Look at me. That's right, your fork, not your fingers."

"I want my chips."

"Give it a rest, Walter," his dad said. "This chicken's great, Ellie."

"It's cold."

"You didn't need to wait," his dad said.

"That's right, Eric. And Danny could have carried his plate down to the basement, never to be seen again, and Sammy could have launched his potatoes off his spoon, and your father could have . . ." His mom looked across the table at Grandpa, who'd found the rocks in his pocket and was now stacking them into a pyramid beside his plate.

Daniel shovelled bites, fast as he could. He was grounded because of his stupid accident and had no place to go except his room. Any place was better than this. He'd texted Melissa ten times today and left three phone messages, and she hadn't answered one. He'd phoned Matt too, who lived across the street from Melissa, begging him to go over and talk to her, but Matt was useless with girls and said no way, definitely not.

Before they moved into his grandparents' old farmhouse last January, they never stayed long enough in any one place for him to have a girlfriend. Melissa was his first, and she was so hot, he could hardly hate it here. Not entirely. But it had seemed like a better place back when he was a kid.

Juice dribbled down his grandpa's chin, and he gave it a swipe with the back of his hand.

"I'm supposed to get a napkin," he yelled.

"I gave you a napkin," his mom said. "Check your lap."

"Tell me about your day, Ellie." His dad leaned toward her.

"My day was fine."

"Can I be excused?" Daniel asked his mother. He could go a few more rounds in his bedroom tonight. He had worked up to repetitions of twelve—biceps curls, chest press, triceps extensions—any more would do nothing to build bulk, and that's what he needed.

"You can stay right here, Dan," his dad said.

"But I'm done."

"And we're not. Your mother put a lot of effort into making this dinner, and you can spend more than two minutes at this table enjoying it."

Just one big happy family. They ate in silence after that.

Finally, his dad turned to his mom. "You didn't go to town, did you? I couldn't remember if you had any appointments today."

Grandpa Walter had a specialist for each one of his body parts. Daniel looked at his mom, who didn't say anything. He wanted to chime in for her: *Actually we didn't leave the house today, thanks so much for asking. We stayed here and rotted.* But he kept the thought to himself.

Sammy choked. He was an excellent choker.

"Slow down there, slugger," his dad said.

His mom patted Sammy's back, which made him give his wild hair a single sharp yank. Then she poured him more milk.

"Ellie?"

"We didn't go anywhere today. We stayed put. In this house. All of us."

"Just as well. Roads were brutal. The worst this week. It's good you didn't have to go out in that. Just a quiet day, then?"

Any quieter and we'd be dead.

His grandpa leaned his hands onto the table, trying to stand. "Can't even get a napkin in this house."

His mom sighed. "Danny, please help your grandfather."

Daniel reached down and yanked the corner of the napkin until it tugged free from under Thorn, dog hair raining everywhere, and then he placed it on his grandpa's lap. Thorn humphed and stretched and flopped back to where he was.

"So, what did you get up to?"

This line of questioning was getting his dad nowhere.

"Look around," his mom said.

His dad looked up at his mom, as if he wasn't sure what he might say that was right. Welcome to my world, Daniel thought.

Then his mom answered, but more softly this time. "I wanted to have the house decorated by now."

"We can do it tomorrow. Right, slugger?"

Sammy was making binoculars with his hands, studying the ceiling.

"You promised to get the tree today."

"I know. I'm sorry. Something came up," his dad said. "I'll get you your tree."

Daniel would go crazy with one more night grounded in this house. "How long am I stuck here?"

"Until we're finished," his dad said.

"Max wants me to go to play video games." Daniel hadn't spoken to Max, but Max never had much going on.

His mom said, "Not my tree. *Our* tree."

"Max's mom says she's got something for us. I think she made us shortbread cookies or something. I told him I'd ask."

Ellie reached toward Sammy and put her hand over his to keep it still. "Families across North America manage to find and decorate a tree before Christmas. I don't know why it's so hard for ours."

"So, can I?" Daniel asked. Both his parents stared at him. He sat up straighter and tried to look credible.

"What do you think?" his dad asked.

"I dunno. That's why I'm asking."

"You're grounded."

"Yeah, I know that, but Mrs. Peterson got a present for us and it'd be rude to not go get it. I don't want to hurt her feelings. I'll be home by eleven. Okay, ten."

His dad put his fork down and crossed his arms. "Is this where I'm supposed to remind you that you cracked up your grandpa's truck?"

"I didn't do it on purpose. That's why it's called an accident."

His mom sighed. "You're not grounded because you had an accident." She hadn't eaten a bite, just pushed her potatoes around her plate. "You're grounded because you took your grandpa's truck out in the first place. You snuck out of the house in the middle of the night for a joyride. You could have been killed."

"A little engine dust never hurt anything," his grandpa piped in, piling rocks back into his pocket. "Got a rattling under the hood. Gonna take a look tomorrow."

Grandpa Walter was long past his driving days. They ended years ago, when Grandma sent him out for flour and he came home with corn-flakes and somebody else's truck. When Daniel got his learner's permit, exactly six weeks ago to the day, his parents told him the truck would be his when he got his licence. Before his pileup with the tree, it was in mint condition—a 1974 Chevy Custom Deluxe 10. Now it was squeezed between the other wrecks down at PoPow's Auto Wrecking and Towing.

"It's not like I stole it," Daniel said. When Grandma was around, she kept the keys locked in the cupboard with the liquor. Grandpa would climb in behind the wheel often enough, but he wasn't allowed to go anywhere. "You told me it was mine."

"Don't feign stupid, Danny," Ellie said. "Yours once you got your licence. You broke the law by taking it out on your own. How do you think this makes your father look? A sergeant who can't keep track of his fourteen-year-old."

"He's not a sergeant anymore, Mom."

"You know exactly what I mean."

"Can someone please tell me what's happened to the pie?" his grandpa yelled, waving his arm.

His dad took a long drink of water and stared at him. His mom sighed. "There's no pie tonight, Walter."

"It was one stupid mistake," Daniel said.

"And look how that turned out," his dad said.

"So I'm stuck here for the rest of my life?"

"Five more days," his dad said. "We discussed this, Dan."

"Dinner's over." His mom stood, whisking bowls and plates and cutlery from the table and slamming them on the kitchen counter. Sammy stood too and headed to his pile of Lego in the living room.

"Now can I be excused?" Daniel mumbled.

"You want out?" His father slapped his hand on the table. "We'll go out."

"Yeah," Daniel said, not trusting this sudden turn. "So you'll drive me?"

"We'll drive out to Gerry's place. You can help me get the tree."

"Tonight?" his mom said, like he was crazy.

"Why not?"

She stood in front of the kitchen sink and turned on the water. "Gerry's not going to want you traipsing through his land tonight. You can't chop down a tree in the dark."

"We'll take the lantern. It will be an adventure."

"You'll chop off a finger. If you don't freeze to death first."

"It's like minus two hundred," Daniel said.

"I'll get you the tree, Ellie. Tonight. And Dan will help."

"No, thanks." Daniel backed away from the table, ready to hightail it to the basement.

His dad stood. "Nonnegotiable, Dan."

Grandpa Walter now sat alone at the table.

"Mom!" Daniel yelled. She wouldn't look at him.

"Get your gear on. You got five minutes."

"You're insane." His mom stormed down the hall, water still running. His dad looked like he wanted to go after her, but he went to the sink instead and cranked the tap off so hard it squealed.

———

Eric had dropped the girl off at Wilson's not four hours before. He hadn't stopped thinking about her since. Daniel was slumped sullenly beside him as he backed down the driveway. He should never have brought him.

"You warm enough?"

Daniel faked a suffocating choke, whipped off his toque and threw it in the back.

When Eric got to the road, he let the car idle, his headlights casting an eerie glow into the trees. Nothing could adapt to this weather, white wrapped close all around on this godforsaken night.

Daniel said, "In case you're having a stroke or something, I'd like to point out that we're not moving."

"We're going to make a quick stop first," Eric said. "Then we'll go to Gerry's and get your mother her tree."

"*Our* tree," Daniel mimicked. "Families all over North America manage to get a damn tree."

Eric snapped, "Don't make fun of her, Dan. It's Christmas. She's having a rough go."

"Ya think? What's the big deal anyway? It's a stupid tree. Who cares?"

"Your mom does."

Daniel smacked his lips. "She's totally lost it, you know. Although you wouldn't 'cause you're never around."

Maybe Dan was right. Maybe Ellie had really lost it this time.

"You haven't exactly made it easy for her," Eric said. He should never have agreed to move his family back here. This is what he'd given up his career for?

"So it's my fault?" Daniel thumped his head against the headrest.

He'd been a handful these past weeks, but Ellie was not his fault. "We're going to do this for her, Dan. And make it nice."

"We're not going anywhere. What's the holdup? Why are we just sitting here?"

Maybe his family was a sorry mess, but the Nyland virus had a chance to cure itself. Christmas would be over soon. Ellie could get back on track. Dan could lose the attitude, if only to get his driving privileges back. Sammy could make some friends at school, boys who saw past his differences. And Walter, well, Walter couldn't live for-ever.

But this girl. This Hannah. He might as well have marked her door with a red X. There was a plague inside that house. Eric could smell it mouldering on Wilson's pressed shirt.

"Dad?"

"Sorry. We're stopping in at Wilson's place. Just for a minute."

Daniel perked up. "Wilson's? You mean the guy across the road? How come?"

He'd make up some bogus excuse for stopping by, see Hannah for himself, find her safe and sound and tucked in bed, and then he'd drop this thing. God knows he didn't need another kid in his head. He didn't need any more excuses to escape his own children.

Daniel said, "I thought you hated that guy."

"I never said that."

Daniel pressed forward against his seat belt and squinted into the night as Eric pulled the car into Wilson's place.

"You forgot to signal," Daniel pointed out.

No, Eric should definitely not have brought Dan with him. "There's a girl living here."

"A girl?" Daniel looked out at the white wasteland beyond the road. "Out here? No way. How old is she?"

"She's eleven."

Wilson's sign was camouflaged in snow, unreadable. There were no lights from the house to guide the way.

Daniel sucked in his breath. "This place is creepy when you get up close. Not much going on at this house."

Eric hoped that was true. He pulled in beside Wilson's car, which hadn't moved, and made a mental note of the time: 6:47 p.m.

"You stay here," Eric said, easing open his door, a frigid gust rushing in. "I'll leave the car running. I won't be long."

"Why can't I come in?"

"I don't know what I'll find here."

Daniel unbuckled his seat belt and leaned toward his father. "Don't you need back up?"

"You watch too much TV. I'll be right back."

The feeble trail Wilson had shovelled to his door had filled in since Eric had last been there. He struggled through snow to the top of his boots to get to the porch. Disoriented by the deafening quiet, he took a deep breath before banging on the door, which surprisingly gave. Eric looked down to see the silver latch had frozen solid, crusted with snow, no longer able to keep out winter. Eric shoved the door, stepped into the glassed-in porch, opened the inside door, and entered the overheated living room, planting his legs wide. He heard nothing except for the grandfather clock's ticking and that voice in the back of his head, telling him to be on guard.

"Wilson," he yelled.

There was movement in the centre of the living room, not ten feet away. Eric steadily circled toward the sound to get a better look: Wilson sprawled across the couch, hair askew, one arm dragging on the floor, the other hiding his face. His pressed shirt, now rumpled and untucked, had a long brownish stain down the front. A bourbon bottle, three-quarters empty, sat on the coffee table's stained doily. The booze smell was foul. Eric felt sickened by it—a little boy's queasiness, Walter sprawled out in front of him from back in the day.

"Wilson," he yelled again, yanking on the floor lamp's tassel beside Wilson's head. Wilson tried to pull himself up some imaginary rope, arms flailing, and then fell back down again.

Eric leaned in close and gave Wilson's shoulder a sharp tug. "Wilson!"

Wilson blinked several times under the light, trying to focus. "Eric. Get outta my house." Wilson smacked his lips, batting his arm, missing Eric. "Get outta my house."

Eric brought his face to within inches of Wilson's, drawing sour air through his nose. "You're drunk."

Wilson closed his eyes again. "It's Chrissas."

"Where's Hannah?"

"No law 'gainst drinkin' at Chrissas."

Eric wanted to squeeze Wilson's red neck. "Where's Hannah?"

Wilson's lips curled into a sick smile. "That's my bisiss."

Eric called loudly, "Hannah! It's Eric Nyland. I just need to talk to you for a minute."

He listened for movement above him. Nothing. No sign of the girl. No sign of the cat.

"Hannah!"

The damn ticking was impossibly loud. He left Wilson to wallow on the couch, gulping air in his drunken stupor. His feet took him to the window. Pushing back the lace curtain, he saw nothing amiss, just Dan's silhouette, head down in the front seat of the car where he left him. He willed his son to stay put—to stay warm and safe and occupied with his cell phone.

Wilson, snoring now, posed no imminent threat, so Eric ascended the stairs, heavy footed, warrantless. She'd been exhausted. Maybe she was in a dreamless sleep, oblivious to the sorry excuse for a parent who had drunk himself stupid. Maybe she'd not heard him call her name.

The top of the landing, at least ten degrees colder than the floor below, led to four closed doors, two per side. Eric opened the closest and switched on the light to Wilson's room, immaculate, worn burgundy carpet, bed made military style, heavy oak dresser with bracket feet, a straight-backed chair, empty garbage can—like a cheap hotel room waiting for its guest. He backed out slowly, leaving wet tracks on the rug with his boots.

The room beside made Eric's heart lurch. The wooden desk in the corner was bare—no papers, pens, files, books, adding machines— nothing for an accountant to count. There was an ironing board set up just inside the entrance, and a metal coil strung the length of the room. Wilson had meticulously lined his shirts on hangers from wall to wall. There were dozens of identical white shirts, each pressed with military precision, collars turned down and buttons fastened. Each facing the same way like headless soldiers.

Eric rushed into the hall and checked the bathroom. There was only one room left. He pushed her door open, hoping to find her asleep, that it was only that.

"Hannah," he whispered. "Hannah, it's Eric Nyland. Your neighbour."

He flipped the light switch. If this was her room, there was no sign of her. There were no clothes heaped on the floor; no posters on the walls or stuffies on her small made bed; no cat on her pillow.

Eric tore down the stairs, past the comatose Wilson, and slammed into the sour-smelling kitchen, the only other room on the main floor. He switched on every light he could find. There were remnants of supper, on the table, on the floor. A china plate had shattered to pieces, and peas had been mushed into the floorboards. If she'd left on foot, that would be the end of her; it was just too damn cold. He methodically opened cupboards and closet doors, sweeping aside brooms, flour bags, checking in corners, and under the sink. Anywhere and everywhere a girl might hide. The door near the mud room was bolted shut. It was one of those nickel flush door bolts that had been added after the house was built, the single addition to an otherwise untouched and outdated kitchen. Eric slid the bolt and pushed open the door to a set of sagging wooden stairs he'd never been down.

He descended, slowly. He reached into the right pocket of his jacket and pulled out his flashlight, smacking it twice before the beam shone a foot in front of him. At the bottom, Eric took several deep breaths, trying to stop his heart from hammering in the cave-like space, barely deep enough to stand up straight. He could feel that familiar ball rising in his throat, his feet itchy to flee. He was afraid of cramped spaces—tunnels, elevators, airplanes. He had slipped an Ativan under his tongue before his one and only MRI.

The bloated angry furnace in the corner groaned and heaved, but it was cold enough to see his breath, tufts of fog clouding around him. A decaying earth smell fanned off the sand walls and sand floor. Eric hunted for a light, found a bulb above him, and pulled the ratty string.

Shadows darted like bats. It took everything he had to stay in this coffin. He could not get his voice to work to call out for Hannah. He turned in circles, pointing his beam toward the filthy furnace, along the empty wooden shelves, and between the vats lined up against the dirt wall.

He missed her with the first pass. Only when he circled again with the beam, he saw a discarded blanket tucked up against a tall stack of metal pails. It was grey and splotched with holes. He patted along the blanket folds and then threw down his flashlight and unwrapped the small, still body curled inside. *Don't let her be dead.* "Hannah, it's Eric Nyland."

He kneeled in front of her and put his arm around her back, lifting her up out of her slump. She roused a little and took swats at his face.

"It's Eric Nyland. From right next door. I'm not going to hurt you." Eric waited while she batted at him, repeating her name until she quieted. "It's okay now. It's okay."

She finally fell back into his arm, panting, blinking into the shadows.

"Let's get you out of here."

"You came back," she said, barely above a whisper.

"Are you hurt?" An asinine question. She was a little girl who'd been thrown into a cellar. God knows what else. Eric had left his phone in the car. He'd left Dan in the car too. He needed to move quickly to get back to his son, to get this girl warm. She wore only thin pajamas, bare toes white as paper. He bent closer and scanned his flashlight along her body, hunting for broken bits, and signs of blood. She had one arm squeezed around her middle, something hard hidden under her pajama top. He untangled her fingers, raised the corner of the flimsy cotton, and sucked in his breath. It was her cat—Mindy, Mandy—rigid as cardboard.

Hannah tried to sit up, crying now, more a gravelly mewing, as if her mouth had filled with dirt. Eric lifted the dead cat from under her shirt and laid it beside them on the floor.

"I c-c-couldn't get her to breathe again," she stuttered, hoarse.

"I'm so sorry, Hannah." Eric whipped off his coat and wrapped it around her. "I'm going to lift you up now. You need to tell me if it hurts."

He grabbed the flashlight and scooped her into his arms, pressing her muffled sobs close to his chest. Then he sidestepped the dead cat and ascended the creaking stairs, whispering assurances. As he brought her into the light of the kitchen, he could hear Wilson's slurred yelling in the next room. Hannah tensed in his arms as he whispered the mantra, *It's okay, it's okay, it's okay.*

But it wasn't. Gripping Hannah tightly, he stepped into the living room to see Dan, eyes wide with fear, staring back at him. Dan had waltzed into this madhouse, right through the front door. He'd even taken his boots off, for God sakes. Wilson was up, right in Dan's face, clinging to the bannister to stop from slithering to the rug, yelling incoherently about Eric being a good-for-nothing loser. The damn clock was striking the hour.

Eric said, "Dan, I want you to back away." Dan bit down on his lip. He didn't move. "Look at me, Dan."

Wilson turned toward Eric, howling, "Get outta my goddamned house."

Hannah quaked in his arms. Eric carried her to the couch and put her down. She cried in his ear and kept on crying as he pulled away.

"Shut up. Shut up. Shut up." Wilson lunged forward, his fist grabbing a handful of Dan's jacket, shaking him like an animal.

Eric flew across the room. He slammed his body against Wilson and drove him to the floor, smashing his fist to his cheek, once, twice, more, until Wilson lay motionless under Eric's knee on his chest, Eric's fingers wrapped around his throat. He stayed on top of Wilson like that until his own breathing slowed down, until he could hear nothing but the sound of the clock and the wind sweeping along the empty road.

When he looked up, Dan was backed against the wall, rocking from foot to foot, toque in his hands.

"Are you all right?"

Dan nodded.

"This wasn't your fault. This would have happened even if you'd stayed in the car." Eric stood stiffly and approached his boy, who moved away slightly.

"Is he dead?" Dan wanted to know.

A weary regret flooded through Eric. *Please state your name for the record. Daniel James Nyland. Please walk us through the sequence of events? Had Mr. Wilson asked you to leave? What was Mr. Wilson's condition at the time? Did Mr. Wilson strike first? Strike ever? And how many times did Eric Nyland strike Mr. Wilson?*

How many times? Eric's knuckles were swollen purple. "He's not dead, Dan. He's drunk. That's all." Hannah had disappeared into the couch. "We have to help her. Can you do that with me?"

Daniel's eyes darted from the couch to Wilson's inert body, back to the couch. "What's wrong with her?"

"She's hurt. Will you help?"

Daniel nodded.

"Good. I'm going to phone the police. You go upstairs. Find some blankets. As many as you can carry. And some of her clothes. And bring them to us. We're going to get her out of here."

four

Ellie curled into Myrtle's mohair velvet chair and stared into the distant night beyond the window. The fields looked overexposed, white on black. Eric and Danny were still out there searching for the damn tree. They should have been home hours ago. Neither one would answer their phone. She tucked her knees to her chest and buried her toes under her housecoat, which was so worn now, she'd be hard-pressed to describe its colour. Muddy grey, perhaps. Like her thoughts.

This Christmas she'd promised herself she would be different, less broken, yet here she was making an unforgivable mess of it. She'd given herself countless deadlines over the years—by spring you will be done, by summer you will have forgotten, by fall you will have moved on. There were days, weeks, when she felt almost normal, like there was a chance she could be a good wife and mother again. Then Christmas came along. It's as though it pulled a trigger that caused her to careen backward, leaving her chest so clamped in pain she thought she was having a heart attack. She wouldn't blame Eric and Danny if they simply kept on driving and never came back.

She listened for the crunch of tires on the driveway, or the sounds of thudding down the hall. But Walter had been blessedly quiet this evening, and Sammy had gone down at 8:15 like always. Each night was the same. She would enter his small bedroom and close the heavy curtains, turn on the air filter with its reliable hum, turn down the plain brown bed covers that were neither scratchy nor fuzzy. Then together they would work through the steps on the bedtime chart over his dresser—put on pajamas, eat cheese string, use toilet, wash hands, brush teeth, drink water, read book, hug mother, go to bed, go to sleep. She would sit beside Sammy on the bed, careful not to touch him or his pillow, and read the now dog-eared book *Are You My Mother?* She turned the pages, the words blurring in front of her. Sammy should have long since outgrown the story—he was happy to thumb through a stack of library books when he got home from kindergarten every afternoon—but he wouldn't have any other at bedtime. He liked the repetition, *Are you my mother? Are you my mother?*, and the predictability of the baby bird's questions as he tried to find his way home. Sometimes she skipped pages, but Sammy would make her go back and stick to the script on a search she now thoroughly despised.

Don't think about them, Ellie said to herself, digging her fingernails into her thighs through the pockets of her housecoat. She felt herself sinking, collapsing in upon herself. Shifting in the chair, she tapped her forehead as hard as she could. She hated when she got like this, when she couldn't muster the strength to push them away.

Lily had been the hardest. Ellie could pinpoint the exact moment of her conception. It was their second month of trying. She was just twenty-four, madly in love with her new husband. Danny was madly in love with him too, four years old and following him moon-eyed from room to room. Once Eric and Ellie started talking about making a baby together, a baby with his genes, his Scandinavian ancestry, he tripped through his days with gusto, his excitement an insatiable, palatable living thing that filled the corners of their home. She'd never been so sure of anything. How lovely to say the words, *well, yes, we are expecting, isn't it wonderful*. She would wear maternity clothes with sayings like *made with love* to highlight her baby bump, her perfect choice. There would be no hiding this time. No teenaged tears.

Ellie felt like she'd willed Lily into being.

"You can't go to sleep now," she whispered to Eric, rolling onto his chest and resting her chin on her crossed arms. "We've just made a baby. I can feel her already."

"That would be some kind of world record. You took health class, right?" He rolled her to her side and wrapped his arm around her.

She moved Eric's hand to her stomach and held it there. "She'll look just like you, Eric. Your eyes. Your wonky baby toenail. She'll have everything that's good in you."

After unsealing the Clearblue box, with its promise of "confidence when you need it most," she took her first pregnancy test in the early morning on the day that her period should have come. Her pee collected in the blue china cup, she dipped the stick like she was stirring a cup of cocoa. Within three minutes, it confirmed what she already knew.

Eric had left for work just moments earlier, so she called him on his cell phone. When he picked up, he said, "What did I forget?"

"You forgot to say goodbye to your baby."

"Ellie?"

"Special delivery."

She could hear Eric's deep sucking-in of air, his fist thumping on the steering wheel, then the piercing sound of the siren.

"You're on a call? Go, we'll talk later."

She'd barely hung up, and Eric was back in the driveway, at the door, and in her arms. Danny stumbled out of bed. Not known for bursts of enthusiasm in the morning, it had taken the siren to wake him. When he heard the news, he looked baffled at first, then embarrassed. *I guess that would be all right,* he said. He would give the baby Mr. Chuckles but not blue bear. He asked if he could tell his grandma. Eric thought it too early, but Ellie said you go right ahead. When Grandma Myrtle got on the phone, she yelled, *Don't tell me that, don't tell me that,* and then she slammed down the phone on the counter and bellowed for Walter to come hear this. Before the day was done, between grocery runs and a trip to the dentist with Danny, Ellie told everyone she knew and many she didn't.

It was a daughter she carried, her name Lily for the flower. Ellie knew this from the first moment, not a mother's wishful thinking but a deep and mysterious knowing.

The family expansion planning encompassed all three. Eric and Danny spent hours in the basement with the Rolling Stones blaring. They banged and sawed and sanded. Their first project was a child's step stool, simple butt joints reinforced with screws. From there, they built a kitchen set: a small table and two chairs.

"She'll need a crib first, Eric. Before she can invite you to tea."

"A high-up bed with a ladder," Danny suggested.

Ellie bought baby magazines and parenting books by the dozen and kept them on the night table beside the bed. She took her prenatal vitamins religiously and stopped drinking coffee. She felt remarkably strong, with little of the nausea or headaches she remembered with Danny.

The end started at twelve weeks, six days, with a small smear of brown. It was the Friday before Christmas. Ellie ignored it. She'd read about just such a thing in her baby books. Her breasts felt so un-tender and un-swollen that she opted for an underwire bra she'd been avoiding for weeks. With happy energy, she raced through her chores before heading to the ultrasound appointment. "It's your drill training day, Eric. You've got a lifetime of listening to her heartbeat. You can come to the next one."

But the technician, who was very quiet, could not find the heartbeat. And neither could the obstetrician.

"No. You're wrong. I'm fine. She's fine. We're fine."

"You'll have to go to the hospital now. It's best to get this over with."

Ellie covered her betraying body and fled the clinic. She drove in the opposite direction of the hospital, not knowing how she got home without cracking up her car. When Eric found her in their bedroom, he knew something was wrong. He drove Danny to his friend's house to spend the night and then cobbled together a dinner of soft foods that could be easily chewed, as if that would make it easier. Ellie sat at the table and played with the food on her plate. She didn't take a bite.

"Why didn't you call me? I would have come. Was it horrible?"

"Was it? Like it's over."

"The procedure, I mean."

"Procedure? I just left, Eric."

"But the baby? What's happened with the baby?"

"I won't have them sucking her out of me, tearing her to pieces."

Eric took the phone into the bedroom and closed the door. He had remarkable tenacity and didn't stop trying until he reached the doctor. When he came out of the room, his skin was the colour of child's glue.

"Ellie. We have to go to the hospital. I've talked to the doctor. You need a D&C. You can't do this alone."

But she did do it alone. She carried the dead body inside her for four days. There was brown blood at first, then black. By Monday night, she felt wet and sticky, something running out of her, contractions coming in waves. She left Eric sleeping fitfully and padded down the hall, dragging an old sheet from the closet and into the bathroom, where she ran herself a bath. She hauled scissors from the drawer, fingers shaking, and spread the sheet across the cramped floor space, covering everything. Then she sank down in the tub and waited. Not knowing what else to do, she reached under the red water, and pulled out the tiny sac, connected to the tiny chord, her baby floating inside. She stabbed with the scissors, the sac as strong as plastic, until it tore open. Her baby was beautiful. Translucent. Arms reaching straight ahead, legs curled under, ribs showing. She had a faultless little head, bumps for ears, a line for a mouth, and huge eyes. She was smaller than a calling card, a perfect fit for Ellie's palm.

Ellie dizzily stood and reached over to the soap dish on top of the counter, and rested her daughter in it. Then she got back into the tub and carried on.

The afterbirth came eventually, an ugly horrid thing. Ellie dumped it into the garbage can. She waited until the cramps subsided, then got out of the tub and stood on the sheet, dripping blood. She scooped out the clots, like saskatoon berries in a sink of water, slipping and sliding from her open palm. She drained the water, a river of red, and ran cold from the shower to get rid of the rest. A sound behind her made her jump, and when she turned, Eric was standing in the bathroom doorway. She couldn't shield him from the mess in the garbage can, so she reached for the soap dish, her daughter resting inside, and passed it to her husband. Their baby was already starting to shrivel, not as perfect as she was just a moment ago.

"Our daughter," Ellie said, her voice hoarse as she choked on the words.

"You're shaking."

"Lily."

"Ellie, let's not do this now. You need a doctor."

"Please. Don't call anyone. This is our family."

Eric wrapped a towel around her and helped her to bed. She couldn't remember what happened after that. When she got up the next morning, the bathroom was clear. The garbage had been removed. There was no sign of the sheet.

Eric brought her breakfast on the wooden tray. Toast and jam and a pot of tea with honey. He'd placed their daughter in his treasured wooden box, the one he'd carved himself with geometric designs along the sides. Sometime in the night, he'd gouged six petals on the lid, a long-necked lily.

"I wrapped her in a washcloth," he said.

"I want to see her."

"No, Ellie, you don't." He held the box away from her. "She's gone now."

But Ellie tore the box from his hands and opened the lid, peering in at the blistered body, her daughter a fraction of the size she was. She would blow away like dust if you breathed on her.

Christmas morning came and went, a sorry affair. They both tried for Danny's sake, feigning interest in the new train set and floor puzzle that Santa brought. As the day wore on, Eric drank too much and then ordered Chinese while she lay on the couch and watched Danny bounce on the floor between them.

It took five more days before she had the strength to bury her daughter. Still weak, pressed down, sick of looking at blood, she and Eric went to the hill beneath the mountain. It had been an unusually mild winter, the ground still pliable. They dug the hole beside the tree where Eric had carved their initials.

Now she heard a noise beyond the window. They were back? She tried to stand, panicky in that dark place, but her legs collapsed and she fell back into Myrtle's chair.

No. It was not her husband and son, just a tendril of ice from the eavestrough, crashing to the ground.

———

His dad put the girl in the front seat for the drive to the Neesley hospital; she was wrapped in blankets from head to toe. Her dead cat was in the car trunk. She wouldn't leave without it, so his dad had said, all right, all right, calm down. He went back into the house and came out again a few minutes later with the cat wrapped in a towel.

Daniel sat in the back beside a green garbage bag stuffed with the girl's clothes: jeans, t-shirts, sweaters, underwear—whatever he could find as he was fumbling through her drawers. He'd never touched a girl's clothing except Melissa's, and only once, her tight sweater with buttons small as red-hot cinnamon hearts, her speckled bra with its lace straps and wire bottom and complicated back hook.

He wanted to ask questions as they raced across the snow and ice. What had happened? What would happen? But when the girl stayed quiet, he did too. He let himself sink down and feel like a child, lulled by his father's soft assurances telling them to hold on, they were almost there, everything would be all right. The words were meant for the girl, but he clung to them anyway.

When they got to the hospital, his dad carried the girl past the nurses' station, his footsteps slapping against linoleum. Daniel wasn't allowed to go behind the maze of curtains, so he sat alone in the emergency waiting room. There were just six chairs in two rows of three, facing each other, as if this town could not imagine a bigger crisis.

His dad came back out once, stopping first at the vending machine down the hall and choosing a can of Coke; he passed it to Daniel as he sat down beside him.

"You okay here?"

He nodded, afraid to look his father in the eye.

"Dan?"

"Yeah. I'm good."

His father dug into his pocket and pulled out a fist of change. "Take it." Daniel opened his palm. "There's chips down there too. Doritos."

"What about Mom?"

"I'll call her."

"How much longer?"

"Not sure. She's in X-rays now. Hang tight, okay?"

"Dad?"

"Yeah?" He'd stood by this point, about to leave.

"What's her name?"

Her name was Hannah. She tried to run away. His dad found her on the road that very afternoon. She got put back and then got taken out again, like milk from the fridge.

After the Coke, his dad disappeared. Daniel could hear the hurt down the hall behind the closed curtains. There was a guy moaning, a woman yelling for something for the goddamned pain, and a baby's endless crying. Fits of coughing and barfing. He imagined sawing noises and a leg coming off. He listened for his dad's voice or the girl's, but they'd disappeared.

His phone sat in his pocket like an empty wallet. He was used to checking in every few minutes, but there were *no cell phone* signs everywhere, and tonight of all nights, he was paranoid about rules and consequences, so he'd turned it off. Oddly, it was his mom's voice he needed to hear. He thought he'd long since grown out of needing her to comfort him.

The smell in that tight room soon became unbearable, his sweat mixing in with that hospital stink rising up off the white-grey walls, same as the equipment room at school only sourer and more antiseptic. He stood, his legs soupy from sitting so long, and wandered out into the hall. The nurse standing behind the main desk looked up from her charts, not bothering to smile, and then returned to her scribbling as if she couldn't see him, so he turned the other way and stomped past the vending machines, past the glass boxes displaying crocheted doll clothes and wooden bird feeders. As he rounded the corner, he crashed straight into a round woman. Her large breasts collided with his rib cage, her clipboard pinging to the floor, papers scattering everywhere.

"Whoa," she yelped.

"Sorry. God. Sorry." He got on his knees to collect the stray papers, postponing the point where he'd need to look her in the eye. She laughed a deep booming laugh. He recognized the sound of it. He looked up to see her adjusting her ruffled self, hands heaving her breasts like bowling balls. That too he'd seen before, a sight he'd found hard to forget.

"My fault," she announced, seemingly satisfied that her lady parts were back where they should be. "I have this ridiculous habit of walking with my head down. Let me just—"

He was still down on the floor. She eyed him closely as he passed up the papers. "Land sakes. Daniel? Daniel Nyland?"

"Yes, ma'am."

She grabbed his arm and yanked him to his feet. "Well, you've grown a mile. Why, you're a strapping young man. Handsome to boot. It's Betty. From Child and Family Services. Not that that's relevant. It's just what I say, I don't know why. I suppose if I worked for the post office, I'd say it's Betty from the post office."

"Hi, Mrs. Holt."

"So you remember. And so polite. Call me Betty. My mother-in-law is the only Mrs. Holt in this town and, Lord knows, you don't want her involved."

She was his dad's school friend. She used to stop by his grandparents' house every Christmas when he was a kid, a walking decoration:

dangly, flashing light-bulb earrings, a red sweater with a huge yellow bow covering her chest. Every time she broke into laughter, jiggling and stomping, Thorn started to howl. She even got his grandpa to slap his knee and laugh out loud.

"Sorry I crashed into you, Mrs. Holt."

"Betty. I'm in at least two crashes a day." She patted her papers into a neat stack and jammed them under the clip, then looked up at him and smiled. "It's been ages. And look what I've missed. You turn around and the future is here."

He only then made the connection. She was here because of the girl.

"Did Dad call?" Did he tell her he almost killed a guy?

She nodded. "You've had quite a night. Nasty business. How's she doing?"

"I don't know. I don't even know where they are."

She laughed again, the boom echoing through the hallway. "Well, this is Neesley. Not even a mouse can hide around here." And with that, she hauled him by his coat sleeve and marched them down the hall.

When they got to the desk, the nurse on duty looked up and sighed. She ignored him and leaned across the desk, rested her chin on her arm, and whispered to Mrs. Holt, "Will this night never end?"

"Marlene. You look like death eating a cracker. That bad?"

"Christmas. It brings in the crazies. We're jammed full. Not one extra bed."

"Jesus had the same problem his first Christmas. So where is she?"

"She's down in—"

In unison, the three turned toward the hall. A cart, wheels squealing, had exploded from a set of giant doors, pushed by a dopey-looking guy in a green smock, Daniel's dad right behind.

The nurse swivelled on her heels to the whiteboard behind her, checking the box beside Hannah Finch's name. "You timed that right. That's her."

He snuck a peek at the girl before Dopey whisked her behind the first curtain. She seemed so small and flat under the hospital blanket.

His father strode toward them. He looked dog-tired, shoulders slumped, much older than he had at their supper table. "Betty. Thank you." He squeezed her hands and she squeezed back. Daniel rocked on his heels, uncomfortable. It felt like there were a million little things he hadn't noticed about his dad before.

"I haven't done anything yet," she said. "Good to see your instincts still work. You were right to go back."

"You remember Dan?"

"Sure I do. Glad to bump into him." She winked at Daniel, who couldn't help smiling.

"Anything broken?" she asked his dad.

"The X-rays were clean. Or at least nothing recent. Swelling and bruising. Some nasty welts. Dan, sorry, just a bit longer. I need to talk to Betty about a couple of things."

And off they went to the waiting room. The nurse at the desk ignored him as he stood in the open area, her head buried in paperwork, so he tiptoed toward the girl's curtain.

She was on her side, facing away from him, her skinny arm cradling her head, the rest of her covered with the blanket. His fingers jangled the curtain, which made a terrible screeching noise. She turned and stared right at him.

"Hi," she said.

"Hi." He jammed his hand into his pockets and fingered the change he found there. "Do you want a Coke?"

"I'd rather have an Orange Crush." Her voice was surprisingly strong considering what she'd been through. There were enormous dark circles under both eyes.

"I don't think the machine has Orange Crush. But I can check." He started to back away.

"No, it's okay. I'm not really thirsty."

"There's chips. Barbecue. Salt and vinegar." He'd never been this close to someone beaten up like this.

"You were at my house. You live across the road."

"I was supposed to wait in the car."

"But you didn't." She was sitting upright now, eyes wide, squeezing her pillow to her chest. "Are you going to get in trouble?"

Daniel couldn't even imagine her kind of trouble. "I banged up my grandpa's truck. I'm kinda already in trouble."

"Oh." She stared at him with concentration, then her shoulders relaxed and she sank back down on her bed. "You don't look banged up."

His accident seemed petty now, and he was embarrassed he'd mentioned it. "How come I've never seen you before? You live right across from us."

"I've seen you driving up and down the road with your dad."

Practice runs, after he got his learner's permit. They should have gone to the same school, taken the same bus. "Where do you go to school?"

"I'm home-schooled," she said, scrunching her nose like it left a bad smell. "Is he taking me back there?"

"Who?" As if he had answers.

"Your dad?"

"He's not my real dad." Why did he tell her that? Eric was the only father he'd ever known. He felt ashamed: was he trying to compete with her for the worst story? He needed a wall to press against. He felt exposed, clutching the folds of the flimsy curtain. "I'll ask him."

As he turned to leave, she called out his name. He couldn't remember even telling it to her.

"Yeah?" he said.

"Nigel Wilson. He's not my real dad either." Then she looked away, pulling the green sheet up to her chin.

Daniel crossed the hall and sank into a waiting-room chair across from his dad and Mrs. Holt sitting against the opposite wall. They were leaning into each other, her lap piled with paper, whispering in hushed tones, when an RCMP guy clipped down the hallway and stopped in front of them.

"Good, you're here," Mrs. Holt said, looking up.

The constable looked too young to shave and too skinny to bring down a bad guy. His dad and Mrs. Holt stood, while Daniel stayed put.

"Constable Bradley King, this is Eric Nyland and over there is his son, Daniel."

"It's an honour to meet you, Sergeant Nyland." The constable shook his dad's hand enthusiastically. "Rolly Adams worked for you up in Griffins. He's a friend of mine."

"Adams is a good man. Just Nyland will do. Not Sergeant," though his dad seemed like he was the one in charge.

"Let's get this mess sorted, shall we," Mrs. Holt said. "You'll need statements, Bradley? We can use the consultation room." And off they went.

They were gone awhile, which gave Daniel plenty of time to think about how his dad had almost killed that guy. He had no point of reference for this. From what he remembered of his dad's cop days, he dealt with fender benders and neighbour disputes and stumbled over rehearsed lines at the front of the school assembly. Now he drove around the gas plant, searching for holes along the fence line. He was the guy who walked in their front door, dropped his keys somewhere inconvenient, and then melted into the backdrop of their family's mess. He was a lot better than some dads, certainly better than Max's, who had a beer gut like Santa with none of the jolly. Daniel wasn't ashamed of his father; he'd simply looked at him so little since they'd moved to Neesley so as to not see him at all.

He replayed his father's actions. The way he held onto the girl. The way his body sprang forward like a lynx. The deep growling from his throat as his fist smashed down. And later, the exactness with which he checked the guy's breathing, rolled him onto his side, and supported his neck. He didn't recognize his father's voice when he phoned 9-1-1, relaying precise details, coordinates, instructions. Or how he drove fast like that, so oblivious to the winter around them, under them, as if he'd spent a lifetime racing down those same tracks.

After an impossibly long time, his dad came back alone to the waiting room and sat in the chair beside him.

"They're talking to Hannah now," he said. "We can go home soon."

"Are you in trouble?"

"No." He leaned forward, elbows on knees, and stared at the floor. "Maybe. It depends on Wilson. He has to give a statement. He's sobering up at the detachment."

The RCMP station in Neesley was just a hole in the wall. Daniel had thought he might get sent there, after his accident, but a constable, an older guy, had come to their house instead. "Is there a jail at the station?"

"There is. Just a couple of cells."

Hannah had asked Daniel if she was going to be sent back. Of course they wouldn't send her back; that would be the world's dumbest idea. "What's going to happen to her?" he asked his dad.

"It's up to Betty and Hannah. They're talking right now. Hannah has to tell Betty and Constable King what happened, before a decision can be made."

Daniel's ears burned. "We know what happened. He hit her. Probably a bunch of times. We were there."

"But we didn't see it. Hannah has to tell. Assumptions aren't good enough."

Adults always missed the obvious. "That's totally stupid. That's why there are so many criminals on the loose."

His dad looked at him and smiled. "At the risk of repeating myself, you watch too much TV, Dan."

"So when she tells them, where will she go?"

He sighed and closed his eyes. "Betty will find something, a foster home, group placement. I don't know, Dan."

His dad stayed slumped forward, flexing the fingers of his right hand, his knuckles swollen and bruised. Daniel wondered why they didn't just go home; it was almost midnight, his mom would be hysterical. But he didn't want to leave and miss what came next. They stayed quiet and waited. When Mrs. Holt came back, his dad stood.

"All sorted then?" he asked.

"Constable King is still with her." Then she lowered her voice, speaking directly into his dad's ear. "Bradley hasn't had much experience with kids."

"I guess we can head out then," his dad said, reaching for his coat on the chair.

Mrs. Holt tilted her head down and stared through the top of her glasses. "There's been a wrinkle," she said.

His dad turned toward her. "Hannah wouldn't make the disclosure?"

She shook her head. "Oh no. Hannah's spilled the whole gruesome story." Mrs. Holt just stood there, lips pressed together as she looked at his dad. Finally, she said, "She's asked to go home with you."

His dad stood stock-still, one arm sticking out, clutching his coat.

"You mean to live with us?" Daniel stood up, unable to keep still.

They glanced over at him, and Mrs. Holt said, "Not live with you, Daniel. Just a few days."

A girl in his house? He couldn't imagine it. "Sammy's not going to want her there. He's gonna explode."

"That's enough, Daniel." His dad turned to Mrs. Holt, red-faced. "You can't be serious. We don't even know her."

Mrs. Holt took hold of his dad's sleeve. "She seems to think you do. You are her only neighbour and she says she trusts you. There's no natural family support. None."

"What about Wilson?"

"Mr. Wilson has no parental rights. He's not her legal guardian. This is your decision, Eric. I'm talking about a few days. I can probably have a foster lined up for Boxing Day. You're off the force so I don't see any conflict here."

"But it's Christmas, Betty," his dad was saying now.

"Exactly my point. I'll check in every day and—"

"Ellie's not herself. It's Christmas."

"Give Ellie some credit. Call her and ask."

His dad shook his head. "You can't just send a child anywhere. You of all people know that."

"Hannah has a say in this. Her statement goes a long way. I've known you, your family, for years."

"You knew me before it got so complicated. Things have changed."

"Not the important bits. But this is your decision. Yours and Ellie's."

Mrs. Holt stared at his dad, who rubbed his temple. They waited for the longest time.

"Dad?"

He put on his coat and announced wearily, "I'll go call Ellie."

Mrs. Holt nodded. "You can use the desk phone, Eric."

"I need some air," his dad said, walking away. "Dan, wait here. This won't take long."

Mrs. Holt beamed. "So that's it then, I'll call my supervisor." She sure seemed confident his mom would say yes. Daniel was doubtful, but what did he know?

———

So many scenarios had come to mind as Ellie twisted in the mohair of Myrtle's beloved chair. But it was nothing she could prepare for. Eric called at half past twelve. She raced to the phone, batting away her feeble inventions about what had kept him so long, ready to forgive whatever had caused the delay. She caught it before the second ring, planning to tell Eric that it was all right, whatever it was. She just wanted him home, to bring her boy home. She didn't want more.

"El," his voice weary and faraway when he said her name. She'd done this to him. She'd made such a childish fuss about his hacking down a tree. He'd failed, obviously. She didn't care; it was not important. She would have told him this, but he didn't give her space.

"There's been a situation," he started slowly, then steamrolled through. "A young girl in trouble. She's eleven. She's been living across the road, at Wilson's place—but she can't stay there. Dan and I checked on her this evening and things were not good. I'd like her to stay with us for a few days until a foster can be worked out. Can we do that?"

What was he saying? She couldn't make sense of it, something about a girl and bringing her home. Here. She couldn't untangle the particulars or think where to begin, like how he'd come to be in her house, or why her son was involved, or why such decisions had to come down to her. When she could think of nothing to say, Eric started over, repeating the rundown, adding more.

"Hannah has been living across the road, at Wilson's place."

That couldn't be true. "There's no girl across the road! The school bus stops right there. We've never seen a girl."

"She's been in that house and she can't stay with him. He's a drunk. Dan and I checked on her this evening. We're at the hospital. She's pretty beat up. He'd locked her in the cellar for God sakes. Killed her cat. She has no other place."

"Danny?" Ellie clapped her hand over her mouth. A cellar. Dead cat. "You took Danny with you? Into that house?"

"Danny's fine. He's fine," he said too quickly to provide any reassurance.

"How could you involve him in something like this, Eric?" She paced the length of the living room, the phone to her ear. When he didn't say anything, she asked again, "How could you?" An edge of hysteria in her voice that she tried to swallow.

"I know" was what he said.

"Where is the girl's mother?" What kind of a woman would let this happen to her child?

"She's dead, Ellie."

As if that was an excuse. She'd left her child in this man's safe-keeping. It always came back to the mother, from either side of the grave.

"You can't bring her here." A hundred obstacles flashed in front of her; she could barely hang on to what she already had. "I can't do this, Eric. It's Christmas. Sammy needs stability, not a stranger in his house."

"Sammy will be fine," he said. He'd used these same flat words with her so many times.

"He's the worst he's ever been." She took a deep breath, exhaling into the phone. "I'm sorry for the girl, I really am, but this is not what she needs. And it's certainly not what Sammy needs. I can't do this."

Eric stayed silent for so long she wondered if he'd hung up. But she could hear the howling wind through the phone line, a car revving in the distance.

When Eric finally cut in, he spoke methodically, like he was addressing one of his less capable constables. "You're overreacting, Ellie. You're perfectly able to do this. We all are. We have a good home. We can provide a safe place for the short term."

She stepped to the window and stared into the blackness.

"Betty and I think it's the best alternative."

Ellie flushed. Betty Holt? Eric's old confidante. His childhood girlfriend. The one Myrtle admired. Of course, she was involved. Betty, the wonder worker, deconstructing families, passing around children like Christmas candy. "So you and Betty worked it out then."

Eric sighed. "It's not like that."

"You make it sound like it's been decided."

"I'm calling you, aren't I?" He'd tipped, no longer able to hide his frustration. "I need you to be with me on this, El. Just a few days. Just until Christmas is over and we can get her into a foster home."

"You and Betty?"

She did not need Betty as the yardstick to which she couldn't measure up. When Eric didn't respond, she hung up the phone.

———

Eric stood outside the hospital, staring at the phone gripped in his frozen fist. The wind whipped tufts of loose snow across the parking lot and between the cars lined up like little glaciers.

You took Danny with you? You want to bring her here? You and Betty? That was all he remembered of her side of that impossible conversation. She'd never before hung up on him. This anger felt different, as though he was standing at a precipice and one wrong step could start a fall that he couldn't climb back from.

Daniel chose right then to come tumbling out of the emergency door exit.

"I thought I told you to wait inside," Eric said.

"I needed some air," Daniel said, fighting with his jacket zipper. "What did she say?"

"We got cut off. It's bad reception out here."

Daniel stomped his feet. "So call back!"

"I'm giving it a minute. Go inside. It's too cold."

Daniel stuffed his hands in his pockets. "Mom said no, didn't she? It's 'cause of Sammy, right? She thinks he'll go nuts."

Eric chose not to answer.

Daniel lifted one foot then the other, like he was warming up for a race. "I thought so too, but maybe he won't. And she babies him too much. Sammy's not a baby anymore."

"We know he's not a baby." Ellie's feelings for Sammy were too layered to explain. God knows, tonight was not the night. "Go back inside. Let me work this out, Dan."

"Sammy might like Hannah. She seems okay. She seems nice." Daniel stopped his fidgeting and looked right at Eric. "And she has nowhere else to go, Dad."

She'd felt so small when he carried her out of that goddamned cellar. "So you'd be okay if she came home with us?"

"Well, yeah, I guess," he said tentatively, as if surprised to be asked. Then he added with conviction, "It's the right thing."

Eric stared at his son, whose view of life still boiled down to comic-book heroes and villains. He wished it would always be this simple for Dan: right versus wrong.

Ellie's ringtone went off in his hand, the sound so jarring that Eric nearly dropped the phone. It took three rings and Daniel's yelling *answer it, answer it* before he could get the phone to his ear.

"Ellie?"

———

"Well, bring the girl home then," she said to him. "And bring my son home too." After she hung up the phone for the second time, she took a great gulp of air. Where to put the girl?

Myrtle's craft room, the one beside Sammy's and across from Walter's. She'd kept that door shut since they'd moved here, unable to face its dizzying array of sparkles and spangles and other crap.

She pushed open the door now and took it in. Here was the place where Myrtle whipped up a sense of wonder to dazzle her adoring family. How could she possibly make it decent?

Working quickly, she stacked piles of boxes under Myrtle's wooden tabletop, shoved the dress form into the closet, dragged the quilting frame over to the corner, and dusted every surface with a wet rag. There was a single bed with metal legs along the far wall. A much smaller Danny used to fall into it after long summer days running behind his grandma. The bed was barely visible now under mounds of needles and wool balls and swatches of fabric. Ellie swept the works into green garbage bags, stripped the bed to its rubber mattress cover, and layered it up again with fresh sheets and blankets. She tiptoed into Walter's room, ignoring the gagging noises he made in his sleep, and seized the wooden folding table crammed behind his bureau. She set up the table beside the single bed and brought down the green glass lamp from the top shelf of the hall closet. Then she rooted through Eric's mismatch of tools in the basement until she found an extension cord that would reach the wall socket. On her knees, stretching her arm to plug in the cord behind the bed, she found a discarded stuffie of Danny's, Gracie the hippo with her ripped pink tongue. Ellie patted away the dust and placed Gracie on the girl's pillow. But then she changed her mind, snatched up the hippo, and shoved it deep into the garbage bag, likely impaling it with a crochet hook.

five

"Of course she said yes," Betty said when he and Daniel got back to the waiting room.

"Ellie's a compassionate woman." Betty pressed a clipboard onto his lap and a Santa pen into his fist. "Sign here and here and here."

That was all it took to bring the girl home. Eric drove slowly, cutting through drifts like a plough horse, both kids slumped in the back seat. He kept his eyes on the road, black ice the least of his worries.

It was the middle of the night, and he was dead tired himself, more tired than he'd ever been. He could be charged for what he'd done to Wilson, who was passed out in one of the four cells at the station. He hoped he could shape the words to help Ellie understand. How he had

72

to get the girl out of that house. How a person only got one or two chances in his whole life to get something like that right.

Eric could hear Daniel squirming behind him. He felt proud of his boy, and this caught him off guard, bringing a tightness to his chest. Tonight, as Eric had pulled the car in front of the hospital's sliding doors to take Hannah home, he'd watched Daniel extend his hand to Betty before she crushed him to her chest. He'd watched his son take Hannah's arm too, shielding her from the wind, guiding her to the car. He'd failed to notice before tonight that his boy was becoming a man.

———

Daniel snuck glances at the girl without turning his head toward her. She was wearing the jeans and sweater he'd hauled out of her drawer and was wrapped in the butterfly blanket he'd pulled from her bed. Daniel thought she might be sleeping, but then her hand reached up from under the wool and rubbed at her eyes.

"We're going to chop down a tree tomorrow," Daniel said, the best he could come up with. "Mr. Hodgins owns a whole forest. He lets us pick any tree we want. We were supposed to go out there tonight, but . . ."

After a pause, Hannah finished for him. "But you got me instead."

"You're safe now," his dad said, looking at the girl in his rear-view mirror. "We passed the town limits quite a ways back. We'll be home before you know it."

Hannah looked right at Daniel then. "Why would you do that?"

Daniel stared at the back of his dad's head, hesitating. "You mean come to get you?"

She shook her head, furrowing her brow. "Chop down a tree."

He exhaled, not even realizing he'd been holding his breath. He almost laughed then, but stopped himself in time. "For Christmas. You know, like the Charlie Brown Christmas tree."

"What day is it?" she asked.

"Friday. No. Saturday. December 21." Daniel held his breath again. He'd done nothing but whine since his accident. He'd gone on and on about the unfairness of his life, about how his grandpa was crackers, how his mom wanted a damn tree, how this damn cold made everything unbearable. And here was this girl who had nothing. She didn't even know what day it was.

They were pulling into the driveway with its layers of new snow. His mom had turned on the porch light, its beam scattering crystals across the road. The house was lit up too, every light, like there was a party going on. His dad cut the engine, and for a moment, the three sat motionless in the car, all eyes focused on the silhouette in the light waiting for them behind the windows.

"We're here," his dad said at last. Then it was unbuckling and doors opening and the tensing of bodies against the cold. Without being asked, Daniel picked up Hannah's bag of belongings from the back seat of the car, and the three trudged single file, Hannah in the middle, toward the light.

———

Ellie stood in bare feet at the screen door as the car pulled into the driveway. Thorn sat beside her, tail thumping the linoleum. When she saw her husband and son and the girl step out of the car, she instinctively backed up. She tried to push Thorn away too, but he wouldn't budge. She would make room out of kindness, so they could enter unfettered and strip out of their coats without falling over each other. But it was the voice from the shiny pamphlet that said that, the one she wished was hers. Beneath, something more true and hateful rose from within her. *I don't want her here. I want her gone.* When the car doors slammed, she had backed all the way to the open kitchen. She stood at the sink in the island, which gave her a clear view of the front door. Picking up a soggy dishrag, she chased it along the countertop. It all still felt dirty, so she threw the rag down and leaned against the sink, fingers pressed against the cold porcelain edges, as if she were waiting to be sick.

She called Thorn over to her, softly, so as not to wake Sammy, but it was no good. The dog stayed at his post at the door. The three entered, the girl wrapped in a tattered butterfly quilt, Daniel and Eric stamping boots, throwing off hats, and ripping open rows of snaps down their bulky jackets. Ellie paid close attention to her son, hunting for signs of damage cropping up like pimples round his boyish heart. But he looked much the same as he had during dinner, if not more peppy and keen.

Thorn circled their feet and drew his big dopey face up one side of the girl's blanket and down the other, sniffing. The girl stood still as a stick for the assault, then poked a small hand out from beneath her blanket, which Thorn licked vigorously.

Ellie should have said something, or at least called off the dog. She should have marched over to the girl and extended her hand. But she was rooted to the kitchen sink, unable to move.

———

Eric, now in sock feet, glanced at his wife and found a look he understood immediately. *How could you bring her here?* If it were simply raw anger staring back at him, he could come up with a plan. He would tell his wife he was sorry—sorry for it all—ride it out beside her, and move forward. But her anger was her outer shell, as fragile and as sturdy as a stubborn egg waiting to be whomped against hard glass.

Beneath Ellie's sulky and sharp-tongued surges, there were layers upon layers he could no longer reach. He used to uncover his own feelings by reflecting back hers. Now he wished he could crawl under her skin to find her again. And he wished she could do the same, even just on this one night, so she could see the tragedy unfolding from inside his head.

I didn't have a choice, he wanted to tell her. Instead, he stated the obvious. "Ellie, this is Hannah." A part of him was relieved to hand her over.

———

Ellie studied the girl, who was too small for the magnitude of the story that Eric had twice doled out on the phone. She had enormous eyes, unblinking, staring right back at her. It was clear she expected Ellie to do something. They all did, standing frozen in the front entrance, waiting.

"Hello, Hannah," she said, her voice harsh in the silent room. "Come in, please. It's cold by the door."

"Where should I put my runners, Mrs. Nyland?"

Ellie wanted to scream. There would be a thousand questions she would be expected to answer. Eric turned and fumbled with the bifold closet door behind him, the heap of jackets and boots jamming it from opening.

"You can just leave your runners right there on the floor," Ellie said, noticing one had no shoelace. "We'll take care of this mess later."

"We didn't get the tree," Danny piped up. He marched past Ellie, grabbed hold of the fridge door, and yanked it hard. Her son looked wired, like he was ready to run a lap around the furniture. Her husband pushed and pulled, kicking boots out of the way. "Eric, just leave the closet door. Please."

The girl crouched to undo her one lace, while Thorn stretched his giant paws over her runners in case she tried to escape. Eric stood beside her, as if his socks were glued to the spot on the floor.

"Do we have any Orange Crush?" Danny called out from behind the fridge door.

Eric looked at Ellie, confused. Their boy had never asked for Orange Crush in his life.

"There's chocolate milk. And chicken," Ellie said, but Danny had already found it. He brought the milk carton and a stack of Tupperware over to the counter, slamming doors and drawers as he got out a plate and fork.

"Want a snack?" he yelled to Hannah.

"Danny, please," Ellie said. "You'll wake Sammy."

What would this do to Sammy? This girl in the house, swaying slightly, runners sitting side by side on the worn hardwood beside her, blanket folded in her arms. Ellie examined her from top to bottom. She might be called pretty, even though she lacked the usual markers. Her long hair was a snarled mess. She looked unkempt and underfed and disconcertingly pale and shadowed. Yet there was a brightness too in that unwavering gaze. She seemed out of sync: too travelled for her small body, too composed given what she'd been through.

Ellie said, "Are you hungry, Hannah? We can make you a sandwich."

The girl shook her head and, as if forcing out the words, said, "No, thank you, Mrs. Nyland."

"You can call me Ellie. Ellie would be fine."

Hannah winced a little, shifting the weight of the quilt from one arm to the other. Ellie still clutched the side of the sink. Bad things had happened to this girl; she was obviously hurt and hurting. Ellie pushed herself forward until she stood in front of her, looking down on glassy eyes, inhaling her dusty drawer smell and a faint trace of urine. One cheek was raised, slightly purple under the hallway light.

"Let me take this." Ellie reached for the quilt, which was surprisingly heavy. The girl's arms dropped to her sides like stones. "Would you like to see your room?"

Hannah looked up. "I have a room?"

Ellie tried to sound light. "Well, of course. Did you think we'd put you in the barn?" She refused to look over to her husband, regretting her words instantly. What else might this girl think? She'd already been put in a cellar.

"What room?" Danny wanted to know. Ellie glanced back at her son. He was ripping into a drumstick without a care in the world. Of course, it would only occur to him now to ask where she would sleep. It likely hadn't occurred to Eric at all. Beds magically made themselves and tables expanded on their own.

"Where's she gonna sleep, Mom?" Danny asked again, his mouth crammed with chicken.

"In the craft room," Ellie said.

"But you said—"

"I've made up the bed," Ellie cut in. Yes, she'd told her children they weren't to go in that room down the hallway, but the ban was meant to be temporary. She had plans. She'd make the room her own, every bit as special as Myrtle's had once been: a hive of activity; a source of pretty projects for home and hearth; a testament to the magnanimousness of motherhood. She only needed to fix herself first.

"That's cool," Danny said between great gulps of chocolate milk, to no one in particular. "Wicked room. Grandma and me used to dress Heidi like a soldier. We made a sword with a yardstick, whittled it pointy and painted it silver."

The girl looked at her boy. Ellie turned to see her son's cheeks crispy red, his body stiff. Heidi was the secret name he and Myrtle had invented for the damn dress form. The pair had secrets galore in that room. He'd embarrassed himself, Ellie knew instantly, by outing his enthusiasm for pretend swords.

"Let's go get you settled," Ellie said, more to rescue her son than the girl. "And you too, Danny. It's been a long night."

Danny pushed his brown-filmed glass down the counter toward the sink but not in it, she noted, although she'd repeatedly asked him to. He rubbed the chicken grease from his fingers on the sides of his jeans.

"Goodbye, Daniel." The girl sounded panicked.

He looked at Hannah, softly, Ellie thought, which shocked her. Not because he'd regained his composure, but because he had the wherewithal to be soft at this moment.

"I'm just going downstairs," he said. "That's where my bedroom is. Yours is up here."

"Okay," she said.

"See you in the morning."

"Okay," she said again, sounding even less sure.

Ellie reached down and grabbed the garbage bag—her things, she assumed—and then led the girl away from Eric, who hadn't said a word this whole time, just stood there at attention, like he was overseeing a disciplinary hearing. He couldn't even manage to grab hold of the dog, who had taken it upon himself to follow, his nose attached to the back of Hannah's knees.

At the end of the hallway, Ellie pushed hard at the dog's chest and whispered, "Go back, Thorn. Go lie down now." He teetered with a harrumph and fell right there at the entrance, farting as he sunk to the floor before stretching full out.

As they stepped into the room, Ellie followed Hannah's gaze as she looked first at the turned-down bed, then at the old-fashioned daisy wallpaper, then the broken pull chain of the ancient lamp, then here and there at the scramble of colours and bits of nonsense poking out in every direction. Ellie wished she could have opened the window a crack, if only for a minute, to let in a blast of new air. But it had been frozen shut since November, like every other damn window in the house.

Ellie hadn't a clue what Hannah felt about this unbearable room, this unbearable situation. But then how could Ellie expect to, she of all people, when time after time she had been judged unfit to bring a girl into her world. She dropped the bag to the floor, cleared her throat, and said matter-of-factly, "So this is your room. For tonight. Or a few nights maybe."

Hannah looked up and nodded.

"These are your things? In the bag?"

"I think so."

Eric must have stuffed the bag for her. "I'll let you sort through your things then." Ellie stepped over to Myrtle's wooden dresser and yanked on the ivory knob with a flourish. The drawer moaned in complaint, dresser legs shaking on upholstered coasters. "I've emptied a drawer for you. You can put your things in here."

"Thank you, Mrs. Nyland."

"Ellie. Just call me that."

She felt an overwhelming urge to tap her forehead. She buried her hand deep into her housecoat pocket and squeezed her fingers as hard as she could. "The bathroom's just down the hall. There's a towel and washcloth on your pillow."

"Thank you, Mrs.—Ellie."

"And we'll keep your door closed so that Thorn won't bother you. He sheds like a bear. You're not allergic, are you?"

"I don't think so. I've never had a dog. He's very nice." Ellie couldn't stand another second in that too-close room. Hannah hadn't moved an inch since she entered, as if by standing still she'd take up the least space possible. There was much more Ellie should have said, but she felt so dried up her skin was starting to crack. She could feel it tear along the edge of her hairline, down the centre of her spine.

"Well, good night then, Hannah." She ran her tongue over her top lip, making it easier to smile. "I hope you'll be comfortable."

She might just as well shake the girl's hand for all the good she'd done, or could do, like a politician sniffing at a doorstep on the night before an election. Ellie turned and left the room, stepping over Thorn, snoring at his guard post.

But Hannah called her name, "Mrs.—Ellie," so she had to look back. *Please, God, don't let her need something more.*

"What is it, Hannah?"

The girl shifted from one socked foot to the other before blurting, "Can you thank the sergeant for me?"

The sergeant? "Yes, of course."

"I forgot to tell him thank you for coming back to get me."

"Excuse me?"

"I wanted him to come back." The girl said this weakly, like she was ready to cry. "And then he was there."

I wanted him to come back too, Ellie thought, and then he was here, except he wasn't really. Here. It was no good asking why he'd gone into that house without telling her first. No good asking how he could stand right beside her and be so far away.

"You don't need to thank him, Hannah. Neighbours should help each other. Good night now. Get some sleep."

The girl stood in a daze like a rabbit about to be shot. Ellie closed the door. Ellie too felt in a daze as she went down the hallway to turn out the bright yellow lights. Around the corner, she found Eric in Walter's chair, the ratty straight back with the sagging upholstered seat, card table in front of him, fingers moving puzzle pieces. The box showed a picture of a grain elevator beside a train track and a mauve sky with galloping white horses in a distant yellow field. It was Walter's favourite, the only puzzle he could get right. Walter fitted the pieces together each afternoon. Eric undid all but the border each night. It was a building up and tearing down as predictable, and as necessary, as the tides.

Ellie looked at her husband, undetected, for more than a minute. "The sergeant," the girl had whispered, with reverence. Ellie thought she noticed Eric's eye twitch, though she was too far away to be sure. She might have heard humming too. Eric often hummed when he felt troubled, a tuneless concoction of white noise to drown out all else. He did this, for example, after he forgot to turn off the tap at the utility sink and flooded the basement, or after his father messed his pants, or after Thorn's back leg gave out on the stairs, or after they fought over Sammy or Walter or Daniel or over no one at all. *Hmm, hmm, hmm, hmm, hmm*, up and down he see-saw sang as he padded between rooms. She held her breath and listened more closely until she could make out the faint sounds. Yes, he was doing it now.

———

Hannah couldn't remember how many times she had stood at her bedroom window and looked across the road and imagined herself running over to their house and banging on their door. But she'd never created a picture of what she might find inside. In her head, she saw the sergeant and Daniel and herself out of the cold—but not in any place specifically, nowhere that could be described. She'd asked to come here—she'd insisted to that woman in the hospital. The sergeant seemed nice, but hadn't Nigel seemed nice too in the beginning? What if the sergeant was a sick, twisted bastard like Nigel said? What if he regretted bringing her here and locked her in his basement and nobody ever came?

Hannah usually felt a burning desire to know what came next, but tonight she was a ghost of herself, too dazed to be curious. She couldn't think straight. By the time they'd pulled into the driveway and stepped out of the car, she was focused on putting one foot in front of the other and that was all.

With a rush of warm air, she was inside instead of out, and the big black dog came right up and said hello with his nose. She looked at the woman in the kitchen and everything changed. It took only a split second, a snap of a finger. There was her mother. She was at the sink, long brown hair pulled back into a ponytail, bangs falling low on her forehead. She had the same beautiful face, same milky white neck rising up from the folds of her much-loved housecoat. Same long fingers. Why wasn't she smiling?

It cracked the wind from Hannah. *Shouldn't you be in bed by now, darling? You've had a bad dream. That's all it was. A bad dream. Here you are, come, get warm in the kitchen.*

Where were her fuzzy blue slippers? *Keep your feet warm, Hannah— cold feet can ruin your day.* But then she remembered Mandy cold in her arms, and her mother stepped out of view, and other pictures flashed by, unasked for, becoming uglier and uglier.

If she could have made her legs work, she would have run and run and run. She heard the banging of her heart, impossibly loud, and tried to hang on. The dog licked her fingers. Yes. Please. Eat me. Swallow me whole.

She was supposed to call her Ellie. How could she? But she nodded anyway—she was not a puddle on the floor. They were taking off their outdoor shoes. She bent and fumbled with her runners. She closed her eyes and held up the mothers' pictures in her head, side by side. Now she could spot the differences, like on the back page of the Saturday paper—a missing belt buckle, an extra polka dot. Mrs. Nyland had a mole above her top lip and a spattering of freckles across her pale cheeks. Her mother's face was a flutter of emotions; Mrs. Nyland's was not. She was taller too, and her housecoat was the wrong colour.

It was just a cruel trick of the light. By the time Hannah had lined up her runners beside her feet and folded the blanket in her arms, she was standing in front of someone else's mother in some other family's house.

———

Eric looked up, startled to see his wife leaning against the wall, staring at him. He stood, knocking the puzzle box lid onto the floor.

"Ellie?" he said. How long had she been standing there? Now acutely aware of his wife watching, he stooped to retrieve the box lid and stood it upright on the table so the quaint prairie scene faced Walter's chair.

He turned. "Will she be all right?" he asked, crossing the room to her. She pressed tight against the wall, arms crossed, fingers digging into the folds of her housecoat.

"Do you think she'll be all right?" he said again. "Has she settled in?"

"It's a horrible room."

"But she's all tucked in?"

She ran her fingers through her hair. "It's drier than any desert in there. We should get her a humidifier."

"She's safe at least." Going back to that house was the first bit of use he'd been to anyone since they'd moved back to Neesley. "I didn't plan for this to happen."

"I know, Eric."

He leaned down close to her ear, one hand on the wall above her head. "Bringing her here was the last resort. Betty and I couldn't think of what else to do."

Ellie flushed. "So glad you and Betty worked it out."

"It wasn't like that."

"You make it sound like the girl is moving in."

"No. Just a few days. Just until Christmas is over and we can get her into a foster home."

"You and Betty?"

"I'm sorry, El."

But it was no good. He didn't have the right words. It was Christmas, and Christmas was the deepest of blue in this house and in all their houses before this. Even if he could erase the last twelve hours, even if he'd brought in the perfect tree instead of Hannah, or the whole damn forest, or the baby Jesus himself, it wouldn't turn Christmas a different colour. When Ellie got like this, whatever this was called, he had no way to make it better.

"And Danny?" she said now. "Will he be all right?"

Eric was quite sure he would be, especially after watching him dig into the leftovers. "I was proud of him tonight. He seemed so . . . grown up."

Ellie pushed him away with the palms of her hand. "But he's not grown up, is he? He's fourteen years old. And you drag him into this."

"I know," Eric said, helpless.

Ellie slid along the wall away from him. "Get Thorn out so he doesn't do his business in the hallway. And turn out the lights when you're done. I'm going to bed."

Then she rounded the corner and was gone.

———

Hannah stayed right where Ellie had left her. It wasn't exactly fear that kept her frozen like a Popsicle—she just didn't know what she should do next.

Ellie had dropped the green garbage bag right here, right beside her left foot. She could nudge it with her toe, but the plastic was gathered into a tight knot at the top. She didn't want to open it anyway. The bag was stuffed with reminders of Nigel's house.

She thought about Sammy. They'd all talked about him in whispers at the hospital. She was supposed to be answering the constable's questions, but when he turned away to answer the phone, she climbed out of her hospital bed and stood hidden by the curtain and tried to catch what the sergeant and Daniel and that lady in the waiting room were saying. Sammy would explode when he saw her. She wasn't supposed to hear that, but Daniel had practically yelled, clear as day. She didn't know who or what Sammy was, only that she had to be careful. She was cold enough to shiver-dance, to clack her teeth and stomp her feet, but then the whole family would sit up straight in their beds and shout out, *What was that?!*

Mostly she wanted to cry. But that would be worse still, because sounds of misery travel far in a house, and there was Sammy to think about. If she started, she might never stop. She was a bad crier too. She was noisy and out of control, with a high-pitched wail that swelled in volume until her ears hurt. Then came hiccups. Then her nose ran like a river and made her collar wet and she swallowed the dripping snot when she gasped for air, and sometimes she choked. Once, she threw up all over her jewellery box.

So, she didn't dare cry, even though she had held Mandy in her arms, impossibly stiff and cold. It was the hardest thing in the world to hold a dead friend, and it was her fault and it had happened so fast she couldn't even say goodbye.

She pressed her fingers along her shirt, feeling each one of her not-broken ribs. She hurt all over: back, front, legs, arms. She tried to ignore the achy parts. She studied the room, turning her body in a perfect slow circle. She'd been in a room like this once before, except it had no bed. It was a store in the city. She'd ducked in to get out of the wind while she waited for Nigel to come out of the pub. The store's bell tinkled when she pushed open the door; a woman with a silver-haired bun on top of her head stood behind the cash register. "Can I help you?" the woman said, not in a mean voice. *Yes, yes, I need help*, Hannah wanted to scream. But she stayed quiet and pretended to eye the displays instead, flexing red, raw fingers that stung as they thawed out. She got so caught up in what she saw, she forgot to pretend. It was a small space, with barely enough room to squeeze between aisles, and very warm. Moist, happy air rose from fancy grates on the floor. She saw rolls of material in giant bins, colourful and shiny, waving like flags; a great long table with scissors as big as hedge trimmers; rows and rows of beautiful buttons; and, sitting high on shelves, felt hats shaped like little canoes, decorated with feathers tucked into ribbons. The woman snuck up from behind and asked again, "Can I help you?" She was less friendly now and much older than she had seemed behind the cash register. Her body tilted forward from the waist up, a hump at the back of her dress. "You know this is a sewing store," she said. Hannah wanted to stay there, but her mother hadn't taught her about sewing. She couldn't think of words beyond buttons and thread, so she stepped back into the wind.

This room had the same kind of feel, like anything might be possible, enough bits and pieces to build a new world from scratch. She took one step, testing the floorboard, then another, then another, until she stood right in front of the wooden table under the window. It was smaller than the one at the store, but there were glass jars lined up of every size and shape, and inside beautiful little bits were sorted—baby pompoms, thread spools—as tempting as candy. She wished she could lift the lids, one by one, reach down, and pull out handfuls from each to spread across the table in a spiral.

She felt dizzy then, like she might topple over and smash her face against the glass jars, so she backtracked soundlessly across the room and sat on the bed's edge, holding her face in her hands, and taking low, deep breaths to stop her head from spinning.

It was very late. Or very early. Maybe the sun was ready to pop its round head over the field, yawning its morning greeting—*I'm here, but I won't keep you warm.*

She stayed there, too tired to think, too tired to move. She had the strange feeling that it had taken her whole life to get here. Her head dropped and bobbed, her body swaying. She was an open gate, forgotten in the wind.

PART TWO

LIKE SOLDIERS WHEN THEY COME HOME FROM WAR

Saturday, December 21

six

Eric spent a few sleepless hours in bed beside Ellie before leaving the house as quietly as he could manage. The thermometer outside their back door read minus twenty-seven Celsius, but that was only the half of it. An ugly wind blew in from the north, slicking up the roads, making it impossible to think straight. He was grateful the car started, despite its squealing objections. After the engine sputtered to life, he opened the trunk and reached for the girl's stiff cat, frozen to the towel, and carried it like a football to the empty barn.

He entered the detachment office at 5:16 a.m. Constable King sat hunched over his desk filling out some paperwork. When he saw Eric, he stood at attention before striding over to greet him.

"Sergeant Nyland," he said, extending his hand.

"Just Nyland. Eric is fine. You've had a long night." There were no other constables in sight. "You alone here?"

"Constable Tanner is picking up Timbits." King's face reddened. "How's the girl?" King asked.

"Sleeping. Has Wilson lawyered up yet?"

"Lawyered up?" King said. "He hasn't even sat up," pointing to the video monitor on his desk.

Eric walked over to King's desk and stared down at the monitor. Wilson was in the furthest cell down the skinny corridor. Eric had trouble making him out on the screen. A big ruddy guy with a straggly beard lay in another bed, his cell door wide open.

"That's just John," King said.

"John Welsh?" Eric recognized the man's great sloping shoulders, his bewildered look even in sleep.

"Yes, sir. They moved him to a group home in Caylee last summer, but he makes his way back often enough. When the group home reported him missing, we found him in the penalty box, over at the arena."

John grew up in Neesley and Eric knew him well. The whole town did. He and his single mother had lived in the matchbox house at the end of 16th Street for fifty-some years, spitting distance from the tracks, their family portraits of two glued to the wall so they wouldn't jolt off their hooks when the daily trains rumbled past. John Welsh could recite the strangest particulars, like times and dates for garbage pickup and town council meetings, but he couldn't count change for a hot dog and Pepsi.

"I was sorry to hear his mother passed," Eric said.

King nodded. "We keep space for his things in the bottom drawer of the filing cabinet—his toothbrush, Spiderman comics, a few of his favourite chocolate bars. We bring him hot chocolate before bed." Eric thought about the John Welshes of the world. All those kids who started out different. Sammy was one of the lucky ones. He might have his oddities, but he would grow up capable. He would not end up in an unlocked cell, a Neesley obligation, evil breathing down his neck from the next bed over.

King shrugged as if there was no getting around it. "John is happy as a clam to stay here. It's kind of a lark for him. We'll run him home after he gets his Timbits."

Eric needed to see Wilson more clearly. When he squinted at the monitor, King hesitated, as if calculating the risk, then reached to the controls and enlarged the image of Wilson's cell.

Wilson was sprawled on his back, arm dangling. Eric watched him wheeze through his nose and imagined a cloud of his booze stench wafting toward the ceiling. No belt or shoes on, and he'd scrunched his shirt under his head for a pillow. The blankets lay heaped on the floor, his undershirt crawling up his soft belly like he was posed for a seedy rag. Eric thought of the long row of pressed shirts in that upstairs room. He wanted to squeeze his hands through the bars and pull Wilson against him with a fistful of undershirt.

But he turned and said to King instead, "Will you need anything more from me today?"

"No, sir," King said, looking as confused as he ought to be. Eric had not been called in; he had no reason to be here at five in the morning. "We've got your statement. Everything's in order."

"Good then. You know where to find me."

"Yes, sir."

Eric got back in the car and drove slowly, unable to get Wilson out of his head, neither the boy he had been nor the man he'd become. He'd wished over the years that he could forget about that afternoon—chalk it up to a childhood prank and let that be the end of it. But on long car rides, anywhere, he could not help but see a hawk perched on a fence post or telephone pole or circling the sky, eyes fixed on him.

The red-tailed hawk had had her babies. That's what Nigel Wilson had said. Nigel wanted to show Eric the nest, so he could see for himself.

Eric should have realized there was something not right in the invitation. They were fourteen years old and it was one of the first warm days in May. When they stepped off the school bus, Nigel tapped him on the back before they separated. That in itself was unusual. They avoided each other for the most part, Eric surrounded by his large, raucous group, Nigel on the edge of their world, the last boy to cross the finish line during track class, the only boy on the sidelines during tag-football games or eating his lunch alone in the cafeteria. He kept to himself, out of sight, out of mind.

"She's had two chicks," Nigel told Eric. "They're getting big and rowdy."

"I got chores," Eric told him. His mother had gone to the city to visit his aunt in the hospital, which meant he was alone with his father, buffer-less; he needed to stay cautious. The chickens needed tending and he had a pile of manure to shovel. But Eric was obsessed with the majesty of the red-tailed hawk soaring in circles above the open fields, a top predator, swooping down and grabbing a rabbit in its talons. He'd said as much just the week before when the English teacher had forced him to stand in front of the class to read his essay out loud, haltingly.

"It's your only chance," Nigel insisted. "They're ready to fly. They'll be gone in a day or two. It won't take long."

How Nigel knew about the nestlings, Eric never asked. They walked along the hot gravel road, awkwardly silent, until they got to where Eric's father's land ended and the clearing began. Beyond it, the patch of trees, mostly spruce but towering poplars as well, their branches dwarfing the others, dappled the ground with dark shadows. The nest was huge, a mess of sticks wedged into a branch fork, so high in the poplar that Eric had to step back and crane his neck to get a good look. He could see the white heads and black eyes of the babies, the pair of them teetering on their stick bed, standing wobbly, falling into each other, pecking each other's heads. It was spectacular.

"They're sure something," Eric said. The parent hawks soared above them, a hoarse, thrilling scream, *kee-eeeee-arr*, the babies rising up, spreading their wings.

"We shouldn't be this close to the nest," Eric whispered, mesmerized by the fierceness of this family. The hawks circled down, their wings beating slow and heavy like great hearts. The mother—the bigger one—perched on the edge of the nest while the father took guard on a nearby branch. "We need to move back."

"Courage," Nigel said, pulling a bottle out of his back pack. Nigel unscrewed the lid and tilted his head backward. He took his time, impressively unflinching, wiping his mouth with the back of his hand when he was done. "Your turn, I dare you," Nigel said.

Eric stood dumbstruck. First the nest, then the tequila. He had no choice. A dare was a dare, even if it was only from Nigel Wilson. He could ill afford to look weak to the dorky boy from across the road, so he took the bottle, the rank liquid burning all the way down.

They backed away from the nesting tree and chose a spot sheltered by branches to protect themselves from being dive-bombed. They sat on green moss, leaning against the dark trunk of a dead aspen, passing the tequila bottle back and forth while they watched the hawks watch them. Looking up, Eric felt small under the hawks' sustained scrutiny, like the earth had shifted and he'd become prey. The mother screamed into the air.

"I gotta do the chickens," Eric might have said out loud, though he knew it was too late to turn it around. Nigel laughed and passed him the bottle and Eric drank until his world became too slippery to hold on to. It was innocent enough, even then.

But then Eric was left in the forest with only the hawks. He might have been unconscious because when his eyes opened at the sound of footsteps, the light had shifted, the sun low in the sky, the air crisp and wet. He was paralyzed, none of his body parts connected to each other. A spurt of nausea rose up in his throat and he leaned forward, his head cracking in two. At first there were two Walters standing before him, two twitchy sets of legs, two black scowls. But they melded into one as Eric got hauled to his feet, kicking and flailing. Nigel Wilson came into focus, standing a safe distance back, arms crossed, a smirk of satisfaction on his face.

———

There were no other cars on the road as Eric drove home from the detachment. It was bitter cold, pitch black. The more he thought about Nigel Wilson, the more he wanted to get back home and watch over his family. It was senseless of him to have gone there in the first place. He no longer had a uniform. He was no longer a man to be looked up to except by those in his house—Ellie, Dan, Sammy. And now Hannah, tucked under the covers in the room down the hall, reminding him of what mattered, of the man he had wanted to be.

He pulled into the long driveway. The house was dark, dead quiet inside. He thought with relief that they might still be asleep and he could just slip in unnoticed, as if he'd never left.

But he saw her in the shadows of the kitchen, his wife, small and alone. He wanted to go to her, but he took the time to hang up his coat, fold his gloves in his pocket, and leave his keys on the hallway table. He wanted to tell Ellie how Nigel Wilson had planned the betrayal. Nigel had waited until Myrtle left town. He had pressed the bottle to his lips, without ever taking a drink. He'd calculated precisely how long to let Eric wallow in his drunkenness before delivering him to his father's fury. Eric wanted to tell Ellie how ashamed he felt that the red-tailed hawks had witnessed what came next.

What is it between you and Nigel Wilson, she'd asked him once. They'd just moved back, not yet even unpacked. When Eric discovered that Wilson had returned too, he told his boys to stay away from him. *You're not to go there under any circumstances, do you understand?*

It would have been simple to describe the events of that afternoon to his practical, no-nonsense wife, then or now. What he couldn't explain was how it had changed him. His father was the one who had beaten him senseless, yet it was Nigel he hadn't seen coming. Nigel the one he feared more. How could she understand it, when he didn't himself?

———

Ellie felt achy all over, like her body was fighting a low-grade flu. She clamped her fingers around the back of her neck's flesh, squeezing so hard she left a trail of red marks. She had not slept. Not a minute.

Eric skipped the couch and came to bed with her last night. He stayed on his side, back turned, motionless, his breathing shallow. They didn't speak. Sometime before five, he lifted the covers and rose to his feet, then dressed in the dark without a word and walked out the door. Ellie heard the car's engine sputter and squeal, the scraper peel back the new ice, the crunch of tires on snow. She assumed he had driven to the detachment. Where else could he go? She supposed he had statements to give, his decades of experience to share in times such as these. He'd be gone the bloody day, leaving her with the turmoil he'd left behind.

But he was back before sunrise, unusually alert and helpful. He found her in the kitchen and told her to go sit; he'd put on a pot of coffee. When they heard Sammy stirring in his room, he raised his hand and said, *no, let me*, then led his son into the bathroom and closed the door. They stayed in there a long time. When they came out, Eric was freshly shaved, and Sammy, hair slicked back, looked not the least bit put out. Eric laid out Sammy's breakfast, cereal and milk, got him his right spoon, and led him to the table without touching.

Walter rumbled down the hallway, plunked himself at the kitchen table, and started to read the old newspaper that Eric had fished out of the recycling box for him. Eric made him two pieces of toast, slathered with butter and farmers' market jam and cut into triangles, and carried them to the table on a good china plate.

"Who you gonna vote for?" Walter shoved a triangle in his mouth. He had an unusually good appetite, especially in the morning. "Election day, don't you know." Walter slammed his hand against the table. "You got to mark a X. And don't try and get out of it. It's your civic duty."

"So it is," he said. "Who do you suggest then?" Walter held an election six days out of seven, and Ellie found it odd, Eric's patience this morning.

"Christ." Walter had a mouthful of toast, and soggy crumbs flew into the air. "None of the sorry bastards worth their salt."

Ellie watched all this, silent on a bar stool at the kitchen island. Eric poured them both a coffee and sat down beside her.

"Morning." It was simple, the way he said it, but it made her feel surer. He glanced toward the hallway. "That dog's been there all night."

Ellie nodded. Ellie had stepped on some part of him, a leg or a tail, when she walked past in the dark. He'd snorted but stayed where he was.

"I feel like I've been run over by a truck," she said.

He pushed her hair off her cheek with the tip of his baby finger. "You look fresh as a buttercup."

She couldn't help but laugh. "A buttercup. Really? You don't even know what one is."

"It's buttery."

Walter scanned through the old headlines while he finished his toast. "Remembrance Day on Thursday," he announced. "Service at the Legion. Ten o'clock. Free coffee. The old coots be expecting a salute, I suppose."

Eric had taken Walter to that Remembrance Day service weeks ago; he caused a ruckus during the minute of silence, precisely the minute he needed the bathroom on the far side of the room.

Sammy finished, got up from the table, and marched past without a word. He sat cross-legged on the carpet in front of the fireplace and chose Lego pieces from the box. Ellie and Eric turned on their stools to watch their son. He had started building with Lego before he was potty trained, conceptualizing complex structures from small basic parts. They had often tried to help him, but Sammy preferred to play alone. This week's project was a series of skyscrapers, New York in a frenzy, buildings racing skyward as fast as his small fingers could click each brick in place.

"Should we warn him now?" Ellie asked, thinking about the girl.

"Let's wait," Eric said. "Sammy is quiet and happy. And we need to let her sleep."

She pictured Hannah as she'd left her, there in Myrtle's room, her used smell and her tangled hair. Ellie had found the girl's motionlessness unnerving. The males in her life were always flapping and fidgeting. Sammy especially, but Daniel squirmed and wriggled too, at the dinner table, in front of the TV, in the van. Walter incessantly scratched the parts he could reach, armpits and balls, his wrinkled, old ass. Eric was at his most restless at night, when his guard let down. Once his mind shut down, his legs twitched and jumped, rocking the whole bed.

"But then what?" Ellie felt her stomach tighten. She should have checked on her in the night. She should check on her right now.

Eric covered Ellie's hand with his. "We feed her. We let her sleep."

"She's not a baby," she said, unable to hide her frustration. "That's not all there is to it. She's eleven?"

Eric nodded, then added, "Almost twelve."

"You don't know the first thing about twelve-year-old girls," she said.

He looked at her, almost shyly. "But you do."

Ellie pulled her hand out from under Eric's, swivelled back on her stool, and cupped her fingers around her mug. She didn't. She didn't know the first thing about girls. Especially this one. She didn't know whether she'd had her first bra or first kiss. At Danny's school, girl packs swaggered by in their too-short skirts and skinny tops, fingering their phones, all whispers and giggles. Ellie wanted nothing to do with any of them.

Ellie had overheard Danny from the other side of his bedroom door, begging for one more chance. It was his first girlfriend. He was so not ready, and neither was she.

She and Eric sat beside each other without speaking then. After a while, Eric reached his large hand up and rubbed her neck. Finally, he asked her, "Ellie, what would you have done? If you were me?"

"I'd have killed the bastard," she said. But then she looked at her husband and saw the sting in his eyes. She could not be the cause of more doubt—he was an insufferably good man—so she tried again. "You've had every reason to detest Nigel Wilson. I see it now. The monster across the road. That young girl in his house. I can't imagine growing up beside someone like him. He must have been a horrible bully when you were kids."

He looked at her oddly. "Not really," he said, turning to watch

Sammy at work with his Legos. "It might have been the other way around. Maybe we bullied him."

This caught her off guard. That he'd think such a thing and, more so, confess this to her. "You? A bully? I don't believe that for a minute."

Eric kept his eyes on Sammy. "We didn't taunt the guy. Or kick the shit out of him. Not that." He sounded far away. "But we didn't go out of our way to include him in anything. That's a form of belittling, I guess."

Ellie touched his hand and waited until he turned back to her. "Or it proves you've got good instincts. Then and now."

It took him a moment to catch up with her words. "Well, I did marry you," he said. His tired smile almost reached his eyes.

"Precisely my point."

He kissed her then, full on her mouth, and the gesture was so unexpected, so rare and charged that her hand jerked forward and knocked over her cup. They separated, disoriented, and watched the milky brown lake spread out in front of them.

Eric stepped down from his stool and grabbed a handful of paper towels to sop up the mess. He poured himself more coffee and reached for Ellie's cup, but she covered its brim with her palm and stood.

"Enough for me," she said. "I'm jittery as it is. Think you can hold down the fort while I get cleaned up?"

"Why don't you have a nap? Or run a hot bath. I'm not going any-where."

Ellie nodded. He stopped her, catching her wrist as she turned. "She's safe with us, Ellie. The system's going to take care of her. We just need a few days to let it get up and running."

She blew a kiss to Sammy and then headed down the hallway, step-ping over the dog on the way.

Ellie crawled into her bed, shut her eyes tightly, and thought about what would cause Eric to kiss her like that. But the longer she lay there, the more Christmas intruded. She was too long married to be fussing over a kiss anyway. She should be making cookies for Santa, rummaging through the bottom drawer of the china cabinet for Dolly Parton's Christmas CD. Who else was going to do it? Eric? And she had the guest down the hall to think about, plunged into the thick of their oddities and outbursts. She could not hide under the covers. So she went into the bathroom and stood in the shower until the water turned cold.

She chose her best jeans and her blouse with silver buttons, the one she had bought three Christmases ago, when this house wasn't hers and she was still making an effort. She hadn't worn it since.

She spent extra time with her hair, adding mousse, working it through with her fingers like a hairdresser had once shown her. She bent over at the waist and circled her head with the blow dryer from every angle until her brown hair fell in waves around her face. She spread out old jars of concealers and blush, half-dried mascara tubes, pencils, and lipsticks. She did her best on the outside. She'd keep the rest to herself.

She emerged from her room at a quarter past ten to filmy air and a smell of burned bacon. Walter, hunched over his puzzle, looked up and yelled, "You got the carrots," then the thought flew out of his head and he was back to work.

Sammy stood on a chair at the kitchen counter, dwarfed by the checkered apron draping around his ankles. Beside him, Eric had flour snowed down his sweater and on the tips of his ears. Thorn lay underfoot, trying to catch the drippings. The countertop was strewn with measuring cups and spoons, the flour canister (lid upside down), the brown baking powder can (tipped over), the electric griddle with its loose cord wedged tight against the wall. A frying pan of lumpy grease sat on the stove, a plate of blackened bacon beside it.

When Eric looked over, he gave an appreciative whistle. The breakfast dishes had been cleared, and now the table was set for six with Myrtle's Old Country Roses china set, pulled out from behind the glass cabinet door. He'd brought down the good china and it was not even noon. She would find new hairline fractures surrounding the roses. Eric had become so clumsy lately with things breakable, cracking two of Myrtle's dinner plates as he carried them to the sink after Thanksgiving dinner. But she wouldn't focus on pending disasters. Her heart lurched, seeing Sammy and his father so close to one another. She wanted to reach out to her son and run her finger along his cheek.

"What are you boys making?" she asked, coming up beside them. Sammy held his wooden spoon, mesmerized by the goop going round and round inside the metal bowl with its wobbled lip.

Eric grinned. "I thought we'd make pancakes. Got a bit out of hand."

"Got a bit out of hand," Sammy repeated.

"I can see that. No sign of Danny yet?" Or the girl.

"He's awake, been rattling round down there for the past half hour. He's had a shower too." He shrugged his shoulders as if he couldn't believe it either. Daniel usually ran up the stairs and raided the fridge within a minute and a half of falling out of bed. "These will be ready in no time. We've got bacon too. An in-betweener to get the day going. Sammy here, he's been a huge help."

Sammy stopped his stirring, just for a second, with the faint trace of a smile. "I'm making the bubbles gone," he said.

"You're doing an excellent job." Ellie smiled down at her son. "Your pancakes are going to be deliciously bubble-less."

"Deliciously bubble-less," Sammy repeated.

"This is your fifteen-minute warning," Eric announced. "Prepare to be dazzled." Eric wouldn't look at her, his banter not as simple as it seemed. He wanted her to go get the girl.

It could not be put off. She would bring the girl out to their kitchen and present her to the Nylands. *Hannah, this is Sammy.* Sammy's earlier calm from stirring round and round the bowl would break like glass. He would see a girl, not where she should be, and he'd rock into orbit and leave this earth. Danny would come up from the basement, fill a plate from the table, and disappear. Walter, oblivious, would shuffle up to her, pockets jangling with the weight of all those rocks, and ask her a pressing question, like if she'd misplaced her husband or remembered to blow out the pipes on the water well. Ellie wouldn't look at her questioning eyes—*What is this place? Get me out of here.*

"I'll go get her then," she said.

Eric nodded, his humming as loud as a wasp's.

———

Ellie knocked lightly, waited, and then opened the door a crack to the black and gloomy room. It was too cold; she should have brought in extra blankets. The heavy brocade curtains, a horrid pea green with floral swirls, pressed together, blocking what weak light might filter through the ice-etched glass on this miserable winter morning. Ellie wanted to back away, to let the girl sleep until Betty came to collect her, but then she saw her outline on the edge of the bed—sitting, not sleeping.

The girl would have a better view of Ellie, who stood in the light of the hallway, than Ellie did of her. She felt a twinge of anger under her ribcage: Why on earth would the girl just sit there like a bump in the dark? Did she need the queen herself to invite her to the table?

Ellie flicked the light switch hard and Myrtle's junk came into view. She took it in now with fresher eyes, the absurdity of this clutter. How could she have imagined her busy dusting and reshuffling had made this room presentable?

The girl sat straight-backed and still on the untouched bed, blinking under the anemic yellow light. She was in the same clothes as last night, her garbage bag of belongings still in the middle of the floor.

"Hello, Hannah."

"Hello, Mrs. Nyland." Perhaps Ellie showed her annoyance because the girl immediately corrected herself. "Ellie, I mean."

"How did you sleep?"

It was clear by the pallor of her cheeks that she hadn't slept well. She had charcoal moons around her eyes, a tinge of blue above her lip.

"I know that bed is lumpy as a bag of rocks. But there wasn't enough notice—" Ellie stopped then, embarrassed. How could there ever be notice for when, precisely, a monster might lock a child in the cellar.

Ellie crossed her arms and started fresh. "We've had this room closed up for a long time now. We should take a match to it is what we should do. But it was either here or the living room couch and that would give you no privacy, and Thorn would have had his nose in your face all night." She looked around, sighing. "But it's awful."

"I think it's beautiful," Hannah said.

"Beautiful? Really?"

Hannah pointed to the trinket-filled jars. "There are so many little things. So many colours."

Ellie stifled a snort. Had she even moved off the bed? She seemed incapable of lifting her feet. "Well, they're all yours. You can open every lid, dump out every bobble and scrap. Do with them what you like."

Thorn wobbled into the room, tail wagging furiously, and stuck his nose in Hannah's lap. Ellie was about to shoo him out, but the girl bent over and wrapped her arms around his neck.

Ellie said, "Thorn is a smelly old dog. Aren't you, Thorn?"

Hannah looked up, face pale. "The sergeant told me he ate a whole bag of dog food one time."

Why did she keep calling him that? What else did Eric tell the girl about their family? "We need to get *you* something to eat. Do you like pancakes?"

She had her fists close to Thorn's ears, rubbing. The dog quivered in delight. "I like pancakes a lot. Thank you."

"Are you hungry?"

"Yes, I am. I'm very hungry."

"Well, the boys are the cooks this morning, so I can't promise how good the pancakes will be. But there's maple syrup and bacon too. We'll go see, why don't we?"

Hannah stood as if favouring her ribs. She looked so pitiful in her ragged jeans and tousled hair. Ellie couldn't let the others see her like that. "Why don't you put on some fresh clothes first and splash some water on your face."

Ellie ripped open the garbage bag and dumped the contents onto the hardwood. There were no fresh clothes here. Nothing that belonged in the dolled-up parade of the junior school's hallways. All Hannah had were lifeless, well-worn utility-grade clothes, right down to the cotton underwear and undershirts.

Thorn watched Hannah as she sorted through the heap, folding as she went. She put aside a purple wool sweater and a pair of jeans, as scruffy as the ones she was wearing.

"Did Eric pack the right things for you?" Clearly there'd been little to choose from. With twenty bucks outlay, Ellie could have chosen better discards at Momma G's Thrift Store. She had no socks or decent pajamas either.

"Daniel did it," Hannah said.

Danny? Not a spectator on the sidelines but rifling through the girl's drawers? Ellie tried to keep her voice even. "Are any of these your favourites?"

"This sweater is the warmest," Hannah said matter-of-factly.

Ellie would have liked to pile the whole lot in the garbage bin out back. She could at least get them into the washing machine on heavy-duty hot.

A chill had seeped up from the floorboards. "Tell you what. You go get washed up and I'll see if I can find you some warm socks."

"Thank you for letting me stay here."

Ellie pushed Hannah into the bathroom and the dog out and closed the door before either could say more. Ellie's legs trembled.

The children's choir version of "Away in a Manger" was floating down the hallway, along with bacon grease vapours. Eric had found the Christmas CDs. The children belted out the words at the top of their lungs. That's all this was. No room at the inn anywhere in this whole world, except at the Nyland house. The girl was passing through, an unintended colliding on her way to someplace better.

Ellie yanked open her third drawer and pulled out fuzzy pink socks with ridiculous pompom strings. She collected a brush and comb and rummaged through her scarf drawer until she found the baggie of old hair doodles and barrettes and went back to the bathroom.

Hannah was leaned over the sink, her face lathered in soap suds. The purple sweater was overstretched, too wide for her shoulders. She rinsed her face and blinked through wet eyelashes at Ellie in the bathroom mirror.

"I brought some things."

Hannah looked at her dirty, tangled hair in the mirror and sighed, shoulders slumping noticeably.

"I'm not very good with my hair," Hannah said.

"It's a pretty colour. I think they call that honey blonde."

Hannah squinted into the mirror and studied her hair. "I thought it was brown. Like a paper bag."

"There are movie actresses who want hair just exactly this colour.

They have to get it from a bottle. And you've got lots of it too, which means you've got options."

What came next was more reflex than choice. Ellie lifted a scoop of heavy hair and brushed gently until the tangles disappeared. Then she selected three strands, right over middle, left over middle, adding to each until her hair was all caught up in a braid down Hannah's back.

"Pass me an elastic from the baggie?"

Hannah reached in and pulled out a red one, not taking her eyes off the mirror. With her hair brushed away from her face, Hannah looked less forlorn. She turned this way and that, eyes wide, trying to get a look from different angles.

"Voila, a French braid," Ellie said, surprised her fingers knew what to do with a young girl's hair. She'd gotten it right, on her first try, as if the bucket of imagined memories she'd filled over the years had guided her through the steps. "Do you like it?"

Hannah nodded. "Jessie said her mom did it too tight every time, and it made her brains squeeze out like toothpaste. Jessie's hair is almost black and it's longer and it gets really kinky when it's wet."

"Who's Jessie?" Ellie asked.

"My friend. From school. Before we moved here." Hannah took a long breath and shook her head back and forth. "It's not too tight."

Ellie passed her the socks and Hannah bent over, wincing, and pulled them on, tying small bows with the pompom strings.

"Let's get breakfast then," Ellie said.

———

Hannah followed Ellie down the dark hallway toward the bright of the house, still tingling from the feel of Ellie's hands in her hair. Thorn had nudged up beside her and kept running into her legs. She felt more grown-up with her French braid and fuzzy pink socks. Ellie knew a lot about style. She was wearing one of the most beautiful blouses Hannah had ever seen. Maybe she worked at the fancy women's shop in Neesley, the one with the mannequins in the window. Or she might be a hairdresser. Maybe Ellie was given the customers with problem heads, a French braid easy as pie compared to what else she could do.

The air smelled delicious and there was music, children singing songs she knew the words to. It had been a long time since she'd heard music and it made the hairs along her arms stand straight up. Her stomach hurt, she was so hungry, and she didn't know if she would be able to stop herself from cramming a pancake down her throat.

At the end of the hallway, Ellie stopped so suddenly that Hannah bumped into her. Thorn sat on his haunches and waited. Ellie just stood there, stock-still.

Hannah peeked around her. She'd forgotten everything beyond her room, even though she'd stood right over there by the front door just a few hours ago. Nothing looked the same as last night. It was a wide-open space, no walls in between to separate one part from another. A squishy couch took up the middle with scattered chairs here and there, a puzzle table beside a brick fireplace with a burnt-up log crackling and spitting. The kitchen sink was in an island shaped like a lightning bolt. There were cupboards along a long wall and glossy ceramic turkeys, six in a row, on the ledge above them. A big wooden table stood over to one side. That's where they were: the sergeant and Daniel with two others, a little boy and an old man, their backs turned to her.

In the dark archway, Ellie stared down at her. Hannah felt a rising panic about someone out there in the light—someone that no one had told her about. And then she remembered. It must be Sammy. Her eyes flitted about, expecting him to jump in front of her.

Finally, Ellie spoke. "There's something I haven't . . ."

Hannah waited for more but it didn't come. "I already know about

Sammy," she whispered, afraid something might hear. "Should I go back to my room?"

Ellie grabbed her arm then, not lightly, and almost dragged her into the open sunlit space and toward the big table, motioning her to sit in the empty chair beside Daniel.

Hannah sat down stiffly. She kept her eyes on the plate of roses in front of her and tried not to fidget. Thorn squeezed himself under the table and laid his head on her feet.

Then everyone talked at once. Even though she had dreamed about not being alone at a table and having people all around her saying things she wanted to hear, she had a sudden longing for silence. The sun poured in from the window behind her, shooting a spray of yellow across the table's wooden slats. She could feel the absolute stillness beyond the glass. If she were on the other side, they could send a hundred people out looking for her and she'd never be found.

But here at this table, their noise was too loud. She sat on her hands to stop from covering her ears. The sergeant was asking if she liked pancakes, and Daniel was asking if the bed screeched every time she moved, and the man wanted to know if she was the nurse, and Ellie was telling them all to be quiet, but they weren't listening.

Then Ellie clapped her hands hard. Suddenly there was no sound but the whoosh of the furnace pushing hot air through the vents in the floor.

Ellie said, "Sammy and Walter, this is Hannah. She'll be staying with us for a few days."

Hannah lifted her eyes without raising her head and glanced across the table. It was a little boy, not a monster, and he looked frightened to see her sitting across from him. His eyes were pale green with a dark-blue rim around the irises. The same as Mandy's.

Hannah knew fear. The little boy was scared of her. He started slapping his arms against his thighs and Daniel said *here we go* and

Ellie reached over to say it's okay, but that made the arms slap harder. He stretched back rigid as a post and the chair tipped back—and then forward with a thunk.

Sammy stood and ran down the hallway and disappeared. Ellie looked at the sergeant, threw her napkin on her plate, and followed. Eric passed Hannah the plate of pancakes. How could she eat pancakes after that? She mechanically lifted her fork and reached for the one on top.

"Thank you, Sergeant Nyland."

"I'm not a sergeant anymore. You can just call me Eric."

Daniel reached for the pancake plate and dug three from the stack.

They all stayed quiet except for the old man named Walter, who said he was going to town for two-by-fours and concrete mix. He had chopped his pancake into a thousand little pieces and was pouring a lake of syrup onto his plate.

Eric took the bottle away. Then he looked at her and said, "Well, now you've met Sammy."

Hannah turned Sammy's face over in her mind, his look of fear, and the way he rocked back and forth until his view of her would be blurred and less real. He was not a monster; he just didn't want her in his house.

"Sometimes Sammy gets like that when he meets someone new," Daniel said. "Especially since he started kindergarten. Now that he's in school he has more to be scared of. They call him a freak."

"Don't say that," Eric said.

"I don't," Daniel said. "I would never call him that. It's those other kids. Like Johnson. He gets Sammy wound up just to watch him spin. They make it into a game. Let's get up in this kid's face and see what he'll do."

Eric shook his head. "We're working on that, Dan. We're talking to the school."

That's not going to help, Hannah wanted to whisper. If people wanted to do bad things, you couldn't stop them. She scooped a small wedge of butter from the bowl to her pancake, which didn't melt even a little, so she smeared it around with her knife.

Thorn licked his way up to under her knees and she reached down and scratched his ears. Eric poured orange juice from a plastic box into small blue glasses and passed two to Daniel, who slid one down to her.

Eric said, "It takes Sammy a while to get used to new things, that's all. I don't blame you if you don't want the bacon. It's beyond burnt."

She reached for a piece. She'd never tasted anything so delicious. And the cold pancakes too—she dipped piece after piece into her syrup, barely stopping to chew before she reached for another.

Daniel's pocket buzzed multiple times and he pulled out his phone, glanced down at the number, and looked at his father.

Eric nodded and then added a warning. "Make it quick. And you do not talk about what's going on here. Not a word. Understood?"

Daniel hopped up and went past Hannah to the window, mumbling words they couldn't hear. When he sunk down in his chair a few minutes later, his mood had changed. He looked gloomy and mad.

"Who was on the phone?" Eric asked.

"Just Matt."

"Everything okay?"

Daniel shrugged. "Why wouldn't it be?"

Hannah had finished her plate, and she wished she had taken more time to taste all her bites. When she looked up, she realized Eric had been watching her. He smiled and asked if she wanted more. She shook her head and wiped her mouth with her napkin. Her stomach had stretched like a balloon filled with water.

The Christmas music had run out and the room was quiet except for Daniel's crunching on bacon, Walter's fork scraping across his plate, Thorn's heavy breathing at her feet.

"I'm sorry Sammy didn't get his pancakes," she said.

Walter looked up, squeezed his eyes tight, and yelled across the table, "Who the hell are you?"

"Jesus," Eric mumbled and curled his fingers into a fist.

Daniel rolled his eyes. "Hannah, Grandpa. Still Hannah."

Walter squinted at her, frowning. "You the nurse?"

"She's only eleven," Daniel said loudly.

"Almost twelve. But I've got my emergency first-aid training." Hannah couldn't bear to have the old man run away from the table too.

Walter eyed her skeptically.

"I know how to check your breathing and find a pulse, and if you're not breathing, I can do CPR, thirty compressions and then two rescue breaths, but first I'd tilt your head and get your tongue out of the way."

"That's cool," Daniel said. "Did you ever have to use it? On a real person."

"Not yet," she said. "But I practise so I won't forget the steps."

"What do you practise on?"

"A pillow."

Daniel laughed, but not a mean laugh.

"And I can do the Heimlich if you're choking, like if a hard candy or a peanut goes down the wrong way."

Daniel grabbed his throat and made gagging noises.

"It's a bear hug mostly and an upward thrust like this." She crossed her arms and gave herself a hard, thumping squeeze.

A searing pain ripped across her chest. It came back to her in a flood then, being swept off her feet and dragged down to the cellar by her hair. Nigel's wet spit. Mandy hissing and jerking and that terrible cry.

She yanked at the neck of her sweater. She couldn't catch her breath, the room spinning round and round. She was drowning from lack of air, her mouth so dry she might choke on her tongue. She had to get out and into the cold to open up her lungs.

Eric lifted her chair with her in it and turned it around, bending in front of her. "Take slow, deep breaths if you can. That's it, just slow and deep." Both Eric and Daniel were counting now. "One, two, three, four . . ."

Her chest burned but she counted along with them. Daniel had hauled his chair away from the table and had swung around too, staring intently at his father and her.

"She's got PTSD," Daniel said. "Like soldiers when they come home from war."

Eric had his hand on her shoulder.

"Just breathe. That's it." *One, two, three, four.*

Thorn paced back and forth, snorting, flashes of black in front of her legs.

"PTSD—post traumatic stress syndrome. No, that would be PTSS. Dysfunction. Disintegration. What's the D for?"

Hannah concentrated on Eric's hand pressing on her shoulder, the weight of his fingers, anchoring her to her chair, breathing. *One, two, three, four.*

Daniel said, "Those guys come out of there and they think they're still on the hill and they hear the wrong noise and they're ready to burn the world down just to stop it from happening again. You get it after you've been traumatized."

"That's enough about PTSD, Dan."

"I studied it in school, Dad." Daniel leaned forward, hands on knees. "When we were doing World War II. Wendy Wilsbee had a fit during Social and had to go to the nurse's office 'cause her mom has PTSD. From her car accident near the Pick-N-Pack. The whole front end smooshed in."

Eric said, "Dan. Hush. "

Hannah wanted him to keep talking. Above her, around her. She felt lulled by the sound of their voices, drawing her out of her cellar.

"Mrs. Wilsbee has nightmares. She jumps whenever she hears a siren or screeching tires. They can't watch TV—not even Wendy's allowed—'cause they might show a car crash. It can happen to anyone."

"That's not what this is." Eric pulled his hand away, stepped back, and looked at her more closely. Her breath was coming steadier now, the spinning nearly stopped, a merry-go-round run out of push.

"You're getting some colour back in your cheeks," Eric said. "Are you feeling better?"

She nodded, less dazed.

Daniel added, "Does your heart feel like it's pounding out of your chest?"

"Give it a rest, Dan. Let Hannah sit quiet for a minute." Then Eric turned to Daniel. "Let's change the subject, shall we. We're going to get the tree this morning. When you're finished breakfast, we'll head out. We can take the van."

She felt almost like herself again, back in her sore body, and calm enough to look at Daniel and his father. She liked having them both so near. She wanted Ellie to come back and tell her that Sammy was okay, that he'd changed his mind about her. She strained to hear down the hall, but there was no noise coming from behind the closed doors.

They were talking now in quiet voices about getting the tree. About getting out and back before the wind picked up, about coming storms and the hardness of winter. Hannah was grateful to them for giving her more breathing room, letting her crawl back into her skin.

Daniel thought Sammy should go too, that he'd get a kick out of trudging through the snow. They talked about what trees were best, spruce or fir, bungee versus rope, ways to keep Sammy away from the axe.

Hannah watched the way Eric looked at Daniel and the way Daniel considered his answers. She wondered how it would feel to be part of this family and to pass food back and forth and talk about the weather or about keeping Sammy safe or about where to put the tree.

She wished she could go get the tree with them. She pictured a row of small figures slogging through the white wilderness in search of a forest. She wanted to swing the axe, hear the echo of the cracking wood, and see the branches crash down and bounce up, flinging snow everywhere. But they wouldn't invite her and she was too worn out anyway.

She felt as if bricks had been strapped to her feet. At least she did not want to burn the world down, which was what the wrecked soldiers would do with a match. She was breathing normally again, no hitch in her side, so if she had the PSTD, it had come and gone as quick as a wink.

Eric turned to her. "You need to rest. Do you think you'll be okay here for a bit?"

Her stomach rolled. Without them beside her, she was sure to make a wrong move. "Should I go back to my room?"

Eric laughed. "You don't have to, but you can if you want. You can go back to bed or flop on the couch here, watch TV or raid the fridge or play *Angry Birds* or . . ." He'd run out of ideas.

Daniel snorted. "*Angry Birds* is for little kids, Dad."

Eric smiled at his son. "Weren't you playing it just the other day?"

"I was helping Sammy," Daniel said, his eyes darting toward hers, then away. He seemed to be studying a piece of lint on his sweater sleeve.

"We won't be gone long," Eric said. "We'll drag the tree in through the front door and stand it up over there and stick decorations on every branch and more all over the place. It's a tradition. You'll see. Christmas at the Nyland house."

Eric went off down the hallway to collect Sammy. Thorn rested his head on her thigh, and as she bent to pat him, she looked across the table to Walter, who had finished his pancakes and was rising unsteadily, both hands on the table, pulling himself up.

"I've got work to do," he announced, reaching for his cane. He thumped toward the table in the far corner of the large room. Weaving his way along the back of the couch, he turned back, looked right at her, and said, "You can take my pulse if you want."

"Okay," Hannah said.

"But you're not getting my blood," he warned her.

"Needles," Daniel told Hannah under his breath. "He says he's allergic, but he really just hates getting his skin poked."

The grandpa had completely missed the to-do on her side of the table. Jessie's grandma was confused like that too. She lived in a home out at Kelby, too far for Jessie's family to visit except on long weekends, when Jessie wouldn't miss a day of school. Jessie hated getting dragged out there. She said the place smelled like diapers and everyone slumped in their wheelchairs like cows in a field and one of the old ladies was wrapped in a blanket from head to toe and held onto a doll for dear life—the kind that was soft like a real baby—and it was all she could do not to run away screaming.

All those times with Jessie, stretched out on Jessie's bed as she ranted about her toothless old grandma, how her grandma babbled to the plastic palm tree beside the nurse's desk, drooled down the bib hung around her skinny neck, fell out of bed onto the mat on the floor each night, gummed her Arrowroot cookies into a soggy mess. All those times, Hannah kept quiet, even though she knew better: her mother had told her to imagine trading places for a day. Imagine needing groceries, your legs too weak to get you to the store. Standing in a crosswalk, too unsteady to step out. Imagine having so much to share and no one left to listen.

Hannah watched the old man make his way to the puzzle table. If he fell down, someone would be right there to pick him back up. She wouldn't have chosen a friend like Jessie, but there had been no other houses along that road. There were no other houses along this road either.

Hannah was left at the table alone then, just the dog at her side. By the front door, Daniel had the phone in his ear, reaching up with one hand to pull down scarves and hats from a shelf in the closet.

She turned in her chair and stared out the window at the grey sky; the trackless white fields stretched out to forever. What a stupid girl she'd been. She'd kept trudging through the snow and not getting anywhere, when all this time she should have just crossed the road.

seven

Ellie followed Sammy into his room and watched him slump on the floor. She had to explain why there was a girl at his table, taking over his house, but how? The snippets of information that Eric had passed along would hardly do. Yet he could not be blamed for this.

"Just for a few days, Sammy," she began. "She's going to stay in Grandma's craft room. We've made her a bed. Hannah doesn't go to your school; she's too big. And she doesn't go to Danny's school because she's too little. She's right in the middle, like Goldilocks."

Sammy turned his back to her.

"She's been having a hard time. And she's very nice." Ellie kept her voice light and even. "Hannah has a kind face, don't you think?

There are things we can do, you and me and Dad and Danny, all of us, to make her feel welcome."

He wouldn't turn to face her. She was making a mess of it.

"Hmm, let's think. Maybe Hannah would like to make special cookies cut into stars with lots of icing and sprinkles on top. Or we could go to the store and buy her a Christmas present and we can wrap it with shiny paper and a bow."

Kindnesses she should have thought of naturally, without needing a five-year-old's tantrum to bring them to mind. How the girl's eyes had lit up when she looked in the mirror at her braided hair.

"What do you say, Sammy?"

"What do you say, Sammy?" he repeated, an edge to his voice.

"Sammy, use your own words. Tell me what you think we should do."

"I don't like words. I like numbers."

"Numbers are excellent, and you're the best numbers boy I know, but we need to use words too. Some words are very nice. Like *jabberwocky*. Or how about *kapow*? That's a good word."

"*Kapow* is too pointy. It's all black."

"How about *bubblicious*?"

"*Bubblicious* is round. And red. *Bubblicious*."

Sammy loved red. She imagined the dial in his brain turned to high. Her son could repeat phrases, full sentences, exact intonations from conversations he'd overheard months ago. How crowded it must be in there.

"Words fly in your head and don't get out," he said, as if he could read her thoughts. "I don't like words."

Sammy was a big boy now, but he'd never been one to be easily fooled by assurances. Cookies and milk wouldn't soak up the school bus taunts. His routines were his comforts, swaddling him like a security blanket, containing the crash. He had one safe place left, here in this house, with people he knew and trusted. Now it too had been invaded, a strange girl invited in, stealing his family's air.

Ellie changed tactics, suddenly and without reservation. "You don't have to talk to her, Sammy. Not one word. She won't come in here. This is your room and you don't have to share it."

"This is your room and you don't have to share it," Sammy repeated.

"That's right."

He thought for a minute before repeating for good measure, "You don't have to share it." Then he added, "I will say *go away*. I will tell Hannah to go away."

By the time Eric looked in on them, they were sitting side by side on the floor, crumpled Christmas wrapping and torn package pieces scattered around them. Eric stared at the balsa wood flyer they'd built. It was an early Christmas present—he could deduce that much. Ellie had given up on a tree dressed with tinsel. She just wanted these next few days to be done with, to go back to the way things were. Her flaws to sort through, her family to stand beside and hold on to for dear life. But Eric, standing in the doorway, was insisting on taking her boys into the frozen forest.

To the surprise of both his parents, Sammy did not put up a fight. He jumped up, as if this were his idea, and squeezed past his father before Ellie could stop him.

———

On his way to Hodgins's place, Eric had planned to talk to Daniel, to analyze what damage he had caused from the night before. To tell him he was sorry. To tell him how proud he felt.

He had planned to talk to Sammy too about the girl in the kitchen. Sammy was stubbornly protective of his space, and Hannah was not part of it. The mean boys at school had given him more reasons to be afraid. Eric wished he could trade places with his son, but all he could do was meet his son halfway—help Sammy translate the world into a language he could understand.

But trapped in the van with his strapped-in boys, the heat blaring, he realized he would not get to the points on his list. Shyness overcame him. Sammy fidgeted in the back, tracing his finger in circles along the window. Daniel sat beside him in the passenger seat, uncharacteristically quiet, cell phone out of sight, and every time Eric looked over, Daniel looked away, seemingly shy himself.

Eric parked on the machinery road at the backside of Hodgins's section. The clump of trees stood less than twenty feet beyond. Eric hauled Walter's chopping axe from the back of the van. Daniel got the tarp and let Sammy out of the back seat, who sprang like a cat, landing on all fours in the deep snow. He was clutching the car brush and wouldn't let it go. The three traipsed toward the trees, Eric and Daniel sinking to their knees, Sammy, lighter, leaving child-sized indents where his boots landed.

They let Sammy choose. A black spruce in a forest of firs—an outsider, off by itself, spindlier than its neighbours. Daniel wanted to swing the axe. Eric showed him how to wedge out pieces from the side they wanted it to fall and then stepped out of the way. His eyes darted from one son to the next: Sammy out of reach, sweeping snow from tree branches; Daniel taking steady, man-sized swings, feeling the weight with his back foot, hurling forward like a pitcher. He swung the axe effortlessly, his cheeks blotched and shiny red. Only yesterday, he was a weightless gangling heap of legs and arms as Eric carried him to his bed.

It took nearly ten minutes before the tree started to groan and crack and lean. Eric told them to stand back while Daniel slapped his knee and yelled, "Here she comes, Sammy!"

"Here she comes, Sammy!" Sammy yelled back.

Christmas came crashing down with a screech that echoed through the forest, then left a quiet so deep, they could hear nothing but the sound of their white breath.

Sammy's teeth chattered where he leaned on his brush. He'd lost one mitten; his fingers were brittle and raw red. Eric found the mitten in the snow and carried Sammy awkwardly to the car, which Sammy didn't like, his small body stiff as a cardboard box. After cranking the heat to high, he put Sammy on lookout, the most important job, and left him there, peering out from behind the icy glass.

When he got back, Daniel had already hauled the felled tree to the edge of the clearing.

"Your first tree. And you had to work for it."

Daniel smiled, rubbing his forehead with his bulky glove. "It wasn't that hard. I could have done a bigger one."

Eric laughed. "But then we couldn't get it in the house."

They dragged the spruce through the deep snow and brought it to the side of the road. Daniel made faces at Sammy through the window, while Eric walked around the van, and the two spread the blue tarp lengthwise along the roof like a picnic tablecloth.

"Do you think she'll like it?" Daniel yelled from his side.

The two of them heaved the tree up top, trunk forward, scattering snow and causing the van to rock back and forth, so that Sammy squealed. Would Ellie like it? It had been a small thing to ask, getting her the tree, and yet he'd managed to find a string of excuses as long as his arm. Why did he do that? Why did he wait until the small requests became impossibly large?

"So, you think?"

"Think what, Dan?"

He was thinking about their kiss that morning, his reaching for her like that before he could talk himself out of it.

Daniel exaggerated every syllable. "Do you think she'll like the tree?"

"I'm sure she'll like it. It's a beaut."

"Do you think she's ever had a Christmas tree? Or Christmas?"

What was Daniel talking about? Eric had missed too many Christmases, dropping Ellie and the boys at the bus station before he sped to the detachment, but there had always been a tree. Cotton-ball Santa heads and papier-mâché bells and cut-out snowflakes. He knew that much. But then it got through to him. Daniel was not talking about his mother. It was Hannah he wanted to get a read on.

Eric gave one final tug on the rope, which didn't budge. "I don't know. We'd better get back and find out."

"What's going to happen to her? Where will she go?"

"To a good home," he said. "A home with good people."

But he wasn't sure. Betty had called while he was making the pancakes, asking if they were all still in one piece, if there had been tears, or worse. She had a place lined up for Boxing Day; she'd pick Hannah up before noon. The Baxter family was out to the west, in Clearwater County. They had a hobby farm, llamas and ostriches, and four foster kids at the moment. The whole lot of them were in the mountains until December 26, visiting a great aunt or second cousin. Betty had been cautious as she described the Baxters, not her typical silver-lining endorsement. But the list had dwindled and she could only do so much.

"We can keep her safe over Christmas," he told Daniel. He could only do so much too.

———

Ellie sat on the floor in Sammy's room, working back through the bleak months since she'd brought them all here. It was a brutal day last January, so ridiculously cold that when they stepped inside, exhausted yet hopeful—*Walter, we made it, we're here!*—their breath rose up like smoke rings. Eric carried the large Rubbermaid container of bedding, the one he had clamped to the top of the van, but the brittle cold had proved too much for it, and its plastic lid snapped right in two, clean sheets and pillow cases tumbling onto the floor. She had looked down at the pile, laughing at first, but then winter stains bled over the sheets, the dog hairs and gravelly wet clumps made by their boots, and a sudden and horrible thought pressed in on her: *this move would fix nothing*.

The others didn't figure this out until later. Except for Walter, who planted himself at the lip of the hallway, not out of the way, but unable and unwilling to stop the procession of boxes and dark rubber boots trudging past like an army of ants. Every so often, he'd raise his cane and bring it down with a wallop, rattling the china.

That first day, Danny moseyed from room to room, touching this and that. Moments from his childhood: the Coca-Cola wall phone with the light-up rotary dial pad; the cat in the gunny sack, its striped tail sticking out, screeching and shaking when he pressed the button. But by evening, he too was sullen. There were only twelve TV stations and no internet.

Sammy kept out of the way of Walter's cane, sitting off to the side on his spot on the carpet as they ate the deviled-egg sandwiches and celery sticks, picnic style, that Ellie had brought in the cooler. Before she and Eric even opened a closet door, they ripped open the boxes labelled *Sammy* in thick black marker to replicate his old room. They made his bed, then lined his racing cars on the dresser in precisely the right order, plugged in his table lamp shaped like a truck, hung his star chart. "My room," he said and then wouldn't come out.

That was nearly a year ago now. A year of changes to the colours and textures of the fields beyond these windows, yet nothing inside her had changed, no matter how often she tapped SOS signals on her forehead. In all that time, she'd not let one visitor through the door.

Several tried, at least at first. Friends of Eric's stopped by with a case of beer or bottle of wine. Friends of Myrtle's, old women with large purses and Kleenexes up their sleeves, showed up with cakes and casseroles. And younger women appeared too, including a pair of welcome-wagon recruits delivering heartiest greetings and free coffee-and-a-muffin coupons. There was even a Daughters of the Empire trio, breathless in their explanation of how Ellie could help make a better country.

She'd never been one to take in stray dogs or birds with broken wings or to suffer prying neighbours, especially since Sammy. She'd given a litany of reasons for why they couldn't pass her doorstep. Her son had a winter cold, a flu bug, spring allergies. They had appointments to keep. She came up with one lame excuse after another—she pictured them swirling about town like snowflakes—until eventually people stopped ringing her bell.

Well, she couldn't stay in Sammy's room all day. She headed back to the kitchen. The girl sat alone at the table with the litter of the pancakes experiment. Walter had fallen asleep in front of his puzzle, shoulders curled forward, head bobbing like a blue jay at the feeder.

She ignored the girl and instead washed away the silty sludge on her tongue with a swig of lukewarm coffee. She went to start the cleanup, but Thorn had begun circling the floor.

"Hold on, Thorn," she yelled on her way to her coat and boots. He was too old for this weather. She didn't need him breaking a hip on the wooden stairs, getting stuck in a mound of frozen snow, haunches spread wide.

"Are you leaving too?" Hannah said.

Ellie turned to the girl. A thread of red, fear perhaps, passed over her cheeks.

"I'm only taking out the dog. And you don't have to stay at the table, Hannah. You can go wherever you want in the house. Would you like to turn on the TV, see if you can find a show?"

"No, that's okay."

Ellie held back Thorn, who was panting through his nose. "Or maybe you'd like to go back to your room and rest for a bit?"

"Can I just sit here for another minute?"

"Do what you like," Ellie said. She zipped her coat in a violent pull and reached back down to grab Thorn's collar. He looked up, shame-faced. A single brown turd had dropped out of his backside onto the hardwood floor.

A stain of disgrace washed over her too then, for what she seemed unable to hold back herself. "It's all right now, old boy." She scratched beneath his grey, whiskered chin, pulled a baggie from her coat pocket, and scooped up the polished stool with a practised efficiency. "Let's go finish what we started."

———

When they got back inside, Ellie stomped the snow from her boots and wiped Thorn's paws one at a time, extra gently, with the old towel they kept by the door. She looked toward the table and saw that Hannah had disappeared. Her relief gave way to an odd sense of déjà vu, as if she had stood on this threshold before, on this very same square of warped wood, looking into an empty room for a girl who was not there.

Ellie threw down her soggy mittens. She could not stand days of this. She needed to pull up her socks, turn it around. That's what she'd do. She'd march down the hall, use her best voice, and come up with something decent. She could tell stories about life on the farm or life before the farm. How she'd plowed through Mitch's fence that time— how embarrassed she'd been, there was no explanation, the steering worked fine. Or about how they got trapped in that godawful corn maze, Sammy wailing in the stroller, the pair of them choking on corn dust in the stifling heat, going round and round until the owner rescued them on his tractor. Or she could tell stories about Thorn chasing the plastic bag in the wind, hooting like a crazed owl. Hannah seemed to like the dog, who stuck to her like a piece of old gum.

And Hannah could tell her things too. She could talk about how cold it was in that awful cellar and how deranged the man was who put her there. Hannah could tell her any number of despicable details and Ellie would listen and nod and squeeze the girl's shoulder, and while she wouldn't say it out loud, she'd think that when you get to a certain age, you'll realize that unfairness is the substance of life, always; that it's only a matter of degree.

Ellie rounded the hallway corner to find Thorn stretched out in front of the closed bathroom door.

She could make up stories if she had to, like she did with Danny when he had chicken pox and needed the distraction, his chest covered in itchy, red bumps.

She slipped into Myrtle's craft room and sat on the lumpy bed and waited for Hannah to come out of the bathroom. She practised the way she might nod and smile and say all the right things, but the longer she studied it, the harder it became. What could the girl be doing in there? She was taking forever.

It crept up on her in notches, tiny tremors at first, then a full-on slap to the face. No. She couldn't do this. She was so poorly equipped for this task that it would be like asking Myrtle to burn the potatoes.

She looked toward the door, hoping Hannah wouldn't come out of the bathroom right then and catch her before she could compose herself. Her eye latched onto the pathetic pile of the girl's things, threadbare and faded, folded neatly into piles on the floor.

She could deal with the pile, if not the girl. Yes, that's what she could do. She would launder her clothes. She would do it right now. It would be a kind gesture, to have everything put in drawers. She'd use extra softener so they'd smell fresh, better than new, like they advertised on TV. You don't just wear clothes; you live life in them.

She scooped up the pile and carried the works to the basement. She sorted darks from lights, taking note of missing buttons and torn hems, making plans to mend them with supplies from Myrtle's room.

Ellie sat on the stool beside the washing machine, thumbing mindlessly through the Maytag manual as the first load cycled through. Then she pulled out Hannah's darks, one at a time, each flat as crinkled paper, and placed them in a stacked heap in the dryer. She threw in two bounce sheets, slammed the dryer door, and turned the water back on for the whites. But she couldn't stay down here through this cycle too, her cold toes turning a bluish grey from standing on the cold concrete. It was rude to leave the girl so long, and the disaster in the kitchen waited. She strained to hear the van's tires crunching over the driveway, the boys stomping feet as they piled into the house. But Eric was taking his sweet time. All she heard was the swishing of the murky water and the thumping round and round.

Ellie dragged herself upstairs to find Hannah at the kitchen sink, skinny arm banging up and down. Remarkably, the table had been cleared of dishes and crumbs, maple syrup blobs wiped up, juice jug and butter dish put away, chairs pushed into place, and china dishes stacked on a rack beside the sink. The counter gleamed: no lingering trace of Eric's big palms in the pancake dust, no dribbles of bacon grease on the stove.

Hannah turned to find Ellie beside her. A little *oh* sound escaped her lips as her arm splashed down into the sudsy sink, soap bubbles flying.

Ellie shouldn't have snuck up on her like that. "What are you doing?" she asked, though it was obvious: Hannah was scrubbing a pot.

"I'm cleaning the bacon pan," she said, leaning closer into the sink and looking over to Walter's bobbing head in his corner, as if she could rely on him to corroborate the facts.

"I can see that." The girl looked so uncomfortable that Ellie unfolded her arms and placed them at her side.

"I didn't know where to put the grease, so I poured it in here." She pointed to the yogourt container, half-filled with brown, sooty bacon drippings. "It hasn't gone hard yet. I can put it in something else if it's wrong."

Danny would have poured it down the sink if left to his own ideas.

"No, the yogourt container is good." Ellie should say something kind, but nothing came to her.

"I found the cutlery drawer. I like how it's divided with the stick-up wood so you know where the forks and knives and spoons should go." Hannah rubbed her forearm across her forehead like a char woman. "I didn't find the cupboard for the plates. I mean, I found the cupboard, but these plates have roses on them, and the ones in the cupboard are just blue. That's why they're on the rack and not put away."

If Myrtle were here, she'd banish them both from her kitchen with a wave of her hand.

"You're a guest in our house, Hannah. Not Cinderella. You don't have to clean up our mess."

"I like cleaning," Hannah said, squinting down at her sudsy fingers.

Ellie found no trace of sarcasm in her. "I haven't met many girls who like cleaning." But she didn't know any girls well enough to know what they liked.

"Mrs. Ellderslie let me be the cleanup monitor for art class for all of grade three. We were supposed to take turns—it went by the alphabet—but after my name came up, I got to stay on. Mrs. Ellderslie said I was the best with the brushes."

"Well, you've done a lovely job with the bacon pan too."

Hannah had laid the heavy fry pan upside down on the spread-out tea towel, which was wet enough to be wrung out. She popped out the sink stopper and wiped her hands on her jeans as the water drained. "I think I'm finished."

"I'd say you are too." Ellie looked about the tidied room, unsure what was expected of her after this gift she'd been given.

———

In the early afternoon, the first snow of the day fell. Harsh wind picked up the fat flakes and swirled them about in all directions, so it was hard to tell if they were falling or rising. Eric watched the wind peak and roar, lift the bird feeder dangling on the dead branch beyond the window, spin it around like a carousel.

The tree now leaned against the wall in the corner of the living room, its grey scaled trunk in a bucket of warm water. Eric and Dan had had to haul it in through the patio door off the dining room. It was a good-sized spruce, over eight feet tall, its needles soft and waxy, silvery green, and if its branches looked flattened a bit on one side, that part could go against the wall.

Ellie had praised the boys affectionately—Sammy for his choice, Danny for his chopping—and if she didn't look Eric in the eye when they marched through the patio door, flinging snow everywhere, she didn't turn away either.

Eric stood at the window and stared at the distant horizon. There was a bleakness to the fields, one dip or swell indistinguishable from the next. He rubbed at the ache beneath his collarbone. *Don't just stand there*, his mother used to say when he was small and at a loss for what to do next. *Plenty of time to do nothing when you're dead.* Myrtle saw inactivity as a sign of weakness, a holy path to hell and a sin more egregious than stealing, which in her mind took gumption, at least in the planning of a good heist. Myrtle lived by her principles. And died by them. Her heart gave out when she was down on her knees in the bowels of the basement, fiddling with the furnace filter on a day as cold as this.

He knew Ellie craved that kind of conviction. That's what brought them back here, her warped belief in the healing powers of Myrtle's busyness. She wanted to be under the protection of Myrtle's roof—not simply a holiday guest arriving sticky and exhausted—but a mother who cared for her family as Myrtle had done before her. It was what they needed, she argued. Fresh air, the country garden. The simplicity of Neesley. They could watch over Walter, keep him clean and fed. It was a good place for the boys, with its wide open spaces, clean dirt, and lack of unsavouriness. *The boys have such fond memories of Neesley, Eric; they deserve this chance.*

Eric had his own memories, which he was not inclined to speak of over the years. By the time Ellie showed up, Walter had ended his drinking days, and though he was never agreeable, she held a romanticized view of the man he had been, if only because Myrtle had chosen him.

He looked across the room to Walter now, slumped harmlessly in his chair, a dried-out fig. Years before, he had watched and waited for his father's body to go slack like that: jaw open, glasses askew, large fists smaller as they dangled at the ends of limp arms. Myrtle had ignored Walter for the most part—his slurred soliloquys and raging torrents. She'd protected Eric from the worst, but Eric resented that she'd never once openly contemplated leaving the man, with her son in tow. When Walter passed out, she hummed while she worked, dusting him with her rag like he was a piece of furniture. For his part, Eric watched and waited for the bottle to empty. Only then could he crawl from his trench, like a soldier at the front.

Since they'd moved back, he felt as if he was living in a museum of who his parents were, with a ghost of a father and a mother who was gone. He had never admitted to Ellie that he hated the man and this house. He didn't argue with her when she came up with the idea. Her enthusiasm gave him hope, and God knows he needed some. He'd discovered the book under their bed at Smoky River, searching for one of Sammy's toys. *Should You Leave?* was the title. Whole paragraphs underlined, passages starred, page corners turned down. He never mentioned it, and neither did she. All he knew was that they needed to start over and this was where she wanted to be. And if the move hadn't yet brought back their earlier happiness, at least they were still under the same roof.

Hannah came and stood beside Eric at the window. She looked pale and tired, her lips as colourless as water.

"I want to bury Mandy," she said.

"Oh." Eric stared down at the top of her head. While he knew she would not just forget that she had a cat—or what that bastard had done to it—he'd hoped she might not dwell on particulars. The winter ground was granite-hard. "The ground is too frozen, Hannah. It has been for weeks. If we tried to dig a space for her, the shovel would break."

"Is she still in your car?" she asked.

Would she want it in the car? "She's in the barn. Near the house."

"It's so cold out there."

"It's not a good idea to bring her inside."

"I know that. You can't keep dead things in a house."

"We could take her into Neesley. Jane's a good vet."

"Mandy's dead already. A veterinarian can't help her."

"But we could get Mandy cremated. That's one of the things that they do at the vet office."

Hannah looked up. "They put the bodies into an oven and burn them up."

How matter-of-fact she was, as though she passed by a crematorium on her way to dance class every day.

"Yes," he said. "And if you ask, you can have the ashes too." For a few dollars more, Barb Delancy, the town's tireless entreprenuer, would fire up her kiln to make a paw-print impression, hand-painted and stuck inside a not-quite-rectangular shadow box. Her husband, no carpenter, made twelve at a time. They were hung crookedly on living room walls all over Neesley.

"They do that when people die too," Hannah said. "They burn up the bodies and give you the ashes in a big vase and you can put them on your dresser if you want."

Maybe that's what they'd done with her mother. Eric recalled her bedroom, the items he'd seen on her rickety wooden dresser. There'd been a jewellery box on top of a faded doily and a hairbrush with a blue handle. No urn.

"I don't want to do that to Mandy," she said. "I don't want her body burnt up. I want her to get buried."

Eric had carved a small wooden box for Lily. He'd stabbed into the wood, then the earth. None of it helped.

Hannah rocked back and forth on her heels, hands clasped behind her back. "I want to say goodbye. I didn't have time. It happened too fast."

He wasn't sure what to say, but then a picture came into his head as if he'd been handed a photograph of his younger self, before Ellie, before Lily, back when he was still a constable stationed up north, green as grass and eager to please, standing on frozen earth beside those not willing to wait to bury their dead. They were suicides most often, or might as well have been—freezing to death after a binge, trying to stagger home.

Silent relatives, old men mostly, cleared snow from the site first, then lit a fire and waited. As the ground became soft enough to dig, the fire was moved aside and the grave chipped away with shovels and pick axes. When the diggers, Eric among them, again hit frozen earth, the fire was moved back into the hole until all that was left was the sound of the earth on the casket, *ka-thud*, *ka-thud*, and the wailing of the women, breaking like ice.

"We can build a fire," Eric said. A cat didn't need much depth.

Hannah touched his sleeve with the ends of her fingers. "Don't burn her."

He was making this worse. "A fire to soften the earth. That's all I meant." He'd find a box to put her cat in. He would dig over by the apple tree, downwind, away from the swing set he'd assembled for Sammy last summer, pile bags of charcoal on the ground, set them alight, and cover them with Walter's old water drum—he'd have to cut that in half first with the bow saw. "It'll take some time to thaw the ground. But we can bury her then."

"How much time," Hannah wanted to know.

"A day. Maybe two. We can keep the fire going through the night."

"Not today?" She looked deflated, all the oomph gone out of her as she stared out at nothing.

"Not today."

What if I'm already gone? That's what she wanted to know. But she asked instead, "Can I go to my room now?"

Eric nodded, although he didn't want to let her go just then.

"I promise," he added as she walked away. "We'll bury your cat. We'll do it together." But she just kept going as if she didn't hear.

———

Sammy lay on the floor in front of his closed bedroom door. He remembered what his mom said. *This is your room and you don't have to share it.* Words stuck in his brains. He didn't like words. He liked numbers the most. His look-out tower got to two hundred and seventy-nine. He needed it built higher to stop the troopers waiting under the couch. Three hundred and seventy-four doubles; ninety-five more. But he couldn't get to the Lego box unless he opened the door.

He lined up his cars, biggest to smallest, blocking the space between the carpet and the door bottom. Black is one. Purple. Blue. Green. Other green. Yellow. Orange. White is eight.

Except his cars were supposed to go on his dresser, not the floor, so he carried them back, biggest to smallest. He didn't want to open his door. In the kitchen, the chairs were wrong. Now there were six and there were supposed to be five. And there were two salts on the table, not one, and it was supposed to be beside the juice jug, not beside the spot for his dad's green cup. It made his stomach hurt.

His mom said that girl would go away. Good.

———

Back in her room, Hannah lay under a heap of blankets, tiny buds in her ears attached by wires, Thorn on the bed at her feet. She kept a tight grip on Daniel's iPad. He'd been excited to hand it over. "This is cool, you gotta see this—and now go here, and if you push your finger up and down, that's right, this does that."

He'd shown her how to blow stuff up and choose the best bombs, but then the phone in his pocket vibrated, and he took one look and stormed away. She stopped the explosions and went to the songs in the store instead, tapping buttons, and letting the sounds fill her ears. She'd forgotten how music made her feel, that fragile buzzing sensation inside her chest, a joy in her throat as thick as a chocolate shake. Each clip lasted just a few seconds, but it was enough to make her forget where she was and why.

Her mother sang songs about love and the moon and yellow sunlight on her face. She kept CDs everywhere—at the bottom of her bag, in messy piles on top of the coffee table and her dresser. She would dance around their tiny kitchen in the trailer park, pulling Hannah along with her, the pair of them belting out tunes, rattling the pots drawer and the nosy neighbours down the row, Mandy perched on top of the fridge, staring down like they were crazy.

After school each day, Hannah used to skip past the playground, past Drucker Pharmacy, past the concrete bench that said *Enjoy Your Day*, past rows of trees spilling pinecones. She looked both ways before she marched through the crosswalk, her arm pointing out like a rifle. Then up the saggy hill, through the parking lot, under the canopy with the *Sunnybrook* sign. She pressed the button to open the wide door, waved at the old people shuffling behind their walkers, and said hello to the striped fish zig-zagging across their tank. She stood on tiptoes to hang her coat on the peg in the staff room. She sat in the flowery chair by the paper towel rack, ate the cookie set for her on a paper plate, drank the juice in the plastic cup, practised her letters and numbers worksheets, and waited for her mother's laugh to burst through.

That's where Nigel Wilson found them, at the Sunnybrook place. He had an old uncle there—Mr. Lambert, a favourite of her mother's—and he had driven up to see him. Mr. Lambert was one hundred and one years old and had butterflies with black and yellow wings mounted on red-headed pins all over his wall. Hannah was not allowed to go past the staff room (*Their rooms are their homes, Hannah, you would not just walk off the street into someone's home!*), but her mother showed her the photo on the bulletin board: Mr. Lambert, not smiling, standing in front of his beige wall in pants too short, butterflies as big as hummingbirds all around, perched on his head and the tips of his shoulders.

Nigel Wilson had come to get his uncle's affairs in order. He was obsessed with order, an uncomfortable and dirty word, Hannah had since found out. He'd just stepped into his uncle's room and was leaning down to take off his wet boots when her mother pushed her cleaning cart through the door, knocking him off balance into the puddle he'd made on the floor. His glasses flew off, skittering all the way into the bathroom.

You've bowled me over, he said, once he'd picked himself up, got his glasses back on, and took a long look at her. That's how it started.

Hannah poked hard on the buttons of Daniel's iPad, trying to find melodies that would bring her mother near. But it was turning against her now, making her think of him instead, the two of them such a tangled mess inside her that she couldn't have one without the other.

He's gone, he's not here, he's not coming. But it was no good, she couldn't get rid of Nigel's face, not even when she squeezed her eyes shut and pulled the blanket over her head. She ripped the buds from her ears.

No man had ever come to their trailer before. He was so quiet at first, hair slicked back, shiny shoes. He'd knock on their door, a *tap-tap-tap* so timid they had to cock their heads and hold their breath to hear it. Her mother would open the screen and press her hands to her chest. Then she'd take the bouquet he held in front of him—*look, Hannah, aren't these lovely.* First carnations, then tulips, then roses, until their trailer became a garden, flowers in every jar that could hold water. If Hannah had known flowers would make her mother so happy, she would have picked every one she could find, filling jars with them herself.

She'd never had to share her mother before. When Nigel showed up at their trailer night after night, Hannah insisted they put on shows for him, the coffee table and the big trunk pushed aside to give them room. She and her mother would wrap themselves in bed sheets for evening gowns, stick flowers in their hair with bobby pins, and clutch wooden spoons for microphones. They would sing just for him, bodies swaying, voices blending together, and he would jump to his feet and clap and whistle. *Bravo, bravo. Encore. Encore.* Sometimes he would take them for a drive to the river to skip flat stones in the green-blue water. He'd escort them to his car, open both their doors, and wait for the metal snap of their seat belt buckles before starting the engine. Hannah sat in the back, her mother's hair in waves in front of her, Palmolive shampoo mixed in with the apple-shaped air freshener dangling from the mirror, her fingers wrapped around the radio dial. When she found a good song, she'd glance back at Hannah, and the two of them would join in the chorus, making up words as they went. They'd bounce along the gravel, a mile-long dust cloud trailing behind them, bugs flying at the windshield. Nigel kept his lips pressed tight, eyes on the road, but every so often his finger tapped out the drumbeat on the steering wheel, her mother exploding in a fit of giggles.

He stayed on for his uncle's funeral service. Hannah begged to keep poor old Mr. Lambert's butterflies, but she was too late; Nigel had already told the night staff to throw them in the trash. She cried like a baby at the thought of their beautiful broken wings, mashed in with dirty Kleenexes and food scraps.

He stayed through the Sunnybrook spring tea and the Jiggy in June school concert. He stayed through the big rainstorm that left frothy waves in the gutters and turned the park down the street into a lake.

But he couldn't stay forever. He said he had a business to run.

Her mother didn't want to leave. She loved the old people and they loved her. In the end, Hannah was the one who clinched the deal. She thought if they moved, her mother wouldn't have to work so much and she wouldn't be so tired. They could spend more time together.

So they went, the whole of their lives squashed into Nigel's car. They didn't need a U-Haul, he told them, because his house was already complete—nice furniture, soft pillows and blankets, pots and pans, everything they'd need to start over—so they took their clothes and Mandy and nothing else. Hannah didn't care. They were headed to his acreage near a town called Bear Creek. She buzzed with excitement along the miles and miles of flat roads, picturing her first real house, a bedroom she could dance in, fields covered in butterflies.

It wasn't the dream she imagined—not one butterfly that whole, long summer. It was lonelier than she thought it would be in a big house, with so many doors she could be closed out of. Every room was bare and tidy, without so much as a drinking glass or a pair of shoes out of place. There were no more shows for Nigel in the evenings; they were now the guests in his world. Those first weeks were filled with tears. Hannah could not find where she belonged and neither could Mandy, who refused to come out of hiding, not even when Hannah shook the treats bag. But her mother seemed so happy that she didn't want to ruin things. Her eyes shone as she held hands with Nigel on the porch step or squeezed beside him on the living room couch. She would tilt her head back and laugh at something Nigel said—the way she used to do with her—and Hannah would go up to her room, close her door, and fling herself on her bed. Her mother found her like that, head buried under the pillow. She held her close and said, *Oh, Hannah, there's plenty of love to go around, you'll see.*

Her mother started taking her on drives in the country every morning, just the two of them side by side in the front seat of Nigel's car. They passed magic forests and unicorns, found clouds shaped like hearts. Hannah treasured those times, her mother beside her, listening so closely to every word Hannah said. Nigel grumbled about their road trips without him—*What is it you two are up to? You have nowhere to go!*—but her mother insisted, and every time she wrapped her arms around him, he handed over the keys.

By August, her bedroom had fairy lights and castle wallpaper, and it became Hannah's and Mandy's favourite place. The cat would sit on her windowsill for hours, staring out at the big world. The house slowly filled with pieces of them, curtains her mother had sewn and Hannah's paintings on the walls. She got to pluck fat red tomatoes from the tangled vines out back and bite into them like apples. She got a bedtime snack every night. Neapolitan ice cream with extra pink or homemade yogourt-and-orange-juice Popsicles. Nigel cooked steaks on the barbecue. On sunny evenings, he would carry a big tray outside, plastic plates and salt and pepper shakers, knives and forks wrapped in napkins. The three of them arranged their wobbly lawn chairs in a triangle under the shade of the aspen tree, plates on their laps. Her mother would sip her glass of wine; Nigel gulping coffee, cup after cup. They made up new lyrics for the tunes in their heads, nonsense really—*Hannah saw a wasp a coming, way in the middle of the air*—and sometimes Nigel would add a few words to the mix, sheepish and out of tune, and she and her mother would laugh so hard their stomachs hurt.

Then her mother crumpled. Just like that. They had been to town for groceries, the two of them, her mother complaining of a headache, dizziness, the light too bright in the fruits and vegetables aisle. When they got back to the house, Hannah had her arms wrapped around the toilet paper rolls; her mother headed into the kitchen balancing all the other bags. One minute she was upright, the next she was bent double, broken egg shells and watery yolk snaking slimy in a trail across the kitchen floor.

Hannah screamed when her mother fell down and screamed again when she wouldn't get up. Nigel tore down the stairs. He wedged his arms under her mother's limp body, got her up off the floor, and ran with her out the door. He laid her out on the back seat and pushed Hannah aside. He said something before he slammed his door, but she was wailing so loud she couldn't hear what. *I want to come too*, she bawled, but he'd already driven off in a pile of dust.

He took her mother away and never brought her back. She had a balloon in her brain, he'd told Hannah, like a berry hanging on a stem, but when she asked what kind of berry and how it had burst, he would not speak of it again. Hannah begged to go to her, read her name on the stone, sing to her the way she had at least a dozen times at the graves of the old people from Sunnybrook, when she and her mother wore their best dresses and Sunday shoes and sang "Amazing Grace" or "Row, Row, Row Your Boat" and her mother would say, *Gently you go, rest sweetly now.*

But he said he had her burnt up, as if she was done with her body. He said she was ashes that he didn't ask to keep. Hannah didn't believe him, but she had no way to find her again.

Nigel searched for a family member he could send her to, even though they both knew there was no one. After that he tried to be good, and she did too. But it didn't last long. He'd take a drink from the bottle and say, *You look nice today, Hannah. Are you excited to see your new school? We'll do a concert another night.* Another drink. *We don't need to talk about heaven anymore. Not now, Hannah. You ask too many questions. Turn that music down please. Turn that music down. Turn that goddamn music off.* Until there was no more music in her ears, her throat rusted shut, their rooms as silent as a church with no people. When Nigel's own mother died, he packed them up, the bottle between his legs, and drove them away.

Hannah listened now for the noises of the family outside her door. She could hear murmuring and the crinkle of a newspaper. She had so many questions and still no answers. What if she had lugged in the heavy grocery bags by herself and let her mother carry the toilet paper instead? What if she'd kept her mouth shut for once and let her mother catch her breath? Mostly she wanted to know how her mother could just give up like that—give her up—without even a goodbye.

Maybe she had been caught by surprise. Maybe the ugly berry

inside her disguised its warning signals, like snow around a chimney, so soft and white, until the next thing you know, the roof comes crashing down. Maybe juice from the ugly thing leaked from her body into his body and bubbled rotten under his skin, until there was nothing left of him but the ugly thing. Maybe some of it had dripped into her own body too. Maybe that's why he couldn't look at her. Maybe that's why he got so mean.

She wished she could make these thoughts go away, but they tumbled about inside her like rags in a dryer. She wished she had someone to talk to, especially her question about the grocery bags. Someone like Ellie. She'd forgotten the little things: a housecoat wrapped tight, the fruity smell of lipstick, sitting on the floor folding clothes. When she thought about Ellie now, concentrating on the shape of her, it felt like a drink of water, the easiness of it, soothing her throat, filling her up.

eight

Eric took a call from Constable King in the early afternoon. Wilson, out of his stupor, had managed to keep down a few bites of toast. King said Wilson looked rough, a swollen eye and a cut above his lip, but nothing that needed stitches and less than he deserved. "He doesn't want a lawyer, doesn't want to press charges. He said he doesn't want the girl either. I thought you would want to know, Sergeant Nyland."

Eric hung up the phone and tried to push Wilson out of his head. He had his family to focus on. He went back into the living room, got down on his knees, and finished tightening the last of the screws into the frozen tree now standing in the corner. He glanced at his wife through the branches; her face was flushed with exertion as she slid the ancient steamer trunk by its leather handle across the floor. She'd been planning this for days—the decorating party, all of them together, a row of matching cups along the counter for hot chocolate afterward.

"Do we all have to be here?" Daniel asked, little beads of sweat on his forehead, wet splashes under his armpits. He had complained he was on his last round with the weights when they'd called him up from the basement.

Eric was willing to handcuff Daniel to a branch if that's what it took. "Look, we already—"

But Ellie interjected, seemingly unfazed. "You did the chopping, Danny. You're the VIP."

She undid the leather straps, letting the lid fall backward. Sammy stepped to the trunk, peered in, and flapped his arms.

"Remember these, Sammy?" She pulled out shoeboxes filled with decorations, reams of shiny tinsel. Sammy reached in and collected tiny tin soldiers in his fists. Daniel flopped on the couch, scattering pillows to the floor.

Eric crawled backward away from the tree and got himself upright. He cocked his head to the side. "Does it look crooked to you?" he asked of no one in particular.

"Where's my chair?" Walter yelled, banging his cane on the floor.

"It *is* crooked," Eric said.

"Yup," Daniel added from the couch.

The tree tilted noticeably to the left. Eric's mother would have clucked and hemmed and shooed them all away before wrestling it straight as a ruler with her iron fists. He needed to get this right— Ellie had been counting on this for so long, the tree no longer just a tree, but layers upon layers of all that had come between them.

"It's perfect," Ellie said. "Perfect the way it is."

"Who stole my chair?" Walter yelled. "What's that tree doing in the living room? Where's my goddamn chair?"

Sammy repeated the tirade word for word, the exact same frenzied pitch, yelling as loud as Walter.

Eric pointed to the far side of the room. "It's right there, Walter. By the window. Your puzzle too." *Who moved my goddamn pen? Where's my goddamn mug?* Eric grew up with these angry demands. It was as if his father believed he lived alone all those years, as if his were the only handprints to touch these walls.

"It's my house," Walter mumbled. He leaned heavily on his cane in front of the couch, eyes glazed, like there were swallows in his head, wings fluttering all at once.

"Help your grandpa to his chair, Danny," Ellie said.

Daniel slid off the couch and took Walter's arm. "It's Christmas, Grandpa. Remember? Ho. Ho. Ho. You and Grandma used to put your tree right there too."

"Ho. Ho. Ho," Sammy repeated. He had taken the tin soldiers from the shoebox, his hands too small to hold them all. They kept falling to the floor. He bent to pick one up, another dropped.

Daniel got Walter into his chair and then flopped back on the couch.

The dog sneezed twice, loud and wet, and when Eric looked over to the hallway, there was Hannah—Thorn at her feet. How long had she been standing there?

"Come help us decorate," Eric said, waving her over. "What do you think, Hannah? Does it look too slanty to you?"

"Not another one," Walter shouted, squinting at the shape in the hallway. "Goddamned trees everywhere."

"That's not a tree, Grandpa." Daniel pushed the puzzle table close to Walter's chest. "It's Hannah." Then he called back over his shoulder, "How far did you get on *Dungeon Hunter?*"

Hannah shrugged without looking up, the dog settling back down over her socks.

"Did you get through the first door?" Daniel sprawled back down on the couch. "The one in the vault?"

When Hannah didn't answer, Eric studied her more closely. Her braid had come loose, stringy strands sticking out everywhere. Why was she being so quiet, standing off on her own like that? He looked at Ellie. Her forehead was creased; her feet already taking her to the girl.

"Come on then," Ellie said, her palm on Hannah's back, guiding her toward the shoeboxes scattered across the floor. "Let's see what we've got."

Hannah knelt in front of the shoeboxes, too close to Sammy, practically rubbing shoulders. Sammy jumped backward, flapped his arms, and scurried all the way to the corner of the room. He dropped a few of his tin soldiers along the way, not stopping to pick them up.

Don't do this, Sammy, not now. Eric wished he could grasp his son's hand, pull him back to the middle. His heart was likely racing, the beginnings of a stomach ache. Sammy hadn't warmed up to Hannah, not one degree, since that fiasco at the breakfast table. He'd managed to avoid her since by hightailing it to his bedroom every time she left hers. *Help him discover the root of his fears,* that's what the therapist said. *Identify the perceived threat, challenge it with evidence.* While it had worked with balloons, grasshoppers, even shave-plate snowblowers, it would not be that simple with this unannounced girl.

Hannah had plopped down, legs crossed, eyes huge, surveying the boxes. In front of her were glittery reindeer as thin as paper, white feather owls with black button eyes, tiny plaid skates, clay candy canes and frosted cupcakes, hearts and stars. Snowflakes. Bells. It was her first spark since she got here—any idiot could see that she was dying to dress this tree.

Eric smiled at her childlike delight, so different from her usual wariness. He turned to Ellie, but she was watching her youngest son, now backed into a corner on the far side of the room.

Eric put his hand on Ellie's shoulder. "He'll come around in a minute," he whispered. She kneaded her lip and said nothing. He had to get these lights up before it all went to hell. "Give me a hand here, will you, Dan?"

Daniel made a production of drawn-out yawns and stretches before getting off the couch and sauntering over.

"We'll start at the top." Eric handed Daniel one end of the coiled mess of lights.

"It looked bigger when it was beside the others," Daniel said, threading the coloured lights through the tips of the branches.

"What looked bigger?" Ellie asked, her eyes still on Sammy as she woodenly unwound tinsel, silver strands jumping with static.

"The tree," Daniel said. "There were some little guys right beside it, buried in snow."

"It's a pretty good size," Eric said. "Look at that trunk."

"All I could think of was one more, one more, one more and it's gotta come down."

Eric reached across for the next loop of lights. "It was a whole lot of thwacking. You did good."

"I'm waiting for the debauchery," Walter announced from his chair.

All of them looked over, except Eric, who pretended not to hear.

Ellie said, "Haven't a clue what you mean, Dad."

"Neither do I," Walter said, a tremble in his voice.

Daniel shouted to his brother. "Sammy chose a good one. Didn't ya, Sammy? You brushed the whole forest clean with the snow brush. You're an excellent brusher. We should call you Brusher Crusher."

Ellie laughed, so he said it again, "Brusher Crusher," his voice a growl. He made a scary face, eyes squeezed together, teeth like a shark. But Sammy wouldn't look up, just kept banging his soldiers together. Hannah's eyes followed Daniel's and landed on Sammy.

"You okay?" Eric asked Hannah. The oomph had gone out of her.

She didn't look up, shoulders sagging, and stated quietly, as if to herself, "Sammy wants me to go away."

"He'll come around," Eric said, wishing he could fix this for the pair of them—for Ellie.

"He thinks I'm going to hurt him," Hannah whispered. "And I'm not!"

"Of course you're not." Eric looked to Ellie for support, but she was rearranging light strings on the other side of the tree. "Sammy just needs a few minutes to warm up. That's all. And this tree needs all the help it can get. You like the decorations?"

Hannah smiled. Eric squatted on the floor beside Daniel, who was weaving the last of the lights along the topside of the low branch.

"That's the end of it," Daniel said.

"Good. Plug 'er in then." Eric stood, clasping his hands.

Daniel jammed the plug into the wall socket, not five inches of cord to spare. The tree lit up, splashes of colour glowing bright. Walter covered his ears, as if waiting for a fireworks boom, but then he looked down at his puzzle, found the right piece, and got back to work.

Daniel came around to face Eric, high-fiving like he'd just run a touchdown. Ellie stood back to take a look at the tree, Eric right beside her, letting their arms touch.

"What do you say?" he whispered close to her ear. What would he have done if the lights hadn't worked? Better not to think about that.

"It's beautiful, Eric." Ellie looked across the room at Sammy, his eyes staring back from the safety of his corner, captivated by the lights. She gave a dramatic wave. Sammy refused to budge.

"This is my fault," she said just loud enough for Eric to hear. "I pushed her practically on top of him."

In Ellie's world, it came back to the mother, always. The small decisions and indecisions. She'd blame herself for the clouds in the sky if she thought they stole light from her children. He squeezed her arm while she stared across the room.

"See any burnt-out bulbs?" he asked, to keep things moving along.

"There's one." Daniel pointed to a light up high.

"And one down there," Hannah piped up.

"Just two gone. Not bad," Daniel said.

"Hannah, reach into the trunk there," Eric said.

She crawled to the trunk and poked her head in.

"See the plastic box? Down at the bottom there. Get out a couple of bulbs, will you?"

Hannah dug through painted toilet-paper rolls with Santa hats before she found the right box, popped off the plastic top, pulled out purple and red and held them up.

Eric took them from her. He unscrewed the dark bulbs and replaced them with the new ones. They lit up instantly.

"Danny, you get to pick the first decoration," Ellie said. Half the tree was now doused in tinsel. "You've earned it."

Daniel rifled through the boxes, until he found the mouse with its little grey ears and long shoelace tail. Years ago, in some other house, Eric remembered him taking that mouse off a Christmas branch, hiding him in his pocket, and feeding him crumbles of cheese.

"Mr. Mouse," Daniel said, running it up Hannah's arm, laughing when she shivered.

"A mouse in the house," Eric added. He'd said those exact same words a long time ago.

Daniel placed the mouse on a thick set of needles close to the top.

Ellie edged toward him and said, "I'll be checking your pockets this time." He shoved her shoulder with more force than he planned. She started to tumble but he grabbed the sleeve of her blouse, pulled her back upright.

"How are those weights working out?" Eric said, and the three of them laughed.

Hannah had lined up five stained-glass angels in a row along the floor.

"Well, let's go then," Eric called out, waving to Sammy. "Get over here, slugger. This tree's not going to decorate itself. You too, Hannah."

Hannah jumped to her feet, angels in her hands. She and Daniel stepped around Eric, tripping over each other, shoulder to shoulder, vying for the same branches, for reindeers and icicles and clusters of bells.

Eric was astonished at how easy they were, nattering nonstop, neither giving an inch, as if they'd spent every Christmas together. Daniel liked having Hannah close by—that much was obvious—making it a competition, bossing her around. And she was no pushover, giving it right back, ordering him to choose a different branch, urging him to think of the whole tree, not just his one little section.

Daniel poked his head out from the side facing the wall. "Bring over a couple of big ones," he yelled. "Got a hole over here."

"Who made you God?" Eric clapped his arm good-naturedly.

"You chop it, you own it," Daniel said.

Hannah picked out a hodgepodge of puffy sewn hearts and red felt stockings with green rims around the top. She passed them to Daniel. "Want any of these?"

He took the handful. "These are butt ugly, but they'll do."

She got down on the floor again, her eye on the cowboy-boot box filled with glitter snowflakes.

"There's so many," she said. "The tree will be coated in snowflakes."

She was on her knees, dragging the box along the floor. She had to maneuver around Ellie, who was not moving at all, who just stood there beside the tree, a coil of tinsel hanging from her wrist, staring at Sammy. Hannah's eyes darted from Ellie to Sammy, back and forth until Sammy spun around and faced the wall so she couldn't look at him anymore.

Hannah stood, a slow-motion unwinding. "I want to go to my room."

Eric came up beside her, holding a clay cupcake. "You're not giving up, are you? There's a whole lot of tree left to go."

Hannah's bottom lip quivered. "Can I go now?"

Ellie was in front of the girl, her arm on her shoulder. "No, don't go."

"A goddamn piece is missing," Walter yelled, his head rising then dipping, close to the puzzle table.

"He doesn't want me here," Hannah said.

"Sammy doesn't want to be like this," Ellie tried to explain. "It's hard for him at the beginning. If someone gets too close. If he doesn't know them very well. When his routine is broken—when something new comes along—it takes him a while to get used to it."

Hannah said nothing, eyes scrunched, lips pressed tight. She stood picture-still for the longest time, and then backed up slowly, away from the tree. "I'll help with the puzzle," she announced. "Sammy can have a turn now."

Ellie looked at Eric—how to choose one child's best interests over another's.

Hannah could back all the way to the barn, and his boy would not budge. Eric wanted to call her back, but her resolute look stopped him as she settled on the arm of Walter's chair. He could drag her to the tree and stuff her hands with snowflakes; it wouldn't matter now, her heart had gone out of it.

Daniel popped out from the backside of the tree. "You can't give up," he yelled at Hannah. "We're not done yet."

"Sammy is going to take over for a while," Eric explained, Ellie heading to the far side of the room.

Daniel blew air out his cheeks, shoulders dropping. He flopped back on the couch and pulled his phone from his pocket.

Eric picked up the tinsel Ellie had let fall to the floor and tossed it into the old suitcase. Ellie guided Sammy back to the tree, stooping to pick up the trail of fallen soldiers on the way. Sammy wouldn't look in Hannah's direction, pretending she was not there.

"So where should we put these, Sammy?" Ellie asked.

Sammy sat cross-legged on the floor, his back to Hannah. He stuck to the branch lowest to the ground. One soldier went up, then another, then another, until all the soldiers hung in a tight cluster, a thicket of tiny helmets and guns.

"Good job, slugger!" Eric said. "I think you've got this area secured."

"Want to do snowflakes next?" Ellie passed him a snowflake by its loop of wire. She guided him to another branch, close to the soldiers.

"We need you over here, Dan," Eric said, knowing Ellie would want it.

"I'm busy right now." Daniel didn't look up from his phone.

All this tactical maneuvering: Hannah's retreat, Daniel's surrender, Sammy and his soldiers marching in, taking over. Eric could hear Walter repeatedly asking her name; Hannah telling him, over and over.

"So what exactly is keeping you so busy, Dan?"

"A tweetstorm about whales crammed in tanks. Abusement parks. There's a documentary about it. And a trailer."

"It's okay," Ellie said. "Let him have a break. We can get this."

Eric followed her lead, throwing decorations on the tree, working quickly, their youngest between them on the floor. Sammy had the feathered owl in his fist, tracing a circle around its black button eye.

"Oh no!" Ellie said, hands on her head. "How could I forget?"

Eric looked around. "It's all here, Ellie." The room was covered with the wearisome business of Christmas. What else could there be?

"Music! We're supposed to have Christmas music."

Eric wished she would stop trying so hard, but he went to the CD player and flipped through the stack. "Which one do you want?"

"One of the choirs. Carols. Something we can sing to."

Music filled the room. "Silent Night." The adult choir. Walter yelled at the nurse to cut out that racket. Eric cranked it up a notch. Daniel was listening to a 9-1-1 call—"a whale has eaten one of the trainers!"—with the phone volume as high as it would go.

All is calm. All is bright. Now you could hear the killer whale, slung in the air by a hoist, crying his one-ton heart out. Eric told Daniel to give it a rest, put his phone away.

Sammy poked out the owl's eye, and the tiny black button skittered along the floor to land in front of Thorn, who rolled out his tongue and snapped it up like a dead fly. Sammy wanted the button back. He flapped his arms.

Ellie announced they were all to sing. "Come on, we know the words. Sammy, you know this one."

Sammy was flat on his stomach, trying to pry Thorn's mouth open with all of his fingers. Ellie sang softly, cheeks red, not willing to quit. Sleep in heavenly peace, damn it. "Danny, help me out here."

"We're not the Jackson family."

Eric swung around and told him to can it, to turn off the damn phone.

"Let's hear you sing then, Dad."

Eric bit his lip and concentrated on the tree. The choir looped back to yet another bloody holy night, Ellie limping along with them.

But then there was a new voice, sweet and clear above the rest. They all turned at once, even the dog.

Hannah stood tall and straight beside Walter's chair, head tilted upward, eyes closed, her voice light as a flute. Second verse. Third verse. The music poured out of her.

The others didn't make a sound, none of the Nylands. Thorn sat grinning sincerely, the rest frozen in place as they listened to the girl sing her song.

When the music faded, Hannah opened her eyes and blinked into the light. "We were supposed to sing?" She sounded unsure, so many pairs of eyes on her.

Ellie stood motionless, not breathing, one arm suspended in midair.

Eric slipped over to the CD player, hit pause, needing a minute to compose himself. He wished the detachment would call and tell him that Nigel Wilson had hung himself.

"Holy shit, Hannah." Daniel snapped her picture with his phone. "You should go on one of those singing shows." He snapped a second time. "I'm serious. You're way better than most of those kids. You could totally win."

"He's right," Eric said. "You have a really pretty voice."

Walter tugged on the sleeve of Hannah's sweater, then handed her a rock pulled from his pocket. "Don't lose it," he warned. Then he saw the rock he'd given her in her hand. He took it from her and slipped it in his pocket with the others.

———

Sammy sat on the floor, button eye forgotten. He recognized her words, shiny and round. They jumped out of her mouth, colours splashing through the air—blue, blue, less blue, red, red, more red, yellow, blue, red—the sounds just right, like a tower of blocks. The room shrank as he listened, a Goldilocks room, not too big, not too small. He was just right too, taking up the best space. She kept her eyes closed. He looked right at her face, and it didn't hurt behind his eyes.

The music stopped. His mom stood too still. Danny took a picture with his phone. His grandpa gave the girl a rock and took it back again. Sammy wanted her to start over; he wanted to sing the words too.

———

Except for the TV noise, the house was quiet, the kids and Walter long since asleep in their rooms, even Daniel. Eric and Ellie had been watching the late-night news, or trying to. Eric couldn't stand the weather lady with her I'm-so-pleased-with-myself tone. Snow and more snow on the prairies. An impending storm. Impossibly cold.

"Come on now, let's call it a night," he said, pulling Ellie from the couch to her feet.

Eric planned to sleep in his own bed tonight, consequences be damned, although he was pretty sure his father would stay put. Walter had been so exhausted by the excitement of the day—the girl, the tree, the angelic voice in his ear—that Ellie had had to help him down the hall and into his pajamas. He hadn't made a peep for hours.

Eric turned off the TV and unplugged the Christmas lights. Ellie blearily followed him into the bedroom, dropped her housecoat on the floor in front of the closet, and flopped down on the queen-sized bed. Her head hit the pillow like a stone. Eric crawled in beside her, spread the extra blanket over both of them, and turned off his bedside lamp. He listened for the sound of Ellie's breathing, a white noise that soothed him, but she was a small ball turned away. He could hear nothing but the creaking of the old roof, the expanding and contracting of the copper pipes.

He thought of the ways he'd belittled his wife. Times when she had called him at work, Sammy still in diapers, a heart-stopping panic in her voice, *I think he might be deaf, Eric* or *I can't calm him down.* He hadn't wanted to hear it. He'd tell her Danny had been strong willed too, and she was overstretching her case. He'd remind her he had a station to run, as if her concerns were petty and had nothing to do with him. Eric felt weak with exhaustion. He couldn't think about them anymore. His father and his sons. The girl. Ellie. He especially couldn't think about Ellie, how she had tried and tried before Sammy came along; the part he played. None were immaculate conceptions: he was complicit in each, exuberantly thrusting and grunting. And after days or weeks, when her normally pale cheeks flushed pink or when she teared up during a Hallmark commercial, neither one of them let on that they'd noticed these changes. Nor in reverse, when she'd gone back to pale, back to rolling her eyes when the TV grandma read the Mother's Day card. Over and over. He'd go to work, come home, and find all the evidence destroyed. She might have trembled a little as she reached for her hairbrush, but she made it easy to turn away, to pretend he had only imagined these things.

He supposed she kept the pregnancies secret after the second to protect him, believing he'd fall apart if he knew. That he'd not be strong enough or weak enough or sensitive enough to do or say or feel the right things. And she was right. He knew every time—the changes in her glaringly undeniable—yet he pretended he didn't. He could have stopped her, become a less willing participant, but he let Ellie carry on, carry the weight of their hope and their grief for the two of them.

Now he just wanted to be alone in his head and feel the sweet pull of nothingness. He couldn't make out what it was at first, coming from such a distance, a pinprick of bright light. One of the constables, or the sun, hurtling toward him, knocking him off course.

It was Ellie, jerking his arm. He shook her off.

"You're doing that thing with your legs." She was sitting up, pillow propped against the headboard, a magazine open-faced across her raised knees. She had turned on the damn light.

He covered his eyes with the crook of his elbow. "Turn off the damn light."

"You're doing that jerking thing again. For the past half hour. Every thirteen seconds. I've been counting. You seem perfectly relaxed one second. Then you do it again."

"El, go to sleep. Turn off the light."

She turned the page. "You need to take the calcium."

He felt a burning urge to kick out his legs, but he gritted his teeth and kept as still as he could.

"I bought you the big bottle. The chewable kind. You could at least give them a try."

"Tomorrow," he said, but then tomorrow flashed before him, so much yet unresolved. Hannah still with them, Wilson bruised and sober in his cell, his house still standing right across the road. He reached across Ellie clumsily and switched off her lamp, knocking her magazine to the floor, the room gone black. He rolled back to his proper place on the big bed, a different country, his indent so worn on the mattress he could trace his body's outline with chalk. But then the strangest thing. Ellie crossed the border. She was beside him now, tucked in close under his arm, her breath on his shoulder.

"It was a good day, wasn't it," she said.

He tried to get his bearings.

"I mean, it's horrible really, if you let yourself think about it. That horrible man. But if you put him out of your mind, it turned out all right, didn't it?"

Eric was still adjusting to the feel of her body, without any warning, pressed tight to him like that.

"Danny was quite sweet really. With the tree. The way he gave her his iPad."

He had forgotten what to do with his hands. *This is your wife, for God sakes. Get it together.*

"And Thorn. He's on the bed with her, you know. Totally smitten. You got him out, didn't you? After supper?"

Uh-huh, he said, or a sound like that, rolling over to face her. He couldn't kiss her now, not on the lips, not with this fragile connection that could so easily break.

"I'm so tired." She let out a drawn-out sigh that ended with a yawn. "I should have listened to you about moving here. About this town. This house."

He didn't think he'd said anything she should listen to about this town, this house. He didn't remember saying anything at all.

"You were so against it in the beginning."

"I said that?" He hadn't shared his feelings about Walter, he knew that for sure, but Ellie had a way of forming her own conclusions.

She stayed quiet for a long time. Eric thought she might already be asleep. Then out of the blue, "You know what I mean."

He wrapped his arm around her, brought her closer still. She yawned again and so he did too.

"I'm just so tired, Eric. So tired all the time."

"Go to sleep, El."

"Take the calcium." She sounded sleepy and far away, lying still on his chest.

His arms slackened around her shoulders, the wind going out of him. But he didn't let go. He thought about falling asleep like this, waking up hours later, Ellie still attached. The possibility seemed startling, like coming to after a bender and finding your body entangled in a stranger's pair of sheets.

"They're gone now," he said about the jerks, his legs bowls of mushed peas.

"A few more days," she answered dreamily, half-asleep.

Only a tiny part of his brain still worked. She'd forced the jerks right out of him. "They're gone now," he might have said again.

"Gone," she repeated. "She'll be gone soon." She was breathing slower now, her mouth slightly open, a trickle of wet on the hairs of his chest.

PART THREE

PLAY IT AGAIN

Sunday, December 22

nine

Hannah couldn't stay in bed a minute longer. She pulled back her covers, causing the dog to jump to the floor. She stepped over him and tiptoed to her bedroom door, opening it by inches, before feeling her way down the black hallway and into the living room. Thorn tangled between her legs as she wove a path around the furniture and over to the decorated tree. She had planned to stand in the dark and wait for her eyes to catch up, but in a brief spurt of courage, she reached over and turned on the lamp so she could find the tree plug.

It was even better than she remembered. Yesterday, with Sammy so near, she'd been afraid to examine the finished tree too closely, but here, all alone in the early morning, she could take her time studying each branch.

There was every colour of bulb you could ask for. Red, blue, green, yellow, purple, white. The tree in her head had just blue lights, tiny as pencil erasers. She and her mother pulled out its box from the trailer's closet each year. The tree's branches folded straight up, its trunk a metal tube, as light as a hollow doll. Hannah got to pull each branch down and poof out the pretend twigs. She got to carry it around too, move it from here to there. Mostly she kept it on the floor beside her at night so that before she went to sleep she could reach out and touch the lights, one at a time, and feel each tiny stab of heat.

This tree was huge. She loved everything about it. The way it smelled like the forest, needles falling to the floor like miniature pick-up sticks. The way the branches curved up at the tips like fingers.

She loved the decorations Daniel and Sammy had made the best. They were ugly really—tattered toilet-paper rolls painted badly, clay sculptures, their shapes unrecognizable, like plops of poop. But they'd been stored in their boxes between Christmases and hung alongside the pretty store-bought ones.

She thought back to her own little tree, not knowing what had happened to it. Was it still in the trailer's closet or had the next family thrown it away?

Thorn had fallen asleep at her feet, his ear flapped backward, a triangle of pink skin. The snowflakes in front of her were too crowded, bunched together on a lower branch. Hannah wanted them to be more spread out, like real snow falling, so she reached down for a handful and rearranged them at different heights.

Her eye caught a movement reflected in one of the stained-glass angels. She whipped around. Sammy glared at her from his hiding spot in the hallway. She froze, her hand mid-air, her teeth clamped tight. It took everything she had to keep still, but she was terrified she'd spook him and he'd wake the whole house.

They stood there, staring at each other like deer on opposite sides of an open field. Whatever she did next, she had to get it right.

———

He'd been caught. She was in her pajamas, staring back at him. Sammy could spin around, so she wouldn't see his face, but then he couldn't see his soldiers. She was too close to them.

He tried to keep his arms still, but they jumped from his sides and flung all around. Hers did too. When he grabbed his from the air and pushed them into his stomach, so did she. Her face was shiny under the lamp. One cheek was fatter than the other, a rainbow you could make with three crayons—blue, purple, green—from the top row of the crayon box. She didn't smile or laugh or sing or move her feet.

His hands escaped and ten fingers flew up at once. Hers did too. He counted the flutters. They were hummingbird wings, same as his.

He counted numbers on his fingers, bouncing up and down, his feet mushing on the wood, air swishing in his ears. Her body did the same thing, exactly like him.

He tried something harder, making all the numbers with his fingers, each one flashing behind his eyeball, lit up in red. When he stopped, she started. Her fingers flew so fast, her numbers crammed together.

Thorn was stretched out in front of her feet. Sammy wanted to keep counting, but she turned her back and he couldn't see her hands anymore. What was she doing? He leaned forward, and when that didn't help, he moved his feet two steps out from the hallway. She didn't turn and look at him. Two more steps. Two more. Five more. Closer. He got right behind her.

"You can't come in my room," Sammy said to her back.

She didn't use her words. She was playing with the lamp.

"I got thirteen soldiers. You can't have them."

She tipped the arm of the lamp, down then up, the ball on the wall a yellow sun bouncing across the sky.

"Are you gonna sing a song today?"

She looked at the light, not his face. "Watch the wall," she said.

He did. Her hand exploded into the sun like Superman.

———

Ellie woke with a start, a fire alarm going off inside her, its unrelenting squeal circling her lungs, pinging through skin and bone. She resisted the urge to jump up, fling off Myrtle's vineyard square quilt, and dive into the heat.

She'd been here before. So many times, in fact, she would sometimes dream about having a dream where she woke with a start, only to find the fat round world sleeping, a shushing finger pressed to its lips, as if she needed a reminder to keep the fucking peace.

Her subconscious liked to play these tricks, a moth's wings beating against her eyeballs, shaking her up for no reason. She knew from weary practice how to coax it back to its jar, slam the lid. She needed to lie flat and breathe in and out, counting backward through all ten little monkeys until the disturbing seconds between sleep and wake evaporated like smoke. Only then would it be safe to blink into the darkness. Take inventory.

She remembered Sunday came next. They were all sleeping. She had drifted off in front of the TV last night, but then Eric had squeezed her shoulder and told her to come to bed. They'd been watching the weather report. Snow and more snow. Now she could feel the weight of the white Sunday layers, caked to the shingles, pressing down from the rooftop. Her flannel pajamas had a tear above the knee—wafts of warm, under-the-covers air pushing against her bare skin through a hole as big as a grape. The toes on her left foot felt tingly cold. Eric beside her under the quilt—Walter must have had a quiet night for once—Eric too far to reach, his breathing raspy and solid. If she could just turn to him and stretch her leg along the flannel sheet, her toes would find his calf, hot as the summer sun.

Instead, she turned away and checked the clock. Seven thirty. She blinked two times to clear her vision and looked again, more alert now. Seven thirty. Morning already? But where was Sammy? He had never slept past seven, not even the morning after they piled into the van and drove out to Boogle Hill and sat without touching on Walter's filthy horse blanket, fireworks popping like corn in the night sky, all of Neesley crammed into the stands at the baseball diamond, miles away, their cheers as faint as a stereo on low.

Something was wrong. Sammy should have needed her by now. He should have already climbed out of his bed and padded across the hallway in his Superman pajamas and pushed open their door and poked her side until she opened her eyes and groggily said the morning words, *It's the one and only S-u-u-uperman.*

She heard whispering sounds from beyond her walls, from beyond any corner she could imagine him to be. In that same woolly second, it came back in a whoosh, a tap opened full. This was no ordinary Sunday. There was a girl in the house with green-grey eyes and a patchwork of bruises. She was to be taken away, but not today. Betty Holt would come galloping to the rescue on her white horse, breasts flopping behind a moose or a flamingo knitted across her sweater.

Then she heard a squeal, almost a high-pitched scream—a sound she recognized but couldn't quite place. Ellie sprang up in a graceless swoop, flinging the quilt over Eric's head. Three long strides and she was turning the door handle, running toward the sounds.

She stopped at the end of the hallway. She stopped breathing too and clamped her hand to her mouth to prevent any sound from leaking out. Her youngest son and the girl were in the far corner of the living room, their backs to her, sitting cross-legged on the floor in their pajamas, so close their knees touched, like ordinary children might do, just a girl and a boy with a fat old dog stretched out in front of them.

They had turned on the goose-neck lamp, the one over by Myrtle's mohair chair—Hannah would have done that, Sammy was still too short to reach the lamp switch. It cast a wide shadow against the wall in the gloomy room. Hannah fiddled with her arms. They were stretched out in front of her, hands together, thumbs up, fingers entangled, and then they went still, stuck up in the air like that. Sammy shook his hands like a madman and squealed. Her son was laughing, a real laugh, so foreign a sound in this house that Ellie had to reach far, far back before she understood it.

There, big as life, thrown against the wall: Hannah had made a dog with her hands, ears perked up inquisitively, mouth gaping, a friendly chomp out of air. Sammy's squeals became remarkably clear now. Short happy bursts coming from his mouth. Thorn lifted his head and woofed halfheartedly, more a clearing of his throat, looking around to see what the fuss was about, then thunking his head back down with a sigh.

Hannah's dog romped along the wall, head up like a coyote in the moon, head down, head all around, sniffing through the tall grass, Ellie's son gyrating madly on his Superman bum, vibrations shooting across the floor and through the soles of Ellie's bare feet. Ellie leaned into the wall for support, her fingers clasped white tight in front of her lips.

Hannah's voice now, quiet and kind, talking to her son. His crazy out-of-control body becoming motionless.

Ellie strained to hear the girl. She used just a sprinkling of words.

The shadow dog's name was Chester and he didn't like being alone and Sammy knew what to do, didn't he, just like they'd practised. He lifted his arm reverently, a symphony conductor, his fingers a perfect crocodile, jaws opening and closing, as if his hands always did his bidding. He brought the crocodile to meet with the dog on the wall, snouts touching, and they stayed there side by side, getting to know each other, neither the least bit afraid.

Hannah's dog turned into an elephant, then a swan, then a long-necked giraffe. *And how are you today, Mr. Crocodile? You have such big jaws*, Sammy asking for all the animals in the zoo. Wanting to make friends with a dinosaur, a penguin, a mouse.

Ellie felt a rumpled heat behind her, Eric's early morning breath on her neck. She reached across her chest and grabbed a handful of Eric's gnarly bicep, squeezing a warning.

"What's up," he said, too loud.

She could have smothered him with her fist in his mouth, but it was too late, the moment shattered. Hannah's animals dropped from the wall like they'd been shot. Her boy turned, a long *aaahhhh* pouring out of him, and when Hannah stood quickly to face them, her arms now just a pair of straight twigs inside her faded pajamas, so did Sammy. Thorn hauled himself up and sat close to the girl's hip, tail thumping.

"I moved the lamp," Hannah confessed, as if she expected to be punished by the adults looking on from the end of the hall.

"That's okay; turn on any light you want," Eric said, deceptively casual, his body now as taut as Saran Wrap stretched over a bowl.

He's rummaging through the evidence, Ellie thought, *like he's at the scene of an accident.* Eleven-year-old girl, five-year-old boy, standing side by side in the cold morning under the light of a goose-necked lamp.

"Were we too loud?" Hannah wanted to know.

Sammy now part of a *we?* Ellie's throat caught; she might never be able to swallow right again.

"That's okay," Eric was saying. "You've been quiet as two little mice."

"Quiet as two little mice," Sammy piped in.

"Haven't slept that long in ages," Eric said. "What have you kids been up to over there?"

Ellie's eyes stayed glued to the other side of the room. Her boy, looking so sure of himself, the beginnings of a smile, and then a raucous series of whoops.

Eric laughed along with him and turned to look at her face. "El?"

They were all examining her now. Hannah, Sammy, Eric, the dog. She had trouble getting her mouth to work. "Nothing's wrong."

"But . . ."

"There's nothing wrong."

"Oh, El."

"The kids were just playing," she said. "Just let them play."

Then she turned on her heel and fled to the bathroom, away from their stares, away from the light of that lamp, pressing her back tight against its locked door, lungs drowning in wet, salty air. It took several minutes before she felt steady enough to step to the sink. What she saw in the mirror scared even her. Her stained mother's face—like she'd been crying for years.

By the time she was able to compose herself, Eric had Hannah and Sammy seated at the breakfast table. Sammy was wolfing down his cereal, looking up between shovels at the girl across from him.

Ellie went to Eric, who was at the sink, changing the faucet filter, something she'd asked him to do weeks ago. He wiped his hands on a tea towel, turning to her.

"Better?" he asked.

"Much," Ellie said. That knot in her gut had loosened. She felt hungry. Ravenous even.

Eric poured her a cup of coffee, smiling ear to ear. "Easier than yesterday's breakfast," he whispered, cocking his head toward the kids.

Ellie kissed him on the cheek and took her coffee to the table. As soon as she sat down, Hannah dropped her eyes. Ellie could imagine what she looked like. Sammy paid her no attention. He was too busy eyeing Hannah, trying to copy the way she tapped her spoon in the cereal milk.

Ellie studied the girl. She looked less haggard than she had when they got her, although the ridge on her cheekbone had turned a deeper shade of purple.

"Where did you learn to do that?" Ellie asked.

"Do what?" Hannah put her spoon beside her bowl.

"Make animals on the wall," Ellie said.

"Animals on the wall," Sammy repeated, his mouth full of Cheerios.

"Brownie camp," Hannah said.

Ellie felt a ping of gratitude. The girl had been taken to a Brownie camp.

"I learned some animals by myself. An elephant is easy." Hannah looked up at Ellie, shaping her finger into a trunk. Sammy tried too, his more like a platypus.

Eric called over from the sink, "Does anyone want toast? Peanut butter and jelly?"

Sammy clapped and nodded. "Peanut butter and jelly!" He never wanted toast.

"I love your shadow puppets," Ellie told Hannah, leaning in. "Maybe we can do a show later. For Grandpa and Danny. Sammy, you can be the dog."

Sammy clapped again. "Chester," he announced, plucking his

word from the air. Chester. A glowy word, rich and smooth, no pointy edges. It gave her courage.

"We should go to church this morning," she pronounced loudly, startling herself. Where on earth had that come from? She'd moved so quickly from thinking the thought, to voicing it out loud, she'd created no space in between to swallow the words back down. She couldn't fathom herself coming up with this notion yesterday. "Why don't we? All of us. For the Christmas Sunday service."

Eric placed Sammy's plate of gooey toast in front of him and turned to her. "Really? Church? You think that's a good idea?"

"Why not," she said, pushing back the reasons why not. Sammy, Walter, Hannah on display—all the moments that could go sideways. "It will do us good to get out of this house. There will be Christmas music. Sammy loves music, and so does Hannah." She turned to the girl. "Do you feel up to it, Hannah?"

Hannah nodded, as if the choice was simple.

"How about you, Sammy? Do you want to go to church?"

Her son repeated back her questions, spitting toast crumbs, "How about you, Sammy? Do you want to go to church?"

Eric smiled. "Let's call that affirmative."

It was settled then. They would go to church, like any other family on a Sunday morning. Ellie left the table before her wits could take charge.

———

His dad told him to quit beaking off. *We're doing this for your mom, okay. It's Christmas.*

But Christmas wasn't until Wednesday. And they weren't a churchy family. They hadn't set foot in a church the whole time they'd lived in Neesley or in any of the other towns before. This Sunday morning exodus was just one more manifestation of his mom's Perfect Christmas campaign, one which he'd definitely rather skip. But then he remembered that Melissa got hauled to church with her parents every week. He hoped his mom would at least pick the right church— Melissa's.

He wore his green shirt and brown pants and a clean pair of socks and slicked his hair back. His mom ran around the house, giving last-minute orders. She was driving him crazy, so he threw on his coat and boots and followed his dad into the cold. He helped brush the snow off the van and scrape the ice off the front windshield.

They left Thorn in the house, pouting, stretched lengthwise against the front door so they couldn't sneak by him if they ever decided to come back. Daniel left his phone behind too. His mom checked to be sure.

His dad drove, obviously. There was no point in asking if he could drive. He would never be allowed again. His dad always got behind the wheel, unless there was a reason he couldn't, like when he cut a chunk out of his thumb with a fishing knife and wrapped it in the bloody washcloth and his mom sobbed *oh Eric, oh Eric* three hundred times as she drove to the hospital.

His grandpa and Sammy got the middle seats. He and Hannah got the back. He showed her how to tilt the seat with the button along the side. She had her hair in a high ponytail with ringlets around her face, and she kept pressing her palm against the curls to check if they were still there.

His mom had done that. First, she ironed Hannah's blouse, one of the pile he had pulled from Hannah's drawer. That shitty night seemed like a thousand years ago and already the details were fuzzy. Like whether a real clock made that horrible *bong, bong, bong* noise, or if it was only in his head.

His mom lent Hannah a red scarf with a clip to hold it down at the front. Then she sat Hannah on the stool at the kitchen island, set up a mirror on a stand like at a beauty parlor. Sammy sat beside her with his colouring page and yelled *ready or not* when the curling iron blinked. Daniel couldn't believe it. Somehow Sammy figured out that Hannah wouldn't bite, and now he wouldn't leave her alone. *Tight or loose*, his mom had asked about the hair. Hannah picked tight. She eyed the mirror the whole time and fiddled with the scarf's clip while each strand steamed and bounced.

Daniel thought she looked cute, like a different girl, but what he liked best was the expression on her face. Their back windows were covered in frost, a map of the world, oceans and mountains, but Hannah leaned forward in her seat belt and peeked through the valley cracks, eyes wide, like she was heading up the big climb on a rollercoaster, waiting for the first drop. They were going to church, not Disneyland, but looking at her now, he almost caught her stomach flips. Except there was Melissa to think about, and that scared him half to death.

He kept his head down when they passed the tree he'd smashed into with the truck. At the church parking lot, he searched for Melissa's mother's car—an ice-silver metallic Subaru Legacy, boxer engine, power everything, and sliding glass sun roof—but there were only Ford trucks and SUVs. He didn't know what her father drove. He'd asked Melissa once. Big and ugly was all she said.

They made a production of getting out of the van. Doors banging. Slipping on ice. They took a few steps between cars before his mom stopped and said, "Where's your cane, Walter?" and his dad had to go back to the van, but he couldn't figure out which pocket his keys were in, so they stood and stomped and froze. His dad got the door open and came back with the cane, but then his mom said, exasperated now, "Sammy's got the snow brush with him," so his dad tugged it out of his hand and patted down his pockets for his keys again, which took forever, while they stood and stomped and froze some more.

Finally, they filed up the wide concrete block of stairs, going slow, slow for Grandpa, who refused to hang on to the railing. Inside the front doors, people milled about noisily. There were little girls in velvet dresses and boys with bow ties, ladies with poinsettia brooches, and lots of Christmas stuffing—fat feet into heels and fat necks into shirts. The volume dropped the minute they were all through the door. It was as if a force field surrounded them. Everyone parted, in slow motion, making too much room. At first, people just looked curious or surprised until, manners chucked out the window, they full-out gawked at Hannah's bruised face. He could hear their sharp intake of breath, holding it there inside their lungs; an organ, far off, was the only other sound.

His shoulders instinctively flexed, making himself big; he moved in front of Hannah. Then his grandpa burst out, "Where's the voting booth?" and all eyes turned to him instead and everything sped up again.

"Walter. Walter Nyland," an old lady said, coming right up to under his grandpa's chin, squinting her eyes. "I never thought I'd see the day."

"A pleasure for you to meet me," Walter said.

The lady laughed and then a few more old ladies squeezed in until his grandpa was engulfed in perfumes and white perms.

"How have you been, Walter," one said. "Out there all that way from town."

"I'll live to tomorrow 'less a tree falls on me," Walter said, looking around. Daniel figured he had his eye out for the ballot box and free coffee.

Some of the men clapped his dad on the back. A few called him sergeant, respectful-like, as if he were their boss.

"We're so glad you chose the Baptist." A younger lady had come right up and grasped her mom's hand in both of hers. Daniel recognized her as the desk nurse from the hospital. She kept sneaking glances at Hannah and raising her ostrich neck, trying to get a view of Sammy. Daniel didn't turn around, but he could feel those little hands flapping behind his back.

A group of girls filed up the staircase. One, two, three, four, a row of ducklings, quivering and quacking. He recognized their sounds from the lockers outside his language arts class. Daniel had never seen these girls close-up. They were usually bunched on the other side of some partition, in the far corner of the cafeteria or behind the library shelf. They were boisterous and today they wore identical white blouses tucked into black skirts. It was remarkable how their lips kept going, all four pairs at once.

Melissa would not be caught dead with these girls. She liked whispers and red lips, feather earrings and Du Maurier cigarettes held high. They'd picked the wrong damn church. He should have put up a real fight and stayed in bed like he wanted to.

But then they were following the crowd, the Nyland family and Hannah, past the bulletin board, past green boughs and red bells piled high on the table, squeezing their coats on the overstuffed rack, doubling up on hangers since there were only a few left. Walter refused to take off his coat. *What for? We moving in?* Sammy wasn't sure, but Hannah held out her hanger and whispered, "Your coat will keep mine warm!" and Sammy went along.

Past the foyer, it looked like the whole town was crammed into the one room. There were rows of wooden pews on each side and an aisle down the middle. They were the last to take their seats. A man in a grey suit, with pants short enough to see his white socks, shoved pamphlets in their hands and led them up the long aisle, painfully slow because of Walter. The man dropped them off at the second row from the front, right side. Daniel kept his eyes on the worn rug that might have once been red. Even if Melissa was out there, he couldn't face her now. It was all too mortifying.

Their family took the whole row, first Grandpa—more shuffling—then his parents. There was some confusion about where Sammy would sit. His mom wanted Sammy beside her and had brought a purse full of stuff to keep him quiet, but she couldn't just grab his hand and pull him toward her, so he ended up between Daniel and Hannah. Hannah got the end seat, closest to the aisle, curls bouncing as she plopped herself down.

The wooden bench had a red fabric seat cover that slid around as they got settled. Daniel landed beside a suspicious brown stain (maybe that's why everyone had avoided this row), so he moved left a few inches, as close as he could get to Sammy without touching. There were Bibles and hymn books stuck into slats of the bench in front of him, worse than school, he thought, but he was glad for the help, since he might need to look up stuff.

The head guy walked to the microphone, swaggering like a rock star. Pastor Mike, with a special welcome to the visitors, which Daniel assumed meant the pew of Nylands. He could hear his grandpa muttering down at the other end, building steam. Then Pastor Mike told everybody to turn to their neighbours and share handshakes and good mornings. The girl in front of them turned and tried to shake Sammy's hand, but he had his head down, checking out the splats they'd made with their boots while swinging his legs back and forth. She turned her attention to Hannah, staring open-mouthed at her bruises, so Daniel folded his arms and scowled at her, a howdy-do to you too, and she swung back again and shrunk in her seat. His parents were shaking hands with the girl's parents, too enthusiastically he thought. *Welcome, welcome, it's the vocal group's program, been practicing for months, in for a treat.* Walter said, "It's hotter than hell's kitchen in here," his shaggy long coat buttoned from knees to neck.

Daniel felt a poke on his shoulder blade from a handshaker behind him. When he flipped his head around, he caught sight of Melissa, a couple of rows back. She was on the other side of the aisle. Bright red lipstick and a red sparkly top he'd never seen before. She had her hair pulled back too, which she never did for school. The lady who had poked him leaned forward, so close he could count her chin-hair sprouts, her breath like burnt toast, asking him his name and if he'd come down from the city. He mumbled a few words but he couldn't take his eyes off Melissa, who glared at him, like they'd never gone at it in the storage room behind the stage, his tongue in her mouth, his hand up her sweater. He tilted his head and shrugged his shoulders. *What was her problem?*

Pastor Mike cleared his throat into his microphone and all mouths snapped shut. Daniel was the only one left facing backward, so he turned himself around again. If he'd done something wrong, she could at least tell him what. Friday was the last he'd heard from her. She'd answered his paragraph-long, pour-his-heart out, need-you-beside-me texts with *later* or *haha*, but then even that stopped. She'd quit answering his texts, his calls, not another word. What was *haha* supposed to mean? She could at least give him a reason, even if it was a lie.

Pastor Mike raised his arms, ready to take the basketball shot, and boomed into the microphone, "Let us pray for one another." The front row lowered their heads. Surprisingly, so did his mom. Hannah closed her eyes. Sammy rocked back and forth, but no more than any other kid with ants in his pants. Daniel half hoped his grandpa would blurt out a good one—*shut your trap already*—but he was noiseless in his spot on the far side of their row, probably nodding off already.

There was a tank at the back of the stage with a wooden cross above it. His friend Ryan told him about this stuff when they lived up in Slave Lake. He said they used to go down to the river, same as Jesus, but it got too sludgy after the chemical spill; you get a white gown and keep your underwear on, and it's better optics if you don't plug your nose when you dunk.

Pastor Mike carried on. Confessing, rejoicing, ceasing, thanking, praising—no end to the -*ings*. And now the heavens were opening and the spirit descending as a dove and a voice coming down from above.

Then it was over and Pastor Mike marched across the stage and sat in the only chair, not ten feet away from the Nyland pew, too close for Daniel's liking, same as getting stuck near the teacher's desk.

He could hear his father sigh when Grandpa's cane clattered to the floor. People filed out of a door on the other side of the church and climbed a few stairs to the stage, an assortment of shapes in white shirts and black bottoms, both frilly and plain, some busting out of buttons, some skinny as wrapped hangers, clutching black binders. There were the gaggle of quackers from his school, all four of them, arranging themselves raucously in the back row in their matching outfits. It took some time to get everybody positioned in two straight lines on either side of the organ. One little old guy shuffled about, lost up there, and a lady stretched out her arm and got him wrangled between two other old guys and behind a pair of springy girls.

That lady stood in front of the group, her back to the audience, and nodded to the organist, who leaned into the keys dramatically, *da da da da*. Then the lady raised her chopstick and they all opened their mouths, binders held up in front of them, and started singing.

He looked sideways at Hannah, who seemed totally enraptured, leaning forward. *They're not that good*, he thought, but then he settled back on the cushioned seat and let the sound wash over him. As soon as church ended, he'd be first down the aisle, grab Melissa's hand, and lead her into a back room somewhere. He'd give her the blue velvet box and wait for her to say sorry.

He'd found the locket at Dave's Pharmacy, in the glass case with the watches. Dr. Dave was helping an old farmer figure out how to ease his arthritis pain without having to pay much, which had given Dan a long time to examine the heart laid open on a piece of red silk bunched at the corners. There was a crowd of people around Dr. Dave, all weighing in on the arthritis issue. The farmer was willing to try anything, like bee-sting therapy—actually sticking his head in a beehive—but Dr. Dave said *no, no, no, that's way too risky.* Ya think?

The locket had a slot inside each half of the heart. He figured he and Melissa could cut out their heads from one of their Facebook photos. He'd let her choose. The pharmacy crowd moved on to diaper rash and stomach bloat. The locket cost thirty bucks, on account of being sterling silver, and came in a blue velvet box that snapped open and shut like a jaw. When the crowd finally scattered and Dr. Dave got around to opening the glass case, Daniel had his wallet out. Dr. Dave threw in a silver see-through pouch with a drawstring ribbon.

The first song ended. The conductor lady raised her stick, fleshy underarm jangling, and off they went again. Daniel thumbed through the pamphlet the guy had given them in the aisle. One, two, three . . . twelve song selections. *You've gotta be kidding.* Also a Boxing Day Social at 4:00 p.m. with the Auxiliary ladies supposed to come early and the Little Mothers' Meeting postponed until January 16.

There was verse after verse, song after song, no clapping between—maybe clapping was a sin for the Baptists—just shuffling of pages and clearing of throats and breathy whispers between the girls in the back row. His mom leaned past him discreetly, to look in on Sammy, but he was preoccupied with copying the shapes Hannah had made with her fingers.

Daniel hadn't mentioned Sammy to Melissa. He'd been waiting for the right time, something sticky cautioning him to tread lightly. Melissa could be kind, but that part of her came and went like gusts of wind. One minute she was sweet-talking with the pimply girl in the puffy sweatsuit, the next she was moving to the other side of the hall so she didn't catch the cooties. He wasn't ashamed of his brother, but he didn't want to choose, didn't know if he could defend Sammy against what might come out of her mouth. A brother is a brother, even a half brother.

———

He had been on his way to see her the night of the accident. He'd woken to his phone pinging, a plate of chicken bones beside him, tacky hot sauce on his fingers and cheeks. He counted twenty-three of her texts, all sent since midnight, the last in all-caps. WHERE ARE U? COME NOW BABY. NEED U BABY!!!!

He piled into his clothes, ran upstairs, threw Thorn some kibble to keep him quiet, and took off in the truck. Snow flew off the hood as he picked up speed on the road into Neesley, wipers cranked, windows fogging as frigid air blasted from the heater. Drifting snow, icy shoulders. He couldn't see much so he kept leaning over the steering wheel and smearing away glaze with his glove. He knew she was high, wired good on the blue pills she had picked up from her greaser cousin the last time he came in from working up north. She said she'd wait for him behind her garage in the alley. God knows if she remembered her coat. He lowered his boot and pressed harder on the pedal.

It was the shape of her breasts, full and round and coming to a small point at the nipple. He was thinking about how perfect they were, their exact fit in his palms, when he hit the track of black ice. The truck bowled sideways to where the tree had been planted, stupidly, a hundred years ago, right there at the intersection that signalled the end of the farmers and the start of the town. His boot smashed on the brake—he'd forgotten the rule to do as little as possible—and the truck spun in circles, around and around. Then after a deafening drawn-out crack, the motion stopped, with a final sputtering before everything went dead quiet. He might have closed his eyes tight or kept them wide open. It happened so fast he couldn't remember. When his vision cleared, he was buried in branches coming right at him through broken glass and felt a rush of cold air. The impact had caved in his door and shattered the rear-view mirror. The truck had turned itself around, facing the way he'd just come, as if it knew all along what a bad idea this was and just wanted to get home.

He brushed the glass to the cab floor, slithered across the seat, opened the passenger door, fell into the cold, and called Melissa. Nobody drove by. He waited through eight rings before he pressed End. Then he called her again and again until she finally answered, sleepy and far away. *Are you inside, Melissa? Are you inside your house?* It took the longest time for her to find the slurred words. She was in bed. Where else would she be?

———

Pastor Mike marched across the stage, waving at the choir, shouting because he hadn't yet made it to the microphone. "Let's have a big round of applause for the vocal group who have worked so hard for this Christmas Sunday program." Everyone clapped, it was not a sin after all, Hannah slapping her palms more wholeheartedly and for longer than the rest.

"Let's bow our heads in prayer."

Melissa later denied pleading with him to come over that night. When he told her to check her text messages, she said he'd been stupid to take her seriously. *You cracked up the truck? You're grounded?* After that, she stopped taking his calls.

Amens echoed between the walls. Pastor Mike lifted his arms and they stood, a stampede of feet hitting wood, a groan in the rafters. Daniel shook out the needles in his legs, looked across his parents to his grandpa, who tilted in his seat, mouth open, eyes closed. It was their turn now, all of them, his mom smiling a real smile as she reached into the slot for the green hymn book. Daniel shared a battered book with Sammy; Hannah reached for her own.

He strained to hear his mom's voice beside him, tentative and slightly off key, and his dad's too, as they clasped their book between them. But Hannah overtook their row—*I once was lost, but now I'm found*—as clean and pure as anything he'd ever heard. Her voice ran like a current from his toes to his ears, everyone else mouthing the words because he could hear only her.

It hit him then—Hannah was taking the whole church thing seriously, the music and the message. He thought about what she'd been through since her mom died, living with that creep in the house across the road. This wasn't just a sappy song to her. He held the shiny pages down to Sammy's height, following the words with his finger to make Sammy feel included. Now it was the chorus again. *Amazing grace how sweet the sound.*

Hannah belted out the words, her voice rising above the others, rising above him. Heads turned. Whole rows looked their way. Pastor Mike was trying to catch Hannah's eye. The girls in the back row strained their necks to find the angel in the crowd. There, she was there, beside a little boy blending into the background.

Daniel turned his head to get a glimpse of Melissa, to see if she heard what he heard. She did. She was sizing up the girl with the red scarf and big voice, her expression sour and cold, without a trace of pretty. He swung back around and sang as loud as he could. Sammy looked up and giggled. Then Sammy gave it everything he had too, pitch perfect, a couple of beats behind because he couldn't read the words.

The song ended too soon. Hymnbooks snapped shut. More sitting. More praying. Then it was over. A rock clanked to the floor from Grandpa's pocket and skittered under the seat in front of them. While his dad bent down to retrieve it, Grandpa yelled, "What did I miss?" loud enough for half the church to hear.

His mom paid no attention as she pressed out the wrinkles of her skirt with her palms. She leaned over Daniel, flushed and happy, and whispered to Sammy, "You've been such a great boy." Then she pushed their ragtag group into the aisle.

They followed the herd single file into the space where they'd left their coats, Sammy in between his parents now, Hannah close to Grandpa as he grumbled about the parade, how it was too disorganized, impossible to see the floats. People milled about, giving praises all round for the choir and their excellent singing.

Melissa stood over to the side, leaning against the emergency exit door, coat on already, glowering at him. He walked up to her, not ready for this conversation, but not willing to put it off.

"Hi," he said.

"You got a smoke?"

He shook his head. It hadn't occurred to him to bring along the pack of Du Mauriers he hid behind the freezer. He couldn't stomach them himself, but she was always running out.

"So who's the gay girl?"

He wasn't supposed to talk about Hannah. His father had reminded him again when they were scraping off the van.

"She's staying with us for a while."

Melissa stared into the crowd, holding up fingers like she already had her smoke. "Like a cousin or something?"

"Nope."

"She from around here?"

"Sort of."

"What happened to her face?"

Daniel bit his lip.

She was losing her patience. "She got a name?"

He kept quiet, wanting to ask the question but afraid of how it might come out.

"Aren't you the mystery man? All dressed up in your fancy pants."

He'd seen her make fun of others a thousand times. He dug deep into his pocket and wrapped his fist around the velvet pouch.

"She's a runaway, okay. It's an RCMP thing."

She stared at Hannah, who was squeezed in against the coats. Her assessment went up a notch, but then her face went blank again. "Shoulda guessed. She doesn't look like she belongs around here. Probably has STDs."

"Really? Really, Melissa?"

She tossed her head back. "It's just a joke. Jeez. Lighten up already."

Daniel felt his cheeks burn, hoping Hannah wouldn't come near. "So how come you haven't answered my calls?"

But Melissa had moved on, her eyes fixated on someone else in the crowd.

Sammy walked up to him and Melissa stepped back, licking her glossed lips. "So. Aren't you going to introduce us?"

Sammy stood beside his big brother, arms hardly twitching. Daniel looked down at the simplicity of that complicated face. He wished the world would warm up and let them run down the road without shoes. Let Sammy win the race.

"Well, what's his name?"

He needed to get his brother away from her. People were filing across the room, toward the main door, his parents among them.

"You ready to go, buddy?" he said to Sammy.

Melissa bent down and got right in Sammy's face. "What's your name, sweetie?"

Sammy said, "What's your name, sweetie," copying her same dripping tone as he backed away from her, flapping his arms.

Melissa squinted and stared. "He's your brother, right? You don't talk about him much." Sammy examined the floor. A long drone escaped from the back of his throat. Melissa covered her mouth to stifle a laugh. "I get why."

Daniel stepped in front of Sammy to block her view. He was inches from her face. Her stale breath made him feel queasy, made him remember the taste of her tongue.

"Careful, Melissa," he said.

She smiled but backed up a step. "I'm always careful."

Hannah came out of nowhere. "Your dad wants to know if you're ready to go?"

Melissa didn't acknowledge Hannah, just turned her head and looked away. Hannah bit her lip and looked at Daniel. He tucked the tips of his fingers into the sides of his mouth, stretching it out like a clown's sad face. Hannah laughed; Sammy too.

Melissa snorted in disgust. "Real mature," she said.

Daniel smiled. "You snort like a pig."

"Like you've got anything to say. You're grounded. Your mommy probably tucks you in at night."

He turned to Hannah then. "Yeah, we're done here,"

"So done," Melissa hissed. "Been done for days. You're just like your brother: too retarded to figure it out."

The trio turned to go, Sammy between them, hopscotch steps. After they crossed the room, Daniel looked back. Melissa made sure no one else was watching before she flipped him the bird and slunk away, through the side door and into the cold.

——

After church, Hannah found her clothes on her bed, folded in two tidy piles. They smelled like Ellie, bright and clean. Her yellowed blouse had a row of new buttons. And her purple sweater looked good as new, its gash stitched up, no more gaping hole in the wool. Ellie had told Hannah that she could use the top dresser drawer, so she filled it with her things, creating neat side-by-side stacks and being careful not to ruin Ellie's creases.

There were two more drawers. Drawer three held stacks of dusty crocheting magazines. The bottom drawer was sticky, so Hannah got down on her knees and pulled both handles as hard as she could, prying the heavy drawer forward a few croaking inches at a time.

Inside, it looked like a baby clothes sandwich—dozens of little outfits wedged between towel folds. There were tiny booties and hats, little crocheted sweaters with teddy bear buttons, and flannel nighties with ribbon drawstrings. Each layer was pink. Some of the baby things at the bottom had scraps of paper pinned to their chests, all with the same handwritten name. The assortment felt pressed down, coated with an out-of-breath metallic smell, like it had been locked up for years.

Ellie poked her head in the room right then and said, "Oh, I've never even opened that drawer. Do you need more space for your clothes?"

Hannah was embarrassed to be caught ransacking the pile. "Thank you for doing my washing. And folding. And for my buttons. And my sweater."

Ellie laughed. "That's a lot of thank-yous. You're so welcome." She smiled big, leaning against the open door.

"There are baby clothes in here," Hannah said. "For a baby girl."

"Really?" Ellie walked toward her and peered into the drawer. "Oh my goodness." Ellie squatted and picked up a bootie. "Myrtle crocheted this. She was Danny and Sammy's grandma. Look at this detail. Wasn't her crochet lovely?"

"It's so tiny. They are all so tiny."

"Newborn size." Ellie got on her knees and ran her finger along the pink edges. "Myrtle certainly kept herself busy. These must have been for a raffle or farmers' market. She must not have got to the giving away part."

Hannah didn't think that was right. "Who's Lily?" she asked.

Ellie dropped the bootie and looked at her sharply. "Pardon me?"

"Lily," Hannah repeated. She dug under the hats and pulled out one of the name-pin sweaters, handing it to Ellie. She was about to search for the other Lilys, but Ellie held the sweater in the palms of both hands, staring down, unblinking, unmoving, her mouth open a bit. It was as if she saw a baby, hidden in the sweater folds.

Hannah held her breath, frozen beside Ellie. She felt foolish doing nothing, like she'd forgotten her line at the school play and needed someone to tell her what to say. But she didn't dare speak, or move, not with Ellie so still beside her. She wanted to know about Lily, if something bad had happened. The longer they sat, the more parts of her hurt—her swollen cheek and bruised back waking up, roaring, like bears from a cave.

"Oh," Ellie said, not so much a word as escaping air. She'd snapped out of her daze, dropping the sweater back in the drawer.

Hannah breathed again, lifting her palm to her cheek.

"I'm sorry," Ellie said, sighing and shaking her head. "You must think I'm mad."

Hannah wished she'd never opened the drawer. "I shouldn't have snooped," she said.

"No. No. Don't be silly." Ellie's fingers clutched the edge of the drawer. "It's just that this is a surprise. I expected more junk, not this."

"Everything's so soft." Hannah wished she'd kept quiet. It was a stupid thing to say.

"Myrtle made her these things. She kept them all this time. Myrtle and I, we never talked about her. We didn't talk about much, to be honest."

Hannah stared down at Lily's little sweater, her own shabby clothes in a drawer above. "What will you do with them?"

Ellie studied the drawer, sighing. "I suppose we'll have to find them another home. But not today. Let's just leave them here for now."

Together they pushed against the wood, baby things disappearing from view as the drawer thudded in place.

Ellie stood and dusted off her jeans. "Beef stroganoff for dinner. How does that sound?"

"Good."

Ellie turned and left in a hurry, Hannah wanting to run after her, to tell her that Lily would have looked pretty.

———

Ellie reached into the Lazy Susan and pulled out the strainer pot. She filled it with cold water and set it on the stove.

All those baby things tucked away in a drawer. It was a layette fit for a princess. Myrtle had never once offered condolences, not one comforting word. How had she even known Lily's name? Ellie must have told her in those first exciting weeks. *We're naming her Lily, Myrtle, for the flower*, she might have said, cockily describing her yoga classes and 10K walks. *This baby's been nothing like Danny. I'm bursting with energy.*

Eric had been the one to tell his mother it was over. *Ellie lost the baby*, she'd heard him whisper into the phone, as if she'd forgotten her daughter on a park bench. As far as Ellie had known, Myrtle hadn't lost a moment's sleep, never gave Lily a second thought.

Ellie stirred the onion and beef chunks browning in the frying pan, her back to the children, who were camped out on the floor in the living room, Lego scattered everywhere.

What about Beatrice? Surely, she hadn't mentioned Beatrice to

Myrtle? Eric had insisted she go to the hospital. She promised him she would. But then he insisted on driving her too, jabbering the whole way about how lucky they were to have Danny and each other. He sped through the streets as if a baby was coming. As if speed could make a difference.

She kept the other pregnancies to herself. She couldn't bear to speak of them, not even to Eric. She got herself to the hospital each time, signed consent forms, and answered doctors' questions with few words and quick nods. She named each without seeing them—Maggie, Catherine, Elizabeth. Five dead baby girls before Sammy came along.

She looked across the room to where he sat on his knees, there on the floor next to Hannah. Their tower was impressive, over four feet tall. She'd made so many mistakes with her son, focusing on all the parts she wanted to be different, yet there he was, showing his new friend how to build things up, how to reinforce the base so none of it would topple over. It would take another ten minutes for the noodles to cook. She'd use the fancy tablecloth and bring down the good china. Sunday best. Myrtle would have liked that.

PART FOUR

NOT QUITE REAL

Monday, December 23

ten

Ellie could not explain what had gummed deep in her chest like half-mixed cake batter. Ever since the girl had shown up, she'd been walking around in a haze of contradictions. The girl would leave the room, and she'd think, *Good, I'll get some peace.* But then she needed her to come right back into view, where she could hear and see her. She had developed a dangerous fondness for Hannah, and fondness was just a stone's throw from feelings that would be hard to let go of. She could not afford to care for this girl.

What she did know for sure was that Christmas morning would not wait. It was less than forty-eight hours away, and there wasn't one package with the girl's name on it. If she didn't do something, her family would soon be tearing through their wrapped gifts, Hannah in the corner watching. It would be like leaving a dog on the wrong side of a glass door.

With Eric called over to Gerry's to boost his dead truck, Ellie would have to drive herself into Neesley to buy Hannah a few things. The roads would likely be awful, but mothers, even damaged ones, have few choices in these matters. Danny was grounded anyway—he could watch over the others; she might even pitch in a few dollars for his time and trouble.

She shooed Hannah out of the kitchen and cleaned up the lunch mess, then waited until the house was quiet: Walter napping in his room, shoes off, drapes shut; Sammy absorbed under the kitchen table with his farm set and a cake pan of water for the pigs and cows to tromp through; Danny lifting weights in the basement.

She was about to slip through the door to scrape off the van when Daniel came up the stairs and asked if he could come too. He sounded earnest and full of purpose, something about needing to get to Dave's Pharmacy.

When was the last time he wanted to go anywhere with her?

Hannah stood right beside him, bolstering his pitch, insisting she didn't mind staying put one bit. Yes, she would let out the dog if he circled. Yes, she would remind Walter to use his cane. Yes, she knew how to turn on the *Cars* movie if Sammy gave up farming. And she had her first-aid training too, don't forget. This girl could stir up a twelve-course meal with one hand and build a swing set with the other, the way she carried on. A pint-sized Myrtle.

So Ellie waltzed out the door, Danny beside her. What was the worst that could happen?

But that was over an hour ago.

"She's still not answering," Ellie said, more urgently now. They were parked badly in front of Peavey Mart, their front tire jutting well into the handicapped space. They'd been in and out of the shabby store already; they'd cruised every aisle. There were snow pants and hard hats and saddles on hay bale displays, but the shelves had been picked clean of knick-knacks and girlie stuff. All of Neesley had been here before her, ransacking the place.

"Danny, we need to go back. She's not picking up."

"You didn't buy her anything yet." He fiddled with the heat controls and then wiped the inside of his window to get rid of the fog.

"I've tried five times." Ellie tucked her scarf into her coat. Winter had sucked all the warmth from the van. "It just rings and rings."

"It's not her phone. When I go to Max's house, I don't answer their phone either."

Ellie ran through her list of instructions. She hadn't told Hannah, *When the phone rings, answer it.* Surely she hadn't needed to spell out such things. Ellie dropped her cell into her purse and jammed the stick shift into reverse. The house was on fire. Walter's fallen and can't get up. Sammy's cut into his own apple and sliced through an artery. She tried to chase these thoughts away, but they skittered back in like spiders. She needed to get home.

"Dave's next," Danny announced. He'd found the Sunny 68 station and cranked the music to high, some old rock song Ellie vaguely recognized.

She managed to get the front end pointed toward the parking lot exit and jammed her foot on the gas. The van jumped and then sputtered to a halt. She held her breath and pumped the pedal. Nothing. She was dangerously hot under her jacket, about to spontaneously combust. Something was wrong with her, with the van. Why wouldn't they move?

He reached out and put a hand on her shoulder, saying words she couldn't hear above the racket coming through the speakers. She punched the radio button and the van went quiet, nothing in the space but her banging heart.

"Mom, you got to put it in park again. Before it will start up."

Yes, of course. That's all she needed to do, but she felt incapable of even that. She yanked off her seat belt and fell out her door in one fell swoop.

"You're driving," she yelled, waving to the lineup of farmers' trucks now behind them. By the time she'd tramped around the van's sludge and into Danny's seat, he'd scooted over and had the engine purring again.

She felt slightly calmer, although she questioned her decision to let him drive, but her son was easing them forward, braking right at the stop sign, signalling like he was supposed to, getting them out of there. He kept both hands on the steering wheel, checking his rear-view mirror every fifteen seconds. "Mom, they're fine. Hannah's smart. Nothing's going to happen," he said, as if she needed a fourteen-year-old's reassurances.

She dug her phone from her purse and tried calling again, the empty ring a hollow sound too loud in her ear. What if Nigel Wilson had come to the house? Eric said he'd made bail yesterday; even monsters got bail. Maybe he had a shotgun and had blown through the door.

Danny rounded the corner and was taking them up Main Street. "Dave's first, then the Style Loft, right?"

She kept her eyes on the phone. "We're skipping the Style Loft." Why hadn't she given Hannah her cell number? What kind of a mother doesn't know to do that much? "The Loft sells junk. They get everything from China."

"But you said . . . I thought you wanted to buy Hannah a new sweater."

"This was a bad idea."

Dave's Pharmacy was straight ahead, a flat red-brick building, one of the street's originals. Danny pulled smoothly into the last spot out front. "They're fine, Mom. I'm going in."

She whipped her head up, but he'd already turned off the engine, removed the keys with the rabbit's foot, and was dangling it in front of her.

She grabbed the furry foot in her fist, thinking she'd leave him there and let Dr. Dave drive him home. She knew she was being ridiculous.

"What's with Dave's? What is it you need so badly here?"

He looked at her, his cheeks splotching like ripened apples. "It's just something . . . I mean, do you think . . ." but then he closed his mouth and opened his door instead.

"What?" Ellie barked.

"Nothing," he said sullenly, stepping out onto the road. "I just gotta return something." He kicked hard at the icicles stuck along the undercarriage.

"You've got five min—" but he slammed the door.

She waited, put the key back into the ignition, fiddled with the radio for breaking news reports and checked her phone settings, the volume of her ring tone, signs of missed messages. They would only have Hannah for five days, not even a full week. It should not be this hard. But what on earth had she been thinking? She'd gone from keeping a watchful eye to giving the girl free reign. Ellie knew nothing about how life with that horrible man had affected Hannah, what persistent aftershocks there might be. She had no right to have entrusted her with a small boy.

And Betty Holt had no right to entrust Ellie with this girl!

Betty had called often the past few days, telling Eric to put her on the phone each time. She'd called just that morning, filling Ellie with more cheery words about her spot-on mothering instincts. It was as if Betty saw her as someone else. Someone capable. As if she'd somehow erased Ellie's "lie downs" during her jovial visits to Myrtle's house in Christmases past. *You just keep doing what you're doing, Ellie. She's in your good hands.*

She needed to call Eric and tell him to get home quickly. But she could hear his steady police voice in her head—*explain that to me again, El*—the sound of it worse than her other imagined scenarios. She could not bear to give him another reason to disguise his worry over his unhinged, hysterical wife.

She got herself out of the van and marched into Dave's. There were happy shoppers scattered about, Myrtle types in knitted scarves, a few she'd seen wandering the aisles at Peavey Mart just moments before. She caught a glimpse of Danny at the back of the store, the bulky down of his jacket, his hair spiked every which way after taking off his toque. He was sidled up to the counter under the pharmacy sign, Dave Sonnenberg on the other side, the two of them shooting the breeze like there was no place else they should be.

She snaked her way past the holiday chatter—news of twenty-five-pound turkeys and old doors on sawhorses to accommodate the Christmas guests—past the shampoos and hairsprays and reading glasses on a revolving shelf. When she came up behind her son, Dr. Dave handed him a small package that he quickly stuffed into his jacket pocket.

"Mrs. Nyland," the man said with a wave, an effeminate gesture, spread fingers, limp wrist. Danny looked over, startled. "Having a nice chat with your boy here."

I bet you are. Was it a package of condoms he'd handed over? The man wasn't even a real doctor. She ignored Dr. Dave, grabbed a fistful of Danny's collar, and pulled him toward her. "I said five minutes."

Her son shook himself free, face red.

"Let's go." She turned without a nod.

Danny clomped behind her. "Aren't you even gonna look? Hannah might like some of this stuff. Barrettes or something."

A fifty-percent-off bin sat near the front exit. She reached in and pulled out the first thing her hand found. Three small hand lotions crammed into a zippered plastic bag. Then she stomped to the checkout and threw the lotions on the counter.

"That will be $3.67 please." The girl wore a Santa hat several sizes too big. She pushed it up her forehead with the tip of her thumb, only to have it slide down again. Ellie fished a five-dollar bill from her wallet and dropped it on the counter. Danny had fled, presumably not willing to be associated with her.

"I mean $3.65. We don't use pennies anymore," the girl chattered on. She'd made a mess of the makeup caked on her pimply chin. "Would you like a—"

"Thank you but I don't need a bag and I don't need a receipt and I don't need change."

Ellie swept the lotions off the counter, threw them in her purse, and walked away.

He was waiting for her in the passenger side of the van. "You're a piece of work, Mom."

They were silent after that. Danny stared out his window without fidgeting, refusing to look in her direction. She followed the centre line as best she could, though it was drifted over in places and she mostly just guessed. Her hands hurt from gripping the wheel too hard, but she kept steady pressure on the gas, even when they rounded the curve before Hodgins's quarter section. She steeled herself at the sight of their house in the distance. There were no flames licking the sky behind their trees, only the billowing grey beard of their chimney stack, the tranquility of the scene making it worse somehow.

She swung the van into their long driveway, sliding into the grooves she'd made on her way out, finding nothing amiss, no stranger's tracks. It was a peculiar light, the world out the window not quite real. The cold west sun ricocheted against the pocks in the glass, making it hard to see ahead as the van eased forward.

He leaned into the dashboard, his head tilted sideways, squinting into the sun. Then he flung himself back again. "Call the fire department. There's your big emergency."

It took a few seconds for Ellie to find them, there, close to the apple tree, near where the bird feeder lay buried in snow, the dog running in circles like his hips weren't arthritic. Sammy was decked out in winter gear like he was made of balloons, every inch of skin covered. Hannah was beside him in her too-thin coat, a scarf wrapped around her ears and tied under her chin.

She eased the van into its usual spot and cut the engine, not taking her eyes off the children. They had two impossibly large balls of wet, white snow piled one on top of the other, forked sticks for arms poking out the sides. Sammy was down on his knees, rolling a third, smaller ball for the head, while Hannah bent, scooped, and helped him along.

"Satisfied?" Danny said.

She'd forgotten there could be snowmen. Forgotten Danny was still there beside her. When she glanced over, he was staring at her in disgust.

"Danny . . . look—"

"Thanks for the *swell* time." He climbed down from his seat and slammed the door.

She got out of the van too, each step an effort, her boots filled with concrete.

"Hey, buddy," Danny called to his brother, traipsing through the yard's deep snow toward him.

"Go back," Sammy yelled, falling sideways in his stuffed suit.

Daniel threw his hands up in mock despair. "Go back? Whaddaya mean? We just got home."

"We're not done." Sammy rolled in the snow before he got to his knees.

Thorn bounded over, butting his nose between Daniel's legs, then turned and pranced back to Sammy, ignoring Ellie, who stopped at the bottom of the stairs, unable to move further.

"Want some help?" Daniel said.

"Got a nose?" Hannah laughed, wading toward him, stomping her feet. "We were having a race. We wanted to finish before you got home."

A heavy knocking sound came from inside the house. They looked up to see Walter's face at the window, the hook of his cane drumming against the glass. Hannah lifted both arms above her head and waved like she was bringing in an aircraft; Sammy too.

"We signal when he bangs on the window," she said. "He likes that."

Ellie stood frozen at the bottom of the stairs, clutching the handrail and her useless purse. It was too much for her, this Norman Rockwell scene, as if everything bad lived only in her head.

Hannah called over to her. "Did you get what you needed? From the store?"

Daniel snorted and mumbled a string of words Ellie thankfully couldn't hear.

Hannah looked from Daniel to Ellie, less sure now. "Is it okay I borrowed a scarf?"

Ellie took a deep breath, the air stinging her lungs. Standing near her two children, the girl looked like some hillbilly's child left out in the cold. The old scarf came from the front closet. She needed a decent coat, boots too. She needed more.

"Why didn't you answer the phone, Hannah?" It was the only thought she had left to cling to. "I called so many times."

Hannah went stiff-still as she felt a change in the air.

"Give it a rest, Mom." Daniel glared at her. "It's a snowman. No one's been bludgeoned with a cleaver."

"I didn't hear it ring," Hannah said, barely above a whisper.

"Help," Sammy yelled, trying to lift the lopsided head on top of his snowman. Thorn leaped and fell over, tried again.

"Are your socks dry inside your boots?" Ellie called over. He was right there, just fine. "Are you warm enough?"

"Too hot." He dropped the head and a piece fell off.

"Come on. Let's finish this thing." Daniel yanked Hannah's arm, pulling her backward through the snow toward Sammy. She didn't take her eyes off Ellie, who started up the stairs.

Ellie turned and called back, "You can hear the phone, even from the yard," which was likely not true, not in the dead of winter, windows shut tight. But she continued anyway, "It's set to the loudest ring. You can hear it clear as a bell."

Ellie didn't know what Hannah had heard, the phone, her words. If she thought too hard, she might explode. She somehow got herself through her door and into the stifling warmth of her kitchen. Walter, an afghan over his knees, was in a chair set up by the window with a view of the yard. Beside him, a TV table held his favourite cup and the blue teapot with the crack along the spout, the bowl of sugar, and a spoon sitting on a paper napkin. Hannah must have arranged all this so she could keep an eye on the demented old man while she somehow stuffed the skittish boy into his snow pants and face mask and led him blindly and without fuss into the great white world.

Ellie moved through the kitchen, opening cupboards for no reason, closing them again. Walter sat forward in his chair, looking out the window with interest. She refused to go near him, refused to look out.

"That nurse . . ." he said. "She's a corker." There was a gentleness in his voice she hadn't heard for a long time.

Ellie sucked air between her teeth. "She's a girl, Dad, not a nurse. Just a perfect little girl who's doing her best." Little girls had no use for purse-sized hand lotions. They needed fruity lip balms and fuzzy socks and a multitude of encouraging words.

Walter cracked against the glass hard with his cane. Ellie could hear the faint hoots and hollers on the other side. The kids were putting on a show for him. She opened the fridge door, broccoli and cabbage fumes filling the back of her throat.

"Now who's that out there?" he yelled.

His eyesight was getting worse by the week. He needed cataract surgery, one more thing she'd put off.

"Sammy and Danny are with Hannah. And Thorn. Thorn's with them too. He'll be stiff tomorrow with all that running around."

"What about that other one? The fellow in the white coat."

"It's a snowman, Dad."

Kids build snowmen and laugh and play.

She closed the fridge door, finding nothing on the crammed shelves she was looking for. She would not call them inside. She didn't trust herself to get the timing right. They could stay out till night if they wanted.

Sammy had left scattered Lego pieces on top of the telephone nook beside the fridge. Ellie scooped them into her palm and looked about the room for their Tupperware container. She found the tray wedged between the wall and the Christmas tree. Crouching low, she pulled it out from its hiding spot, popped off its top, and dropped the pieces into their slots, colour by colour, the wheels to the dip in the centre.

It occurred to her then what was missing. The phone. It was not on its cradle.

She whipped around, spilling the tray, Lego bricks pinging across the floor.

"Dad, have you done something with the phone?"

"I gotta make a call," Walter yelled back, his eyes on the window. "Where's the phone?"

"I'm asking you. Do *you* know where the phone is?" Of course not. The answer clung to a misfiring neuron. Why did this not come to her before now? At the Peavey Mart parking lot, when she was making such a fool of herself. Or at Dave's, when she stood behind her son, watching him slip the God-knows-what package into his pocket.

Walter repeatedly called the 5-1-1 number, enamored with the voice-activated Road Reporting Service. *Bare, dry, wet. Fog, snow, ice. Partly covered. Poor visibility. No visibility. Driving not recommended.* He relished the gritty details, shouting his opinions to the automated voice on the other end of the line.

Ellie marched to the empty cradle, pressed the half-moon locator button, and listened for the pinging noise that would lead her to the phone. She followed the muffled sound, moving forward, backing up, heading down the hallway into Walter's room, getting hotter now, each ping more grating as she rooted through the bed covers and flung open the drawers. There. It had been buried under a pile of the old man's undershirts, a string of eight missed messages on the caller list, each one from her.

——

Later that afternoon, Ellie knocked and waited. When she got no response, she tried again, then inched open Danny's door and stepped into his territory. Her son was on the floor, leaning against the wall between his bed and dresser, legs stretched in front of him, iPad on his lap.

"Mind if I come in?"

He shrugged without looking up. "It's your house. And you already did."

She took a few steps and sat on the edge of the rumpled bed. The air smelled of sweaty shirts and sour socks and expired chicken bits. How long had it been since she'd bulldozed through with a pail and the vacuum? Weeks? Months? She sat without moving for as long as she could, resisting the urge to sweep the room with her eyes.

"So what are you doing down here?" she asked.

His finger kept swooshing across the small screen. "Not burning down the house."

"Hope I'm not interrupting a game." She tried to sound light and unintentional, but her voice cracked midway.

"What do you want, Mom?"

"I want to start over."

Nothing.

"I was a witch today. In the van. At Dave's. I had no right to treat you like that."

"Ya think?" He still wouldn't look at her, but his response was a start.

She leaned forward, planting her hands on her knees. "I do. This is not your fault. You did nothing wrong, and I ruined it for us. I'm really sorry, Danny."

He shoved his iPad out of the way and raised his knees to his chest. "You go crazy for no reason. Not just today."

She took a deep breath and nodded. "I know it must seem like that. Like Jekyll and Hyde."

"Yep." He was still for a minute and then asked, "Is that the one with Christian Bale?"

"Um, I think that was Batman."

"Which one's the monster—Jekyll or Hyde?"

"I always get them mixed up. The doctor is the professor. But there really is no Mr. Hyde, that's the point. Hyde is just Jekyll, who has turned his body into something ugly."

"We got a lot better monsters since then."

"I know. They're everywhere. On TV. In your phone. Sitting beside you in the front of the van."

Daniel laughed in spite of himself. "You make a crappy monster. You're not scary enough." Then his face went dark again. "But you can be crazy. Lately, a lot. Sorry."

"I know. Like a momma bear who keeps losing her cub."

"It's stupid. Sammy's gonna be okay. And hello, I exist."

She began to suspect that she would always be apologizing, a withered old lady choking on dried-up words.

Her son rubbed his forehead in a way that reminded her of Eric. Then he looked up and asked, "Are you getting a divorce?"

God. "Where did that come from?"

He picked at the lint on his sweater. "Every time a parent sits down with their kid and says *this is not your fault*, the next thing out of their mouth is *Daddy's leaving, but he loves you very much, we'll get you a puppy, yada yada*. Everybody knows that."

"That is certainly not—"

"I'm not completely stupid." He rose up off the floor and flounced on the bed behind her. "You can't even look at him without finding his flaws. You're mad that he brought Hannah here. You're mad that he brought us here, even though it was *your* idea. You're mad that it's Christmas. You're mad about everything."

Her regret was too great; she was doubled over with the weight of it.

"I'm going to do better, Danny," she said, turning to face him. "We're not getting a divorce; of course we're not." Although she had thought about it, back when Eric was gone day and night dousing other families' fires. She'd even ordered that damn used book from Amazon. She didn't read past the first few pages; neither its words, nor the world, made any sense to her without Eric. She couldn't imagine waking up in an empty bed, no more jangling keys, the silence deafening. "I love your father very much," she told her son now.

"What about Hannah?"

His question caught her off guard.

"She's the one you should apologize to. You were so mean out there in the yard. *You know you can hear the phone ringing. Any idiot can hear the phone ringing.*"

Shame washed over her. "Is that how I sounded?"

"Pretty much."

"Okay, just shoot me now." She raised a hand to her head and pulled the trigger finger.

He threw his head back on the pillow. "She probably didn't even hear."

"She didn't say anything, did she?"

"Nope."

Of course she didn't. If the girl could live life in that vile house, she could certainly manage to keep her thoughts to herself.

Ellie grabbed hold of his socked foot and squeezed. "I'm going to do better. Can we start over?"

He tried to wrestle his foot out of her grasp while she held on tight.

"Pretty please?" she pleaded.

"I guess," he said. He seemed to mean it.

"Okay, deal." Ellie stood. "Are you coming up soon?"

"In a minute."

When she got to the door, she turned and looked back. He seemed so innocent, a little boy waking up from his nap. Her boy.

"Danny, what were you looking for at Dave's? You don't have to tell me if you don't want to."

"I wasn't looking for anything. I was taking something back."

"Oh. You okay?"

He shrugged, his shoulders defeated. "I guess."

"Does it have something to do with that girl?" There was a girl, she was sure.

His eyes narrowed. "What girl?"

"The one you were going to see the night you had your . . . accident. You never told us her name."

"What are you talking about?"

"I'm not completely stupid either, Danny. You were going to see a girl."

Daniel stared at her for a full ten seconds. Finally, he said, "She texted a whole bunch of times. She sounded like she was in trouble."

"You thought this girl needed help, so you went to her. Or at least you tried. Have I got that right?"

He nodded, cheeks reddening.

"Well, I'd say that's pretty honourable. It didn't turn out the way you wanted, but your intentions were good, and that's where goodness starts."

"Her name's Melissa," he said. "She dumped me."

She hung on to the doorframe to keep from running back to him. "Oh. That sucks. When?"

"I don't know. Maybe I dumped her. Anyway, it's over. It was inevitable. I got her a necklace for Christmas. That's why I needed to go to Dave's. To take it back."

"A smart decision."

"She was a jerk. I don't know what I ever saw in her. I feel kind of relieved actually."

Ellie felt no small relief herself. "Then I'm glad. She doesn't deserve you."

"That's what Hannah said."

Ellie stopped cold, incredulous. Her son's shattered heart—the girl had found her way even in there? "You talked to Hannah about Melissa?"

"She saw us together at church."

"Melissa was at church?" She'd missed this too.

"Yeah. I told Hannah she was my girlfriend and that we broke up, and she said I could pick better friends. She seems older than eleven."

Yes, she does. Ellie decided she should say nothing else—not about Hannah, not about that package she'd seen Danny slip back into his pocket before leaving the store. If she was starting over she could start right here and keep her mouth shut, so she blew her son a kiss and walked away.

eleven

Eric's high beams lit up a snowman when he pulled into the driveway at a quarter past five. He'd taken longer than he'd planned with Gerry, whose truck battery was too fried to come back to life. On his way home, he'd phoned Betty. She'd just left the station where, she said, the constables seemed on edge. Of course they did. Assaults on little girls had a way of taxing resources. Wilson was out on bail, back home, and likely ironing more shirts, his preliminary court date set for February 16.

Instead of going straight home, Eric stopped in at the Style Loft to pick up a few Christmas gifts for Hannah. He should have consulted Ellie first, but something stopped him from having the conversation.

Ellie somehow knew the right things. How to do the girl's hair, make her a nice room, or tease out a smile. But for that, he'd had to repeatedly assure her, *just for a few days, that's all this is,* as if his promise was the duct tape holding her together. No, he couldn't allow her to find out just how consumed his thoughts were by the girl and what was to happen to her.

Laurie Haddon, the shop's owner, was another kind of problem, poking and prying as she rang up his purchases, stealing sideways glances at his still-swollen knuckles.

"A lovely sweater choice, Sergeant Nyland."

"Not a sergeant, Laurie. Just Eric."

"And such a beautiful coat. It came in with last week's order. She'll love the faux-fur trim, and if she wants a different look, the hood zips on and off—here like this. Who did you say it was for?"

He changed the subject by asking Laurie about her dimwitted son, the one who'd been caught twice spray-painting the word *vagina*—spelled v-e-g-i-n-a—on the stone wall in front of the seniors' complex. That shut her up, although he presumed she had already plucked Hannah's story off the street as it rolled through town.

He entered the house empty-handed, leaving the packages in the trunk of the car where the dead cat had been just a few nights before. He took off his coat, patting his pocket to be sure his keys were still there and patting the dog who ambled into the entryway to say hello.

"Something smells good," he said.

"Macaroni and cheese," Ellie called over, pulling the casserole from the oven, nothing else in her voice other than macaroni and cheese, which bolstered his courage considerably.

There was a strange calm about the place. They were all in the same room, the kids and Walter gathered around the supper table, already set for their family of six. Sammy bopped up and down in his seat, but he was right there beside them, not off in a corner staring into space. Hannah leaned forward on her elbows on either side of her knife and fork, her hands under her chin.

"And then what happened?" she asked Walter, who was digging in his pocket for a rock.

"Finish the story, Grandpa," Daniel said.

"What story?" Walter blinked like the lights had just come on.

"The one about the duck!" Daniel could barely contain himself. "You lowered the bucket . . ."

Walter smacked his lips. "That's just what we did. We lowered the bucket and that duck hopped right in, we hoisted her up and out, and she shook herself off and waddled away, as if falling down a well happened every other day."

Hannah laughed unabashedly. Walter looked up, surprised, as if he'd heard nothing like the sound of it in his sixty-some years in this house. Daniel smiled, hands folded across his chest in satisfaction, although he'd heard his grandpa's stories a thousand times. Eric could not remember the last time his son took such interest.

"We're eating early tonight," Ellie said cheerily, brushing her hair off her face with her oven-mitted hand. "We're all starving."

"No wonder." Eric walked up to her and kissed her on the cheek. "Pretty handsome snowman out there. Anyone know how he got here?"

"Sammy," Daniel and Hannah piped up in unison.

"Is that right? Sammy, you invited him here?"

Sammy simply said, "I made him."

Eric felt his shoulders relax for the first time all day. "Really? Who knew you were such a great snowman maker? What's his name?"

"Robert," Sammy yelled. The other kids chuckled. Thorn was back under Hannah's chair, licking her bare toes.

"They were all in on it." Ellie carried the casserole dish to the table and plopped it down on the hot-mat. "It was Hannah's idea." She caught his eye and shrugged her shoulders, as if she had no say in the matter.

Eric stood at the sink and washed up, hot water stinging his bruised fists. "Well, I'm thinking Robert the Snowman will be with us a long time. There's a whole lot of winter ahead. Maybe he needs a brother to hang out with. Or a son. Robert Junior."

"Or a girlfriend," Daniel said, drawing a curvy figure with his hands. "I'd like to see Sammy make that one."

Sammy jumped out of his seat and ran to the front closet.

"Whoa, not now, slugger." Eric strode over to collect him. "We've got to have supper first. Maybe tomorrow, okay?"

Eric maneuvered Sammy back to his seat by getting up close, stretching his arms wide, and taking small steps forward while Sammy backed up. That same technique had worked with Stump too, Eric's favourite among the horses that had trotted in and out of his childhood. "Will one of you kids get a glass of water for everybody?" Ellie was back at the counter, tossing the salad with the giant wooden hands.

Hannah sprinted over to the exact right cupboard.

"Danny, you get the ketchup and the salad dressings." Daniel jumped right up too. "And the mayonnaise for your grandpa."

By this point, Walter had stuffed his napkin in his collar, waiting, fork in one fist, knife in the other. There was nothing for Eric to do but to sink into his place at the table, grateful, while the others zinged past, each with their jobs.

The table was ready, everyone seated except Hannah, who was transporting the last glass of water, Eric's, taking small careful steps as she passed behind Sammy and Walter, so as not to spill. But then her toe caught an edge, Eric couldn't see on what, and she started to go down, grabbing the back of Walter's chair to keep from falling. The glass jumped out of her hand, shattering on the floor into an obscene array of pieces.

Eric leapt up and commanded her to stand still. He heard nothing at all, not Ellie's gasp or Sammy banging on the table. He was seeing her small toes, glass shards glistening in the lake on the floor. But he spoke too harshly, may have screamed, in fact, because she was cowering now, backing away from him; she had that exact same look she'd had in the back seat of the car as they rounded the curve toward Nigel's house.

With chunks of glass all around her, behind her, she was about to step down and slice a hole in her heel. There was nothing else to do but reach out for her. When she threw her arms up to fend off the blow, anger splashed through him. He saw himself in her actions—his arms had shot up like that, a long time ago, Walter coming at him. He hoisted her off the floor, out of harm's way. She weighed less than air.

"Sorry, kiddo." He set her down on the kitchen counter. "I didn't mean to yell. I didn't want you to cut your bare feet, that's all."

Hannah hugged her chest, looking down. He turned around to see his family at the table. They were staring wide-eyed to see what he would do next, as if he'd thrown the glass himself just to hear it crack.

"I'll get the broom," Ellie said, not moving.

"Why isn't she wearing socks?" His voice lashed out, gruff and uneven. He reached down, a hot sting between his toes, and plucked a diamond dipped in red out of his work sock.

"They were wet, Eric. From building the snowman. They're hanging in the bathroom. Is that all right with you?"

"It was not an accusation."

Ellie sighed. "Well, what was it then?"

Hannah threw her hands over her face and burst into noisy sobs, the same desperate wet sound he'd heard come out of her at Wilson's house.

He didn't dare touch her heaving body, perched on the counter where he'd dropped her. He scanned the breadth of his table for reinforcement, the picture unsettling him even more. Sammy perfectly still—choosing this precise moment to be unflappable—and Daniel too, suddenly devoid of teenaged counsel. Thorn under the table, right where Hannah should be, licking her chair leg furiously. Walter stretching his arm across the table, furtively inching the macaroni dish toward him by the loop on the hot mat.

Ellie stood, but instead of going to Hannah, or finding her a Kleenex at least, she went to fetch the broom. Hannah didn't let up crying as Ellie swept around her with long, efficient strokes, pushing the wet splinters into the dustpan and getting down on her knees to sop up the spill and scoop the tiniest bits into a swirl of paper towel. She gingerly tweezed the tips of her fingers for a few wayward slivers, Eric backing up to get out of her way. Then she threw the soggy ruins into the garbage can under the kitchen sink and leaned on the broom, scanning the floor closely.

"I think I got it all," she said above Hannah's sobs. "Can anyone see more pieces?"

Not a sound from the table. Hannah, face still covered, replaced the worst of the racket with man-sized hiccups mixed in with noisy sniffing and gulping noises.

Ellie took her time putting the broom away before she stepped in front of the girl. "Would you like to come to the table now?" she asked breezily. "Hannah, look at me."

Hannah gulped and sniffed and croaked like a dying frog, watery eyes blinking at Ellie. Her face was a spectacular patchwork of Christmas red, snot dripping from her nose.

"Can, can I go to my room?"

Eric moved in beside Ellie. "Come on now. It was just a little accident. It's all fixed now."

Ellie dug her fingernails through the arm of his sweater. "You go right ahead, Hannah. Take as long as you need." She lifted her down and whispered, "I'll save you some supper." Hannah scampered off, Thorn's claws scrambling on the linoleum, doing his best to catch up.

Ellie sat down at the table, placed her napkin on her lap, and took a long drink of water. Eric slumped against the counter. He was astounded by how fast things could turn.

"Earth to Danny," Ellie was saying. His son looked dazed, like he was waking from a coma. "Why don't you get your macaroni and then slide the dish to me. I'll help Sammy."

Daniel started to reach for it, then changed his mind and thumped his arms down hard, rattling his empty plate. "May I please be excused?" he asked defiantly, as if expecting a fight.

"You certainly may," Ellie answered without a second's delay.

Sammy shot up, knees on his seat, staring after his brother now striding toward the hallway.

"And you too, Sammy. You can go with your brother if you want."

He hopped down off his chair and ran after Daniel, holding his undone drawstring to keep his sweatpants from sliding down.

Ellie wrestled the macaroni dish from Walter, who had polished off a fair chunk already, and scooped a spoonful onto her plate.

They had all gone into Hannah's room, the kids, the dog. Eric could feel the wet under his armpits soak into the wool of his sweater.

"Maybe I should go check on them," he said.

"Or come eat your dinner," she answered, still readying her plate.

"What kind of pie?" Walter chimed in.

"We're not having pie tonight, Dad," Ellie said. "Would you like some salad? There's mayonnaise."

Eric heard an odd sound coming from his own throat, a humming noise that he swallowed back down.

"What about the lemon meringue?" Walter said.

"That was yesterday," Ellie lied. She never made pies, certainly not a lemon meringue. "Tonight it's chocolate ice cream. With cherries on top if you like. But you should have some salad first, Dad."

How could his wife be so insensitive about Hannah? Eric strained to hear noises coming from behind her door. Was she still crying? What were the boys doing in there?

Ellie spooned a blob of mayonnaise on top of Walter's lettuce, laughing at something he said to her. Eric left them to their supper and went down the hallway until he was leaning his ear against the cold wood of her door, a sliver of white light from the other side washing over his socked feet.

He heard whispers and laughter, Daniel's, a rustling and then a series of thumps, Sammy jumping on her bed maybe, Thorn moaning, like he did when he managed to flip on his back and stick his paws in the air. Then he heard the girl, a torrent of words that he couldn't make out. There was no lingering misery in that voice, not a gulp in the mix. Daniel laughed again, a deep sturdy sound; Sammy yelling *more, more.*

He thought about sisters and brothers and their dogs, holed up in bedrooms all over the world, teetering on the edge of another universe, one that adults were not privy to. It didn't make a damn difference if you were an ex-cop, a trained investigator, you would always be one step behind. He backtracked to the kitchen and sat at the table.

"They're okay." He stared at his plate.

"I know," Ellie said.

How? He looked at her closely. "How did you know?"

She was staring back at him, clear eyed, giving nothing away. "Would you like me to get you a glass of water?" she asked.

"God no." He could feel his forehead heat up.

She covered her mouth but couldn't hide the sound, snorting into her hand. He could tell she was trying, really trying, to be delicate and failing miserably. Her laughter floated above him, around him, rising to full volume. He caught the sound in the air and let himself go, the pair of them hee-hawing like jackasses getting out of the rain.

"What's got your buns in a knot," Walter scoffed. He'd lined up his rocks in the shape of a smile.

That set them off again. Finally, Ellie wiped her eyes, patted her face, and straightened her blouse. Eric swung his legs out from under his chair and strode over to her side of the table. He wanted to lift her up and feel her in his arms, but the moment had clearly passed. He rested his hand on the curve of her shoulder. She covered it with her own and gave it a squeeze. He could have stayed like that all night, his hand under hers.

"I bought her a few things at the Style Loft today," he whispered, overly cautious. If their hullabaloo hadn't brought the kids out yet, nothing would. "A sweater. And a coat. I thought we could wrap them for under the tree."

She tensed, or he imagined it, a slight shudder beneath his fingers, but then she stood quickly. "Help me serve up, Eric," she said, all business again.

"What?"

"We'll make it a picnic. They can eat in Hannah's room."

She flapped around the table, stacking plates, bringing dishes together like a church buffet. His beautiful wife, another unsolved case he would have to let stand.

———

Eric snuck the gifts into the house after Ellie had tucked Sammy in, and while Daniel and Hannah sat side by side at the kitchen table, distracted by noisy YouTube videos of Mr. Bean getting a Christmas turkey stuck on his head.

Coming in from the cold with the large package in his arms, Eric grabbed Ellie's hand and hauled her down the hall and into their bedroom. When he first pulled the jacket and sweater out of the frozen Style Loft bag, holding them up to her expectantly, she sucked in her breath and tried not to think about her disgusting scene in the drugstore. All she could say was "We don't know her taste."

She hated herself in that moment, that silly "sticks and stones" rhyme popping into her head. She would have preferred broken bones to the slump she'd made of his shoulders, the way his eyes refused to meet hers. "Sorry," she said. "These are very nice."

"I thought we should get her a few presents," Eric said, as if this wouldn't have occurred to her. "Laurie Haddon was her usual piece of work. She wanted the juicy details to serve up with her Christmas turkey."

Ellie smiled, rolling her eyes. "That woman lives for gossip. Hannah is none of her business."

"Of course not."

"And neither are we."

He sighed. "That's right, El. Neither are we."

Of course, he knew she was thinking of Sammy, the unanswered questions that followed them everywhere. Ellie wanted to reach out and touch the side of her husband's cheek, but she went over to her dresser instead. "We'll need to come up with a stocking too," she said, her back to him. "And some little presents. We must have some things here we can give her."

She rummaged through drawers, through the closet, through the shoebox of junk they kept under the chair, while Eric sat on the bed and watched. She found a new clear nail polish, a package of glitter stickers, heart keychain, a sample perfume in a vial, and a Kleenex packet covered in daisies. She dug through her purse for the fifty-percent-off hand lotions too.

Eric fingered through the pile that she'd dumped on his lap. "This is good, right?" he asked. "She'll like this stuff?"

He needed her to tell him it was enough, as if he could not see the stinginess of her heart, as if she had actually earned the right to make such a pronouncement. His trust in her was astounding.

She tried anyway, to sound convincing. "We can use Sammy's old stocking with the hole in the toe, stuff in some tissue. It's at the bottom of the decoration box."

"I'll get it," he said, slipping out their bedroom door. She sat down where he'd sat, letting the warmth that he'd left seep under her skin.

When he got back, they wrapped the last of the presents. Ellie was humbled by Eric's choices, the perfectness of the colours and how he'd selected the right size.

For the sweater, they dug up an old Sears box and used the end-of-the-roll mistletoe paper. Ellie folded the ruby red cardigan in tissue, soft as a dove with its velvet piping and patch pockets. Hannah's jacket went into a large Gala Apples box wrapped in silver glitter paper and a sparkly bow. The jacket was a lovely aqua blue with fur around the collar, a zipper and snaps to keep the cold from seeping through, and extra deep pockets to hide treasures.

After several false starts, Eric wrote on the tag, "To keep you warm. Your friends, The Nylands." There was no room for more and no right words anyway.

PART FIVE

THIS INEXPLICABLE AND TITANIC SHIFT

Tuesday, December 24

twelve

Ellie looked out their frosted bedroom window at the driving snow. A single raven perched on the telephone line, head tucked in close, feathers fanning behind like a peacock's. The ruthless north wind had risen with the sun, hours ago now, its bitter bite of eddies and undertows, gorging on anything not properly tied down. Eric had strung a safety line between the house and the barn for times such as these, times when you could so easily lose your way. God knows it had happened before in this county: Erdman Croeger got his Ski-Doo turned around in a blizzard and drove it in circles until it ran out of gas. They found him the next morning, miles from the Ski-Doo, trudging through the deep snow, half-naked, recognizing nothing and no one.

He survived another week before his frozen heart stopped beating, just days before his seventy-first birthday.

Ellie stared at the tattered raven. She couldn't understand the mechanics, how the bird stayed upright, its skinny claws attached to the wire. Or the cows out further in the Jorgensen field, beached whales, still as ice sculptures. How did they endure it, hour after hour, no barn or windbreak to protect them from the worst? She was grateful for their solid walls, as dry as brushwood, and the warm air wheezing through the ducts from the overworked furnace.

It had been a good day, finer than she ever imagined. Sammy and Hannah spent the morning building a fence around his Lego city with a stack of alphabet blocks they found in the closet of Hannah's room. (Odd how Ellie thought of it as Hannah's room now, Myrtle pushed against the wall like her straight-backed mannequin.) It thrilled Sammy to no end to create a barrier between what was his and the world's. Hannah could not know this—she was not even twelve—but her instincts were uncanny when it came to Ellie's youngest son.

Daniel too seemed surprisingly merry. He had a spring in his step and a silly grin he didn't try to hide. He kept running up and down the stairs, first for a box, then scissors, then scotch tape, then a ballpoint pen, yelling each time, *No one come down, don't come down*, as if he hoped for a skirmish in front of his closed door.

Eric had stayed unusually close, hovering over Sammy and Hannah, making excuses to stay near. He admired their alphabet fence, knocking on the gate, huffing and puffing like the big bad wolf. He spread old newspaper on top of the coffee table and glued the ear back on the old reindeer that Myrtle had hammered out of wood decades ago.

Every time Ellie glanced his way, Eric was busying himself with something new. First, he rearranged the lights on the highest branches, blues beside green, purples with yellows. Then he prowled about, stops and starts, filling the basin under the tree with the Pyrex cup and adding a splash to the poinsettias against the wall. He even got down on his knees and fiddled with Walter's wobbling table leg.

When he looked around to see what might come next, she asked him to give her a hand, and he rushed to the kitchen, grateful to have a job. They worked side by side, hips swaying to the classics, Hannah belting out the words in the background. "Let It Snow." "Have Yourself a Merry Little Christmas." They peeled potatoes and turnips; sliced onions and carrots; mixed the bag of cranberries with sugar and orange juice and a splash of bourbon, stealing swigs from the bottle and stirring the mix over the burner until berries popped like little guns going off. Eric brought the giant roasting pan out from under Walter's bed and scrubbed it shiny with an S.O.S pad. The turkey was downstairs, dunked under cold water in the utility sink with a brick on top to keep it submerged.

Ellie had crossed off almost everything on her two-page list, her movements uncomplicated and weightless as she glided through her morning from cupboard to drawer, fridge to stove, pantry to closet, Eric underfoot, the comings and goings of the children working through their important business. She forgot to tap her forehead or chant her ridiculous mantras, forgot to worry about Sammy's future or Daniel's collision course to manhood.

Now she stood in front of their bed, surveying the stack of presents piled on the quilt. She had held back the stocking stuffers from Santa, bringing the rest out of hiding from the back of her closet. All that was left was to put them under the tree.

At some small noise, she turned and found Hannah at the bedroom door, staring wide eyed, mouth open, not breathing. Hannah's wonder made her laugh.

"Come in. I could sure use your help."

Hannah stepped forward tentatively. "There's so many," she said.

"I know, I know, it's crazy." Ellie threw up her hands. "We went kind of overboard this year."

"The paper is so pretty." Hannah came nearer to the bed.

Ellie smiled at her. "Don't look too close. I'm not good with corners. We need to get all these under the tree. Want to help carry them into the living room?"

Hannah jumped forward and scooped up a load of wrapped boxes and odd-shaped packages and shot off down the hall. She moved so fast that Ellie couldn't fit in a word about where they should go under the tree: Sammy's spaced so they were not touching; Walter's hiding in the back, in case he started poking around with his cane, recognized his name, and started tearing off the paper. No matter, she could rearrange the gifts tonight after Hannah and the others had been put to bed.

A piece of wrapping had come undone on Sammy's new pajama box, so she searched through the drawer of her night table for a roll of scotch tape.

Hannah was back in an instant, ready to fetch more.

"What's Sammy doing?" Ellie had her head in the drawer. It was a delicate balance with Sammy. She did not want him so overwhelmed by glitz that he'd turn sour on the whole idea. "Is he sniffing around the tree?"

"Is he allowed?" Hannah asked.

"Of course he's allowed." Ellie thought it strange to be asked, as if she ruled over every little thing. She found the tape at last and turned to face the girl.

Hannah could not tear her eyes from the pile of gifts on the bed. "Sammy is in his room. He's drawing another picture. Should I go get him?" she asked, clearly not wanting to, as if the presents might disappear.

"No, no, just wondering, that's all." Ellie wasn't used to a girl underfoot, pointing out ribbon and bows, scrambling to be helpful. *Should I wash the dishes? Does the cheese go in a Ziploc? Which knife should I use? Where do these newspapers go? Should I go get Sammy?* Her questions were exhausting. But then it was more than that: they required Ellie's attention, all of it, forcing her back into this world.

The jacket box had caught Hannah's eye, the largest of the gifts, and Hannah reached out to test its weight. "I'll take this one by itself," she announced before skipping away.

Ellie ripped off a piece of tape and pressed it into the fold of Sammy's pajama paper. When she pulled it taut, it tore a jagged hole right down Rudolf's flank. Cursing, she started over with a new piece of snowflake-patterned paper from the box under the bed.

It took several minutes to get the wrapping just right. And Hannah? The girl was taking so long she could have marched into the forest and back out by now. When she finally re-entered the room, Ellie saw her spark had disappeared, her steps heavy and dragging.

"That present had my name on it," Hannah said, more a question.

Ellie smiled. "It did? Imagine that."

Hannah stared at Ellie without blinking, then leaned over and checked the rest of the tags. "And this one does too." Her cheeks were pale and shadowed. What on earth could be wrong with her?

"Are you okay, Hannah?"

She was biting her lip. "You got me a present," she announced, a warble in her voice. "You got me two."

"Of course we got you a present." Ellie tried to ignore the mounting disappointment, both hers and the girl's. She had wanted this to be a nice surprise. "It's nothing much. Just a little something for Christmas this year."

Hannah seemed unable to move, uninterested in carrying another armload to the tree.

"If we had more time, we would have done more," Ellie said.

Would she? Or would she have let her petty fears, wrapped round and round and round, leave no extra room under the tree?

They didn't look at each other, Hannah rocking back and forth on the balls of her feet, Ellie biting her lip, drumming her twitchy fingers along the sides of her thighs.

Finally, Hannah said, "Do you know where Eric is?"

"He's not in the living room?"

Hannah shook her head, running her finger along the top of the quilt. "I need to ask him something."

Ellie blushed. It was as if she'd been caught on video throwing the goddamn lotions on the checkout counter.

"Hannah, what is it? You can ask me. You can ask me anything."

Hannah stood next to Ellie for the longest time, her pointy elbows sticking out, hands cupping her chin. She sucked air through her teeth, lips parted.

"That's okay," she said with conviction. "I'll go find him."

Ellie watched her go, the world spinning a little, pulling her sideways.

———

Eric was not one of those idiots who thought, *We'll have a kid, it will fix the marriage.* God knows, that's what wrecked them in the first place, all their relentless trying. But this was more. It wasn't this girl herself, or where she'd come from, but the string of moments between before-her and now. It was this inexplicable and titanic shift in their world as he knew it, and in the people he loved, as if they had collectively dropped into a new country like tourists. The boys seemed to have a renewed interest in each other and the things around them. There were whispers, teasing, high-fives in the air. Sammy had found his pastels, no longer satisfied to draw amoebas in caves. Since the shadow puppets, he'd become interested in animals again, stringing happy cows and tigers along sunlit fields. He took his time, adding crooked but bold Sammy signatures before shooting each coloured page under Hannah's door.

Daniel had crawled into the cramped space under the stairs in search of the old Crokinole game. Then he'd lugged it up to the kitchen table, insisting they play in teams, Daniel and Hannah against the parents, and then mixing it up, girls against boys.

But it was the changes in Ellie that unsettled Eric the most. She would announce matter-of-fact things like *It's only another few days* or *Of course she'll be gone soon*. But there was a glaring incongruence between her tossed-off words and the way her eyes followed Hannah from room to room, the way her shoulders relaxed and her face softened when Hannah was down on the floor with Sammy, or huddled beside Daniel and the iPad, or hovering over Walter and his puzzle.

It was nothing he could articulate on a witness stand. *My wife is different, Your Honour. There's a girl in my house and it's changed her. I'm afraid of what will happen when we send her away.* A judge could question his hypothesis ad nauseam, but Eric could not be more precise. He could only stare into the future blankly, the most unreliable of witnesses.

Now here he was in the van, Hannah seated beside him with her hands on her lap. It was the day before Christmas and he was taking her back to that house. Every cell in his body screamed *bad idea*, but by this point, the girl could have asked him to pluck down a star and he'd have found a way.

She would only say she needed to get a few things. She said it was important or she wouldn't have asked.

He offered to take her into town instead, to buy whatever it was she wanted, but she adamantly declined. It was her bedroom she needed to get to.

When he'd called Betty, she'd said, *Well, of course, Hannah has the right to retrieve her belongings. But she should go with one of the constables!* When he told Betty that Hannah didn't want that, Betty said more sternly, *She's the child, Eric. You need to tell her what's best.*

He'd already tried that. He'd explained to Hannah that the police had to escort her; he could call them right away. When she shook her head, he reminded her that Nigel Wilson would be there. She had just looked at him without blinking and said, *But you'll be there too.*

———

Hannah could barely breathe. She told herself she would not be scared because she was doing the right thing. Eric was unhappy about taking her back, Ellie even more so, and their disapproval had nearly stopped her. But they'd gone to so much trouble to make her feel special. There were presents under the tree, beautifully wrapped and just for her. Two, not one.

They were only going across the road, driving not walking, so that she could load up with as much stuff as she wanted. She promised herself she wouldn't cry. She'd get in and out, quick as a wink; steer clear of Nigel as she ran up the stairs. She knew exactly what to look for and where to find it. Eric had promised to stand guard at the front door, although he hadn't said a word since they'd stepped into the van. She wished he would promise one more time.

As they pulled into the driveway, Eric blew air out of his mouth and stopped the engine. "Are you sure about this?" He didn't take his eyes off the house. "It's not too late to change your mind."

Hannah undid her seat belt and pushed open her door. She placed both feet on the uneven ground, lungs filling with frozen air. Eric was beside her then—she would not cry—and as they walked side by side to the front door, she reached for his hand.

She didn't ring the bell, just walked right in, Eric now behind her, his hand on her shoulder.

Nigel came out of the kitchen but just barely. He stayed on the far side of the living room. His eye was ringed with purples and greens, and the side of his face bulged like he had stuffed an orange in his cheek. There was a cut above his lip. He looked frightened to see them standing there. Whether he was afraid of what he'd done to her in the cellar, or what Eric might do to him now, she had no way of knowing. She felt a moment of guilt seeing him like that, so shrivelled, but then she thought about Mandy and her teeth clenched.

Nigel kneaded a tea towel in his hands. She wanted to run upstairs, like she'd planned from the get-go, but she couldn't make her legs move.

"You're not supposed to be here," Nigel said. "I'm not allowed to be around her. Or you."

"She's not staying." Eric squeezed her shoulder to let her know he was still there. "She just needs to pick up a few things."

Nigel wouldn't look at her; he focused instead on Eric, who towered behind her. "So she's with the Nylands now. One big happy family."

"She's with us over Christmas." Eric's voice sounded different. Mean. "You didn't leave her a choice."

Nigel cupped his hand over his swollen cheek. "You always did get what you wanted, Eric. Things always turn out for you in the end."

Eric moved beside her, feet planted wide. She could see his hand clenched into a tight fist. Nigel could see it too, dropping the tea towel, stepping back until he stood pressed against the grandfather clock. None of them said a word. Eric and Nigel just stared at each other, until Nigel finally said, "Hannah, take your reindeer sweater. It's Christmas and you always liked that one best."

She wanted to scream at him. It was the sweater her mother had knit her. She'd outgrown it ages ago. She didn't even have it anymore. Eric pushed her a little. "Go," he said. "Go get your things now."

That was all her legs needed. She flew up the stairs and into her room, shut her door, and leaned against it, panting. She could hear no thumping below, no creaking on the stairs, no Mandy there to greet her. *Move, Hannah.* She dug her nails into her palms until she winced. Then she was down on her knees, pulling out the box from under her bed, then at her dresser, opening drawers, the lid of her jewellery box. She worked quickly, lining her treasures in a row along her mattress.

For Ellie, her most prized possession: *150 of the Most Beautiful Songs Ever,* the book her mother had saved weeks for. When it arrived in the mail, her mother cried out, *It's here, it's here,* which made Hannah cry too. Every night before bed, her mother let Hannah choose which songs to sing. "Climb Ev'ry Mountain," "Fly Me to the Moon," "A Dream Is a Wish Your Heart Makes," "These Are a Few of My Favourite Things." Her mother seemed so close she could feel her breath in her ear.

For Eric, the wooden key holder she'd made at Brownie camp. Her painted hearts were less than perfect, not nearly enough, but there were three solid hooks for his always-missing keys.

Her toy kaleidoscope was for Sammy, a present from a man in a broken wheelchair at Sunnybrook. She put her eye to the hole and turned the cylinder to be sure it still worked. They were all still inside, bits of spinning glass Sammy could find patterns in.

She spent several minutes digging through her rock box for Grandpa Walter. She and her mother had collected these from that day at the beach. She chose one small enough to fit in his pocket beside his others, pink tinged and shiny smooth, like it had been baked in an oven.

Daniel was the hardest. She decided on her angel on the chain, the one she kept in her jewellery box. When she was younger, she wore it all the time. It made her feel safe having an angel next to her heart. Until it didn't anymore. She didn't expect Daniel to wear it, but she hoped it would keep him safe, even if it stayed in a drawer and he had no idea where the feeling came from.

She looked over the possessions she'd scattered across her bed, feeling small and unworthy. She'd tried so hard to be on her best behaviour since she got to their house, but she'd made so many stupid mistakes. Not answering the phone when they were building the snowman. Having a fit at breakfast. Another at supper. Crying like a baby over spilled water. Talking too much, too little, too loud, too quiet.

When she was little, she had made pacts with God. *I'll always be good if you bring her back to me. I'll never make a peep if you make him nice again.* She used her favourites as bargaining chips: ice cream, her singing voice. It didn't work then and it probably wouldn't work now.

She found an empty box in her closet and placed the gifts inside. Before she turned to go back downstairs, she reached for the small pillow she kept tucked under her covers. The fairy pillow her mother had made her, *I Love You Most* embroidered across the top. She would keep this close, whatever bed she ended up in.

Hannah looked around the room one last time. There was nothing more to take with her. It might be a silly pile of stuff, but it was everything she had.

———

For the sixth time that afternoon, Daniel snapped closed the lid of the velvet box. A charm with no bracelet was probably too dumb a present to give, but it was Christmas tomorrow, and then she'd be gone. The charm was a straight-across exchange for Melissa's locket, which didn't seem like such a hot deal since it was as small as his thumbnail and minus the chain. But Dr. Dave had said it was their most expensive line, that girls held on to these for years, generations even, adding charm after charm until their bracelets were heavy as silver bricks.

It was called the Birdbox—a tiny little bird sat on the detailed roof of a square birdhouse with a heart-shaped hole, its head raised up, beak opened wide.

"What kinda bird is this?" he'd asked Dr. Dave, who held it in front of his nose, peering down from the bottom half of his glasses.

"If I had to guess, I'd go with robin. Or some kind of thrush."

"Robins sing, right? Like in the morning. They have good singing voices?"

"It's called dawn song," Dr. Dave said. "They're famous for it. First birds to sing in the morning. They like to tell everyone within hearing distance that they were strong and healthy enough to survive the night. They're quite territorial—"

"I'll take it. And the velvet box too."

Dr. Dave started a slow explanation about how the box went with the locket, not the charm, but then he glanced at the growing lineup at the pharmacy counter and shook his head and said, "All right then, you can have the box."

And just in time too, since Daniel's mom reared up behind him like a madwoman the second he had shoved it in his pocket.

Now that he'd had time to think, Hannah didn't seem like the kind of girl to go in for collecting stuff, much less charms. When he'd gone into her bedroom to grab her things, it was bare and neat, like a cleaning lady had just swept through. No extra anything lying around. Either she liked it that way or she didn't have a choice.

All he knew was that he liked being a brother more with her in the house. Sammy had been the focus for as long as he could remember, overriding everything else going on. It seemed easier with Hannah beside him. She'd taught Sammy a clapping game that morning, his busy hands pounding out the music alongside hers, laughing and hooting like a regular kid.

He couldn't make a big deal of it. He would pass Hannah the gift like it was a package of Kleenex; her expression would tell him if he'd made the right choice.

PART SIX

THOSE WORDS COULD MEAN ANYTHING

Wednesday, December 25

thirteen

Hannah felt a scream rising in her throat. He'd somehow found her, crept out of her dreams and to the side of her bed, clammy fingers pressing down on her mouth, hot breath wheezing in her ear. She tried to lunge forward, get away from what came next, but she hit a mesh of warm fur, a wet nose nuzzling her cheek.

It was only the dog, not Nigel. She lay there blinking in the darkness, waiting for the ugly shape to disappear, for her heart to stop thumping.

"It's okay, Thorn." She threw her arms around the dog while he slurped her face. "You're a good boy."

The clock beside her bed read ten after three. Christmas morning.

It would be hours until the others would wake; hours before she could reach under her bed for the gifts she would give them. She'd used the brown paper from the roll beside her window, different coloured ribbon for each one, and glitter stars for Sammy.

"It's not time yet," she told the dog. "Be quiet. It's still night."

She tried to make Thorn lie down beside her, but he refused to be still. He whined and yipped and jumped down from her bed and back up, then down again, which must have hurt because then he paced in circles on three legs instead of four.

"You have to go to the bathroom?"

She'd never seen him this crazy, not even when he helped build the snowman. A gale beat against the window like a living thing.

She looked closely at Thorn as he limped back and forth. "All right then, I'll take you outside." She lifted the covers and let her toes touch the cold floor. She could dress in layers, cover every inch of skin, and be as quiet as a mouse so as not to wake the others. She threw her jeans on top of her pajama bottoms, and added two pairs of socks and her heaviest sweater. She would lead Thorn to the front door, help him with the stairs as she'd seen Ellie do.

"Come on then, silly dog," she whispered, stepping into the hallway of doors, all closed except for Grandpa Walter's. She patted her thigh encouragingly as she tiptoed backward toward the kitchen. But Thorn would not be coaxed into coming with her. He went the other way, through Grandpa's open doorway and back out again. In and out he went, while she stayed in her spot, praying all his clicking and clacking wouldn't wake the whole house.

She had not dared go into Grandpa Walter's room—*their rooms are their homes, Hannah, you would not just walk off the street into some-one's home.* She could poke her head in, check on Grandpa, and back away with the dog by grabbing his collar.

Except Grandpa Walter was gone. She snuck up to the side of

his bed, that Sunnybrook smell filling her nose. She patted her palm against the tangle of covers, lifting pillows and sheets. Thorn sat on his haunches and stared, head tilted to one side, as if he expected more from her than just this. She could hear nothing but the wind, the crackling of branches as they fought with the storm.

She ran then, as fast as her legs would take her, flicking lights along the way. She spun in circles in the big room, his usual places flashing in front of her. His favourite chair with the sunken seat, the half-done puzzle, his place at the table. She ran to the window, trying to look through the trees for a shape in the snow, but all she could see was her face staring back.

Thorn sat with his nose pressed to the front door. Panic tore through her, a prickling at the back of her neck that moved to her chest. Grandpa Walter was out there somewhere. Alone. The wind would lift him up and swallow him whole.

She bolted toward Ellie and Eric's room and threw open their door. She found them pushed together, close to the edge of the bed.

"Wake up. Please, wake up."

There was shuffling and an untwisting of arms. They weren't moving fast enough, so she ran to the bed and pounded the covers. Eric lunged forward, flinging his arm, nearly hitting her. She didn't jump back, just lifted her heels to make herself taller.

Ellie propped herself on an elbow, blinking into the yellow light spilling in from the hallway. "It's okay, honey," she whispered groggily. "It's just a bad dream."

"He's run away." She tried not to cry.

Eric flung off the blanket and swung his legs to the floor, while Ellie reached out and pulled Hannah close to her.

"It was just a bad dream," Ellie said again, holding her close, her breath in her ear.

Hannah wanted to stay like that, next to Ellie, but she could not waste more precious time. She broke free, took a deep breath, and spoke slowly, enunciating each word. "He's not in his room. Not anywhere. He's disappeared. Thorn . . ."

As if he heard his name, Thorn barked from his post at the door. Ellie, sitting and wide awake now, held Hannah away from her, gripping her shoulders to get a closer look at her face. "Sammy?"

"Walter." Eric cursed. He'd wrestled into his jeans and yanked a sweater over his head. "She means Walter."

"Oh God." Ellie pushed Hannah to the side and jumped to her feet. "He can't have gone out there!" The wind crashed in waves against the side of the house.

"He'll be heading for the barn," Eric said. "I'll get him." Then he was pounding down the hall like an army of men, Thorn barking furiously. The commotion had woken Sammy, who called for his mother. "I'll help," Hannah said, not wanting to go, not able to stand still. She could feel the cold bite her toes, bite the old man's skin. Did he remember gloves? A scarf?

"You will do no such thing!" Ellie flung on her housecoat and then stripped it off again. Sammy's calls were getting louder. "I'm not going to lose you too."

Hannah kept her eyes on the floor while Ellie tore off her nightie and threw legs into sweatpants, arms into Eric's huge sweater. *I'm not going to lose you too.* Stupid, stupid, stupid. Those words could mean anything. She pulled at the rug's scruffy fringes with her pointed toe. She was just a girl to keep track of until she could be delivered somewhere else.

Now Sammy could be heard sobbing in his room, a feverish calling that could crack the moon.

"I have to calm Sammy down," Ellie said, an edge of panic in her voice as she headed toward the door. "You go get Danny. His father might need him." Then Ellie came back and bent down in front of her, grabbing her shoulders. "You don't go out there, Hannah. You don't know your way around, and it's too easy to get lost. Promise me you won't go out there."

Hannah winced under the pressure of Ellie's fingers. "I promise," she whispered.

Then she flew too, down the hall, down the stairs, down the length of the cold concrete floor. Hannah hadn't been in Daniel's room; she hadn't been in any boy's room before this. She flicked on the light. There was crap everywhere—covering the walls, the floor. She hopped over piles of clothes, pulled back his blanket, and shook his bare shoulder.

"Wake up!" she yelled, panting. "Grandpa Walter is lost."

Daniel was dead weight, unmoving except for the up and down of his chest. She dragged his blankets to the floor—he wore only shorts—and shook harder. "Daniel! Get up! Right now!"

He stretched out his hand, eyes squeezed shut, grabbing for something to fight against the cold. "What? What's going on?" His voice cracked with sleep.

"Wake up. It's Grandpa Walter. He's lost in the storm."

Daniel bolted up, rearing out of sleep, and saw Hannah standing right there beside his bed, looking down at him.

"Grandpa got out?" he yelled, grabbing his pillow to cover his nakedness. "Holy shit. What time is it?"

"Hurry. Get dressed. You have to come now."

She didn't know where to look as he pulled on pants, a sweater.

"Go tell my dad," he said.

"He's already out there."

They tore up the stairs. Hannah watched at the front door as Daniel threw on boots, jacket, hat, gloves, and scarf. Thorn whined and yelped, getting tangled in their feet. They could hear Sammy behind his closed door, Ellie's muffled shushing.

"Aren't you coming?" Daniel asked, breathless under his scarf. Thorn pushed his nose through his legs. "Not you, old boy. You have to stay here."

"Ellie says no." Hannah watched as he reached for a flashlight from the boot box in the closet. "Your dad's heading for the barn."

"I know," Daniel said. "That's where Grandpa goes." Hannah held tight to Thorn's collar as Daniel opened the door and was eaten by the night, the whistling cold striking her before she pushed the door closed.

She paced up and down the entryway, Thorn pacing with her, favouring his hind leg. She counted the steps she imagined would get Daniel to the barn and back with Grandpa beside him. Hypothermia could kill. The first aid teacher said so. If a body's temperature drops too low, a person starts shivering at first, then confusion sets in and they can't remember who they are and they stumble around, and then they turn blue and their heart pumps slower and slower until it doesn't work at all. Especially an old heart, already worn out.

Sammy had stopped crying. Hannah strained to hear Ellie in the stillness of the house. She wanted to go to her, to sit beside Sammy on his bed and let Ellie's voice wash over her, but she was stuck on what the teacher said about treating a hypothermia victim. Get him inside, of course. Then she supposed a warm bath or hot tea or a pile of blankets. Eric would know what to do. Except they weren't back—none of them. Years had passed since Thorn butted her awake, since they set off in search of him. It shouldn't take this long to sweep the barn, to help an old man make his way home.

Then it came to her. All those muddled repetitions at the puzzle table, more insistent each time. Grandpa Walter had said he needed to change the spark plugs. He needed to fix the carburetor. He needed to get down to PoPow's and get his truck back. PoPow's was in Neesley. If Grandpa Walter got that much straight, he was headed toward the road, not the barn.

Hannah ran to Sammy's room and pushed open the door, but Ellie held up her hand, warning her to stay back. Ellie was on the bed next to Sammy, who was rocking wildly back and forth.

Ellie mouthed the word *Go*, waving her away. Hannah closed the door and paced the hallway, waiting for Sammy to get right again. The thought hit her like a stone hurled at her chest. She knew how to get to the road. It wouldn't be that hard. She would find Walter herself, take his hand, and lead him home. And once Walter was back where he belonged, safe and warm, wouldn't she be more special in Ellie's eyes, in all their eyes—someone worth hanging on to?

She ran back to the front closet and grabbed an old down-filled jacket with a tear in one sleeve and a striped toque too big for her head. There was one flashlight left in the boot box and when she pressed its sticky black button, a feeble beam danced along the wall. She buried it in the jacket's pocket beside an old package of gum. The tattered butterfly quilt—the one from her bedroom she'd come wrapped in— lay folded in the closet corner. She scooped it up and whispered to Thorn, "You have to stay here. I'll bring him back."

She opened the door, struggling to keep a grip on the metal handle, the gale ripping it from her grasp before she could push it closed again using the weight of her whole body. Despite her two pairs of socks and heaviest sweater and the too-big jacket, the cold shocked her senseless. She hoisted the blanket under one arm and clung to the railing as she stumbled blindly down the steps. The porch light was no help, its beam too weak against the driving snow.

She tripped over a solid and unexpected mound at the bottom step and heard Thorn's yip. He was beside her, had somehow slunk through the door and laid himself down for her to stumble over out there in the storm.

"You have to go back," she cried, her voice devoured by the deafening wind, tornadoes of white rising all around. "Thorn, please."

She grabbed his collar and tried to lead him up the stairs, but he backed away, pulling in the opposite direction.

"Eric! Danny!" she yelled, although she'd already given up trying to see or be heard. The world had shrunk to the two feet in front of her. The barn, the van, their snowman—it was as if they never were. Thorn pulled her along, head close to the ground, as she clung dizzily to his collar, bits of ice stinging her cheeks. She didn't dare let go or he'd disappear too, and she'd be alone.

She looked back as often as she could manage in the driving wind, trying to keep the porch light in view, but it was becoming more a pinprick, a distant star. She could still make out the blur of gauzy light through the kitchen window, but they were moving farther and farther from it, slogging toward the open road, though she couldn't be sure with nothing real or solid to focus on but the razor-sharp swirls. Thorn forged ahead, his bad leg working again, shoulders hunched low like he was pulling a heavy cart up a steep hill, muzzle white with crusted snow.

She placed one foot in front of the other. Her fingers had numbed inside the heavy gloves, no longer willing to do what she wanted. As they slipped out from under Thorn's collar, she lunged forward to grab onto his neck, but all that she found was a piece of the wind. He'd moved on already, left her behind.

"Thorn," she screamed, dropping the weighty blanket in the snow. She turned to get her bearings, to measure the distance from here to the house, but the lights behind the window had been swallowed without a trace. The house was gone.

She swung her head in all directions, desperate to see past the thick wall of lifting snow. What if she'd gotten turned around? What if she'd been traipsing round and round in circles, the house ahead not behind? Which way was which? She shook uncontrollably, waterfalls streaming down her cheeks, under her nose, teeth clattering behind tight lips. She was no hero. She'd done the exact opposite of what she'd promised Ellie, the person in this world she wanted most to please. She'd lost everything and everyone, including herself. She couldn't find her nose much less Grandpa Walter—or Thorn either, who was probably buried under a mountain of snow by now, his old legs buckling beneath him.

She couldn't stay in this spot or the storm would tie her into itself, but she didn't have a clue where to go from here. Fists inside gloves, gloves inside pockets, her hand scraped against the cold metal of the flashlight she'd stuffed deep into the pocket's lining. She pulled it out and clumsily stabbed at the button until the world lit up, or at least a piece of it no bigger than a slide under a microscope, a fury of pelting ice flakes angrier than ants getting poked. She shot the shaky beam all around, but it was no good, she could see nothing but sideways snow—not the house, not the dog—the world was erased and her with it. Her breath thickened like porridge on its way to her chest. The soles of her feet, sharp crackles of hurt, melded into the frozen earth.

There was a faint volley of barks behind her. She swung around, batting away snow with her useless glove, screaming the dog's name. She heard nothing more from Thorn, just her own cries, her panicked breath like the clopping of hooves, until finally she made herself stop, the first aid teacher in her head nodding knowingly at her confusion.

But then he was real, a muddle of legs, not a dream. She dropped. Such a good old dog, panting and quivering, right there beside her, utterly unruffled to find her down on her knees, as if she'd been waiting for him to bring back the stick.

She hoisted the jumbled blanket under her arm, then hauled herself upright, leaning against Thorn's frosted body so as to not lose him again. They were in agreement on this. Every time he pushed ahead a few steps, he stopped and waited until she caught up, barking shrilly to get her to hurry. Her flashlight banged against her pant leg, its trembling light no help at all.

They trudged to the end of the long driveway. She could tell this now by the way the ground beneath her feet came up solid underneath. They were on open road, the wind whipping madly. She was no longer sinking as deep with each step, her runners dipping into ragged ruts of ice and snow that tires had made between plow runs. The Nylands had driven over this exact spot, the weight of their vehicles pressing down winter. It made her feel better, knowing they'd been here too, until she looked back toward where the house should be and was not.

She could not feel her toes, peering down to see if they were still there. Thorn pulled away, woofing and yowling. The blanket, impossibly heavy, was making her too slow. She was about to drop it when the dog stopped, not a body length ahead. She could see the faint outline of his wagging tail.

Walter hadn't made it far, just a few feet down the road. He'd turned right instead of left, away from Neesley not toward it, going down in the snowy bank, bent at the waist, his top half tilting to one side, legs sprawled out in front. He was still, too still, ignoring the dog that was slobbering all over him.

Afraid to get close, terrified he'd be dead, she still stumbled and skidded forward, dropping to her knees in front of him.

"Grandpa. Grandpa Walter!" she cried, her words torn away in the wind. She lowered her ear close to his mouth to listen for signs of breath. *Please, please, please breathe.*

He swung out and hit her squarely on her numb cheek, causing her to fall back in the snow. Awake now, he batted his arms as he struggled to stand.

Get him inside. Get him out of the storm. Thorn had moved off, his job done, poking his nose in the pile of snow built up beside the road.

She wrapped her blanket around Walter's head and shoulders, gripped his arms, and tried to pull him up.

"Get up!" she screamed, yanking hard on his sleeves, dragging him upward. "Get up now."

She could not get enough traction to bring him to his feet. Thorn was barking again, lifting his paws. Get him up. Get him up. Pull. Pull harder. But it was no good. He was too old, too heavy.

She couldn't think straight. Couldn't leave him behind. Couldn't take him with her. Couldn't get her legs to work. She tried one more time to haul him out of the snow. Then she sat—there was nothing else to do—tucking herself against him under the blanket until he stopped struggling and leaned into her. Thorn stood guard in front of the pair, barking endlessly.

A year passed, or a minute, before the shouts, faint at first but then clear and sure, getting nearer. She still had enough wits to bawl out hoarsely, "Here. We're here."

———

The storm had caused a power outage, likely from a falling branch or downed tree. Ellie couldn't get the backup generator going, the switch too stubborn for her to trigger by herself. But she found the hurricane lantern with its stub of a wick and got the candles from the emergency box, arranging them in clusters on tabletops and window ledges. The room glowed with tiny trembling flames, corners filled with mauve-tipped shadows.

Ellie put Sammy in his grandpa's chair, where he rocked back and forth. She had explained in half sentences how Grandpa had gone into the storm, and Dad and Hannah and Danny too, and they needed to wait patiently for everyone to come back. Sammy seemed to understand the enormity of their circumstances, ear cocked to the bad night noises coming from outside their window.

"Will they come now?" he kept asking, to which she repeatedly said, "Soon, buddy, soon," praying she was right.

Finally, she heard a commotion out front. Ellie ran to the door, opened it, and thrust her arms forward, preparing herself to catch what waited. They fell inside—one, two, three, all four—brittle, wind-whipped, the dog in front, silver with frost. Ellie covered her mouth with her palm at the sight of them all.

"He made it to the road," Danny stuttered, face blotched and swollen from the cold.

Hannah looked so small in Danny's old jacket, hunched inwards and shuddering. She wore her runners. She had no boots to wear.

"Get away from the door!" Ellie cried. "Quickly now. Don't worry about your shoes."

"Dan, build up the fire," Eric ordered as he half carried, half dragged Walter into the living room and laid him on the couch; he looked alarmingly frail and crumpled lying there, his brash mouth still, lips pale and bloodless.

"Hannah, stay close to Dan and get warm. Get those runners off."

Walter had started to revive, now struggling with Eric, as if Eric was a thief, trying to steal his clothes.

"Stop hitting, Dad," Eric told him. "I need to get your coat off."

Ellie clapped eyes on Eric. He'd called him *Dad*, not Walter. She dragged Myrtle's chair in front of the fireplace. "Hannah, sit here." She bent in front of the girl, fighting with her frozen laces, so desperate to get Hannah's runners off that she grabbed the heels and pulled. The girl's socks were rock solid, like slabs of meat from the freezer.

"I'm sorry," Hannah stuttered, barely moving her lips.

It didn't matter one fig to Ellie what the girl had promised; she'd come back in one piece.

"Do they hurt?" she asked, pulling off Hannah's socks.

"I'm sorry," Hannah said again, shivering uncontrollably.

"Oh, darling." Ellie surprised herself: *darling* was a word she never used. "You're safe. Everyone is safe." Hannah's toes were only milky white, not spongy or blue, but Ellie needed Eric to take a look before she could be sure.

Danny built up the fire, adding kindling and three logs from the wooden box. "Will Grandpa be okay? We thought he'd gone to the barn like he always does." He looked truly rattled, as if he'd never considered an option where his grandpa could be irreversibly lost. The times before, Danny had grumped about what a nuisance these searches were. "Thorn went crazy. Good thing he's such a loud barker, or Grandpa would still be in the snowbank."

Ellie squeezed Danny's hand. "You're very brave, Danny. Both you and Hannah."

She looked over her shoulder to the scene on the couch, Eric still fending off kicks as he tried to remove Walter's boots.

"At least he's fighting back." Danny unzipped his coat and threw off his hat. "That's good, right?"

"Grandpa will be fine," Ellie said. Walter had to pull through for Eric's sake.

Danny's cheeks had already lost their mottled look, although it was hard to distinguish colours in the quivering light. He hadn't taken off his boots, good to minus forty. His toes would be fine—and the rest of him too.

Ellie looked from one son to the other. Sammy hadn't moved from his chair by the window, his concerned face tipped toward his grandpa.

Ellie was most concerned about Hannah, who had not stopped

shivering. She wrapped the girl in one of the blankets she'd gathered from their bedroom and threw another over Danny's shoulders. Ice cold herself, Ellie felt anchored, steadier on her feet when she looked at her husband's solid frame kneeling beside Walter. More convinced they could get through this.

fourteen

Eric concentrated on the tasks before him. His mind had slowed, calculating next moves like he was dismantling a bomb. Warm his father, not too quickly; focus on the chest, neck, head, groin; check extremities, the strength of his heartbeat. Hannah too—toes, fingers, cheeks.

He'd managed to wrestle Walter out of his coat and boots, but he needed more heat. More light.

"Ellie, get the thermometer. And the electric blanket. And Hannah, move back a little, you're too close to that fire." If her skin had been damaged, she could burn herself without feeling it.

"I'll be right back," he told them. "I'm going downstairs to get the generator working."

Flashlight in hand, Eric made his way down the narrow staircase to the basement. He followed the beam along the concrete wall, past the shelves of his mother's dwindling preserves, past the washer and dryer and the Christmas turkey bulging out of the sink. When he got to the panel, he used two hands to throw the stiff transfer switch, disconnecting from the grid and shooting power through the circuits. The furnace spit and groaned as a circle of light spilled out of Dan's bedroom.

He had failed in vigilance. Tonight of all nights. Christmas. And the goddamn howling wind, enough to freeze a body from the inside out. Walter might have been a nasty brute his whole life, but what remained of him was a diminished old man in need of protection—protection that Eric had failed to provide. How long had he been out there?

And Hannah! When he had seen her in that snowbank, bunched under the blanket with Walter, he thought he'd been plunged into a nightmare, none of it real. But then she threw herself at him, clinging to his jacket, mumbling through clattering teeth about how Grandpa was after his truck. Not finding Walter in time would have haunted him. But losing Hannah—he was terrified to even imagine that.

When he got back upstairs, Christmas bulbs sparkled, illuminating an enormous stack of gaily wrapped presents. The kids sat side by side on the floor, a safe distance from the raging fire. Dan, stripped down to his shirt, was flipping logs with the poker, yakking nonstop. Hannah was wrapped like a cocoon in her blanket, her feet nudging out, tucked into Ellie's joke gorilla slippers. Sammy sat unusually still over on Walter's chair, clutching his red truck with both hands, his eyes focused on the covered lump that was his grandpa.

"I tried to cover Thorn, but he wouldn't have it," Ellie said. She had plugged the extension cord into the Christmas tree socket, dragged it across the floor, and attached it to the electric blanket over Walter.

"Is it turned to low?" Eric asked. "We can't thaw him out too fast."

Ellie hovered over Walter, fiddling with the blanket's control button. "I've taken his temperature." She held out the thermometer to Eric, biting her lip. "Thirty-five degrees, Eric."

"We can work with that," Eric said. "He'll be okay."

Ellie felt a gust of relief. She'd been worried Walter would need to be taken to the hospital, and they could not get him there, not in time.

Eric bent over his father, leaning awkwardly because of the dog, and pressed his fingers against Walter's scrawny neck.

"He's got a weak but steady pulse, not likely to stop anytime soon." He lifted the blanket, searching for discoloured blotches, feeling the texture of his paper-thin skin. "There's no trace of frostbite that I can see."

"He said he wants his supper," Ellie whispered. She was the one who'd said no to a lock for his door. "I'll make him a pie—billows of meringue."

Eric turned to her, smiling weakly. "Walter should lose himself more often." He squeezed her shoulder. "He's sleeping now. He just needs some rest."

Walter opened his eyes, banging his arm against the couch to get everyone's attention. "Crack a window, Myrtle," he ordered. "It's too goddamned close in here."

Ellie saw Eric take a deep, slow breath. If his father was not ready to go, perhaps Eric was not ready to let him.

He looked at the kids, who'd turned on their blankets to face him, their backs to the snapping fire. "You all right? Warm yet?"

Daniel pulled his shirt away from his chest, panting. "Are you kidding? I got three logs going."

"How about you, Hannah?" he asked. "Are you warm?"

Daniel answered for her: "She's warm as toast. Right, Hannah?"

"Blow out the candles, will you," Eric said to Daniel, who jumped up and stomped around the room, leaving tiny smoke signals everywhere he went.

Eric asked Hannah, "Have you got feeling in your toes and fingers?"

Hannah nodded without looking up.

Ellie had been watching Eric closely, the steadiness of his hands, the way his eyes swept the room, absorbing the smallest of details. He functioned best when he had something on the line. She loved him for that. She loved him more in this moment than ever before.

Hannah hadn't said a word since *I'm sorry*. Ellie knelt in front of the girl and cupped her hands around Hannah's, blowing on the tips of her fingers.

"Danny was right. They feel warm as toast." Hannah did not take her hands away. "And your teeth have stopped chattering."

Eric came toward them and bent down on one knee, his fingers reaching under Ellie's, finding Hannah's wrist, counting her heartbeats.

"You okay, kiddo? Let's get a look at those toes."

Ellie watched as he pulled off one gorilla, then the other, bending Hannah's toes this way and that, pressing along the bottom of her soles.

"You're okay," Eric said. Then he added, "But I don't want you doing that again. Not ever."

Hannah looked up. "You're mad at me?"

"Of course not!" Eric and Ellie said at once, pressing into each other.

Without consciously thinking about it, all this time Ellie had been counting the hours until Hannah would leave. Twenty-nine, twenty-eight. Barely more than a day. A dread overcame her. How could she have wasted a second of their time together? While she'd been fretting over the minutiae of her family's everyday lives—worst-case scenarios—the girl had been standing right there in front of her self-absorbed fog, as bright as the sun.

"I could use your help," Ellie said to her. "We need warm drinks. Hot chocolate or tea? What do you think?"

"Hot chocolate," Hannah said, some of her colour regained.

"Good choice," Ellie said, taking Hannah's hand and lifting her up, Sammy beside her now, the three solemnly proceeding to the kitchen.

"I'm starving," Daniel yelled after them.

"Where the hell's supper?" Walter said. "I want my chips."

Eric laughed. "It's settled then. Dan's starving, Walter wants his chips. The Nylands are back in business."

The kitchen became a beehive of activity. They raided the fridge, sliced up cheese and pickles. Eric helped make a heaping plate of sandwiches and hot chocolate with marshmallows melting like little snowballs. The family ate with plates on laps, arms reaching, knees touching, breadcrumbs skittering in all directions, Hannah cushioned in the thick of it.

It was not yet six in the morning when they packed tightly near the warmth of the fire. Stomachs full, a drowsiness overcame them. Walter stretched out the length of the couch under the electric blanket, his temperature rising, snoring in synchrony with the dog, who hadn't moved from his spot since he'd come in from the cold, not even when Daniel dropped ham from his sandwich in front of his nose.

"Merry Christmas," Ellie said. She was facing the tree, between Eric's knees, his arms wrapped across her chest.

Eric squeezed tighter. "Let's open presents. See what Santa brought."

Sammy put down his truck. Walter snorted and grumbled in his sleep. Daniel darted to the edge of the tree, reached beneath branches, grabbed the small gift he'd hidden under the skirt, and dumped it unceremoniously on Hannah's lap.

Hannah stood suddenly, clutching her present from Daniel. "Wait! Please wait!" she begged, running off, too-big slippers slapping against the floorboards.

———

The tempest petered out as if it had all been a joke, leaving nothing but a harmless blue sky over a desert of snow, shiny and blinding under the too-bright sun.

Betty called on Christmas Day a little before noon. She'd stopped in at the station to hand out chocolates and gave Eric the Neesley rundown. John Welsh had escaped from his group home again. The group home staff called the station at 8:15 a.m., unable to confirm exactly how long he'd been missing. Constables King and Cruikshank were well into their search when some out-of-towner from B.C., a Christmas visitor, called 9-1-1 on her cell phone. She'd crashed into John as she was jogging through Memorial Park. Jogging! As if it were a reasonable pastime in this kind of weather. John reared up from the garbage can beside the picnic shelter, big as a bear, scaring the bejesus out of the woman. The constables collected them both and drove the shaken and cold out-of-towner to a house on 13th Street, and then dropped John back at the station, where they gave him a few candy canes pilfered from their stash of Christmas paraphernalia.

Then, if that wasn't enough, Bill and Audrey's yelping chihuahua, home alone, set off their useless new security alarm. The constables were called out so often they had memorized the security code. They'd learned to stay upright in the house at all times, their noses a safe distance from that leaping excuse for a dog.

Albert Finning, ninety-six and still on his own, called in a self-diagnosed bout of appendicitis a little after ten. King and Cruikshank showed up before the ambulance and loosened Albert's belt buckle. Problem solved. On the way back to the station, they confiscated George Lundy's potato launcher, which he was loading and reloading as fast as he could in Peavey Mart's empty parking lot.

Beyond that, Betty said over the phone, little else had come through. Not one frozen limb. Not a car wreck or a single reported blow between spouses. The good people of Neesley had had a surprisingly quiet time, the violence of winter knocking the wind right out of them.

Eric laughed at Betty's stories, feeling relieved he wasn't the one making the rounds. All those Christmases he'd missed out on while he sorted others' problems. When Betty asked for an update about the goings-on at the Nyland house, he didn't tell her about their harrowing night. It seemed too intimate, a family matter that he didn't want to share.

The utility truck arrived just after one as Eric was shovelling the last few feet of driveway. Larry Turner stepped down from his cab, wobbling slightly—red-eyed, stubble-chinned. He looked like an accident waiting to happen.

"Quite the storm," Eric said. He'd known Larry since his school days, a sullen sort who hadn't amounted to much. Two failed marriages. A son who wouldn't speak to him. "How are things?"

"'Bout what you'd expect," Larry grumbled. "Damned lines down along Lincoln Road all the way to the tree farm."

"At least the town grid stayed up."

The sun's rays bounced off Larry's bald scalp and scraped cheek, highlighting the start of another shiner. The whole town knew that Larry had been pulled out of several bar fights the past year.

Eric said, "Appreciate you getting here so fast. Christmas Day and all."

Larry shrugged his shoulders, turning away, one day as bad as any other.

While Larry worked on the line, Eric headed to the barn. A bird circled above. Eric looked up unwillingly. It was a red-tailed hawk—the real thing. He cranked his head back, studying the oatmeal belly, magnificent wings, and wide, fanned tail. He felt boyhood wonder—nothing more, nothing less. The hawk soared effortlessly on an air current, until it caught an updraft and climbed into the sky and out of view.

Eric had to take a moment to catch his breath. Then he grabbed the pick axe from the barn and waded through crusted snow to the far side of the yard. The apple tree stood lifeless and bloated in its coat of white, Walter's old water drum half buried beside it.

Eric had been at it for four days, chiselling away the earth to make a resting place for Hannah's cat. He'd managed to keep the fire burning day and night, the drum protecting the heat from the worst of the wind. He'd gone back again and again, each time shovelling the smoldering charcoals aside as the ground became soft, and then chipping away with the pick axe. By yesterday, he'd cleared off over two feet of black earth, more than enough, but he'd kept on swinging anyway, picturing Wilson beneath him as the ground cracked open. God only knew what he'd find now. The damn storm might have decided to seal the empty grave back up during the night.

Eric shovelled around the water drum and then tipped it on its side, peering down to find the hole still a hole, the ground still warm to the touch, a spray of ash and powder.

He'd done all he could do to get ready for this. The dead cat was in a small Borden Cheese crate he'd found in the barn, wood streaked black, the box ancient enough to be worth cash to the collectors who flocked to Neesley's antique sale every year. He'd shaken out the dead flies and crammed in the brittle carcass. After he slid the wooden lid shut, he banged in a few finishing nails to keep it that way. Hannah didn't need to see inside.

The system would take care of her. That's what he'd repeated to Ellie over the last few days: the lie he told to protect his wife. He'd seen kids get bounced so many places they couldn't remember the names of their street or their keepers. In truth, the girl would be better off right here, on this plot of land, where she would be safe. An impossibility, of course. He had to hide this line of thinking, bury it along with the cat.

Eric stabbed the shovel hard into a deep wedge of snow and headed toward the house. The sky was gay and bright, not a whisper of wind, the right kind of conditions for a cat's quiet send-off. But it didn't feel right, not today, not on Christmas.

He heard Larry's engine start up and turned to see him back behind the wheel. Somehow he'd managed to repair the line without frying himself in the process. It was remarkable how life carried on. Despite stupidity and wickedness, worry and remorse.

The cat could wait. Tomorrow, he would stand beside the girl under the apple tree and try to find a few right words.

———

The whole family went to bed early. Hannah wished she would fall asleep, but her stomach hurt. She couldn't stop her thoughts from frothing around and battering her insides.

It had been a happy Christmas Day, her happiest in a long, long time. They fed Thorn treats all day long, brushing his coat while he farted up a storm. Grandpa Walter was back to his old self, not remembering one thing about being lost in that storm. She wished she could forget too. She wished she could snap her fingers and make the past go away.

There were so many presents. Ellie cried when she unwrapped her songbook, just like her mother had when it arrived in the mail.

Once Ellie was able to talk again, she asked, "Do you play the piano, Hannah?"

No. At Sunnybrook she'd been allowed to turn the pages for Mrs. Humble at hymn sing, but she'd hardly seen a piano since.

"What a shame!" Ellie's eyes were still teary. "A voice like yours. You should have lessons."

Eric slapped his knee and said, "Just what I need! How did you know?" Then he found the hammer and a nail and pounded the key holder to the wall by the front closet.

Sammy jammed his eye to the kaleidoscope's rim, tilted his head toward the ceiling, and marched around in circles, crashing into the coffee table and almost knocking over the tree.

"Hey, buster, watch where you're going," Ellie said, but Sammy announced, "The world's in here," and everyone laughed.

Hannah and Daniel opened their presents at exactly the same time. "It's an angel," she said, wanting to grab it back before he had time to react.

"Cool," he said, smiling big. Then his face turned red, even the tips of his ears. "Yours is a bird. A robin."

"It's so tiny!" A tiny bird on top of its own little house.

"You're supposed to have a bracelet to put it on," Daniel said, redder still. "It's a charm. Girls collect them."

"Or I could put it on a chain, like a necklace." Her present to him wasn't nearly enough. "You don't have to wear yours!" she burst out. "You can put it in your drawer." But when she looked up, her angel was around his neck.

The Nylands gave her more presents than she'd ever had at one time. A fuzzy sweater and a new jacket with soft fur. A nail polish. Lotions that she'd rubbed over her arms and neck until she smelled like a garden.

So why did such a growing ache run right through her middle?

It was this family. It was finding everything she'd missed out on, seeing their lives framed in happy poses along the mantel and then playing out in front of her. The warmth of the fire; the concern on their faces; Ellie's careful, kind tone—none of it fooled Hannah. Being with the Nylands had brought a new kind of loneliness. She didn't belong here. Tomorrow morning, she would be sent away. She might as well have stayed lost in the storm.

PART SEVEN

THURSDAY'S CHILD HAS FAR TO GO

Thursday, December 26

fifteen

Ellie woke early. She dressed in the dark, so as not to wake Eric, and closed the door soundlessly as she left their room. Turkey and stuffing spice lingered in the hallway; she could smell it in the walls and blowing up through the heat ducts.

She turned on the lamp in the corner of the living room and sat in Myrtle's overstuffed chair, wrapping Myrtle's afghan around her cold ankles. Christmas detritus lay scattered about, wayward bows and bits of ribbon clinging to the skirt under the tree. A bag with wads of torn wrapping paper was still under the coffee table.

The lamp cast jagged shadows along the wall, poinsettia leaves in their red crepe basket. She reached out her arm, extending her fingers into the light, but she couldn't get their shape right as they skulked around the poinsettia's silhouette. Her fingers looked obscenely long, like black daggers piercing the leaves, so she curled them into a fist and brought them back to her lap.

That old English poem floated into her head: *Monday's child is fair of face, Tuesday's child is full of grace, Wednesday's child is full of woe.* She got stuck on Thursday's child. What did it mean to have far to go? How does one find where they're meant to be?

And what could she offer Hannah? She'd been up half the night thinking about it. Legally, it could work. Betty had said as much, when they'd talked on the phone yesterday, reciting a long list of conditions—paperwork, criminal checks, interviews, home visits—before blurting out, *Are you seriously considering this, Ellie?* Ellie assured her she wasn't, just curious about the machinations of a system that Hannah was now a part of.

She was foolish to have asked the question, wrenching the thought out of her and into the open. Sammy's and Walter's complications were piled as high as a chimney stack, her own craziness on top. Look what it had done to her, wanting something so bad only to lose it again. No, as much as she might fantasize about keeping Hannah—singing lessons, movie nights, book clubs for two—the child would be better off in professional care.

Betty would come for her today. She'd be at their door in a few hours, bright eyed and ready for business. It would be a good day to travel far, to get to wherever she was taking Hannah without a storm hurling through the fields.

Walter had left his Ag Society pen and paper set on the table beside the chair, the top page littered with his spillage—loopy doodling and scribbled words that had nothing to do with each other, *moldings, shotgun, dominoos, bateries*. Ellie ripped off a clean page and started writing a list of her own. Milk, eggs, cottage cheese. A ham might be nice to break up the days left of turkey. She could pick up some of the green mint jelly that Walter liked so much. They kept stacks of jars in the back cooler at Dave's Pharmacy, almost like the kind that Myrtle used to make. Animal crackers for Sammy. Protein bars for Danny.

But it was no good. Even as the pen formed the words, she knew her list was as ridiculous as Walter's. It included none of what they needed. She folded the paper over and over and over again, until it was as small as a love note in a teenager's pocket.

——

Eric woke when Ellie slipped out of bed, but instead of getting to his feet, he wrestled with the covers and dug himself in deeper. The house was hauntingly quiet in that black hour before dawn, not a hint of wind beyond the window.

They had no plans for Boxing Day other than to bury the cat, find Hannah a suitcase, and then give her away.

He should get up right now. Betty would do the handover before noon and he needed to be sharp for the ensuing fallout. But he couldn't move his legs, couldn't let go of all that had happened. If he lay still in the dark, he could play back their Christmas, a moment-by-moment recap. It was the only way he knew how to make it stay real—make it mean something.

Somehow, they had tunnelled their way through the storm, the easiness of it almost absurd. Walter on the couch, in and out of sleep, as cantankerous as ever; Thorn on the floor beside him; Ellie staying close, bringing him everything he asked for—extra pillows, the cordless phone, chips crispy not mushed.

They'd opened their presents slowly, one at a time. Afterward, they huddled around the tree, at turns silent and then talking all at once. There were naps on the floor, a heap of pillows and blankets and bodies sprawled messily like at a child's sleepover. They started the turkey using the backup generator, browned it after Larry finished repairing the wire, but instead of fussing with fancy Christmas place settings, they piled around the table with their everyday plates.

Years from now, they would still be telling stories about this Christmas, the one when Grandpa got it in his head to walk to town in the middle of the night during a record-breaking wind chill, the worst storm of the decade. Daniel would exaggerate the specifics, Sammy going along with the story: how long it took to find him; how deep the snow; how the power was down for days; how Grandpa bounced back, like a child who'd been playing in the snow.

And while they would keep it to themselves, they would think of Hannah too. They might be staring out a window on a bitterly cold night; listening to a clear, sweet voice on the radio; or walking down a sidewalk, a girl in a too-small, shabby coat coming toward them, and they would see her.

———

The three of them walked single file along the narrow path Eric had cleared from the house to the far side of the yard. Hannah was between Daniel and Eric, the wooden box in her arms. Daniel had hoped to see inside—he'd never examined a dead cat before—but the lid was nailed shut and his dad had said *absolutely not*. He'd asked him three times how Hannah's cat ended up dead. His dad never answered, so he figured it had to be bad.

Before they reached the apple tree, they passed by the remains of Robert the Snowman, now just jagged peaks in the mountain of new snow. A strange fog had rolled in, greying out the white world, and as they solemnly marched forward, the thick air ran across their cheeks like wet tongues.

Before today, Daniel had only been to one funeral, his grandma's. At the chapel, they had her in an open box. She looked nothing like she had in life, her face too caved in and shiny. It was shocking to see her so still, hands folded, lying there in her blue dress and dark stockings. In real life, she never stopped moving. She used to tilt her head and lean toward him when he spoke, as though he was worth listening to, but when he stood beside her casket and stared at her waxy eyelids and powdered cheeks, he couldn't think of one thing to say.

Daniel had wanted his mom to come into the yard with them, but she didn't want to leave Grandpa after his big escape, and Sammy had a sore throat and wasn't allowed out.

When they lined up around the hole in the ground, the three of them looked down. The air smelled like a campfire drowning in sand. It was an impressive-sized crater, the shovel wedged in the snowdrift beside it. Daniel wished he could have done the digging, but his dad had never asked for his help.

"Will this be okay, Hannah?" his dad asked her.

She didn't say a word, just banged the toe of one of Daniel's old boots into a chunk of ice, hugging her box while she stared into the hole.

"That tree was just a twig when we first planted it," his dad said. "I was your age when I dug the hole for it. You can't tell now, but in the summer those branches will be loaded with green apples."

"It's a good place to sit and think," Daniel said. "Well, not now. In the summer. When it's shady." He sucked air through his teeth, determined not to say anything else stupid. Why did she have to leave? It's not like she was going to live with a nice aunt or with anyone else she wanted to be with.

Hannah quit kicking the ice, her whole body stiffening. "Nigel says that cats don't have souls."

"He's wrong," Daniel jumped in, not knowing about souls but

knowing she'd want her cat to have one. He hated everything about that man.

His dad took off his glove and pressed his fingers to his forehead like he was trying to push away a headache.

"We can't prove that animals have souls," he said. "But we can't prove they don't either. I've seen a cat run back into a burning home not once, not twice, but five times to save every one of her kittens. That cat got badly singed—her paws, the tips of her ears—but she didn't give up. Who's to say she didn't have a soul?"

His dad put his hand on Hannah's shoulder. Daniel didn't know what to say next. After his grandma's service at the funeral chapel, they got into cars and drove to the seniors' recreation centre for sandwiches and cake. His dad had asked if anyone in the crowd wanted to share a few words. One after another sprang out of their chairs and stepped up to the microphone. One lady recited his grandma's secret recipe for double-fudge brownies. Another pointed to the stage's ceiling and yelled, "You can thank Myrtle Nyland for this paint job! She was the only one of us willing to get up on that scaffolding."

Daniel wished he could tell a story about Hannah's cat. "What was she like?" he asked, turning to her. Hannah stared into the hole, so he asked again. "Your cat? What was she like?" He didn't know the cat's name, and it was too late to ask now.

Hannah didn't answer, so his dad stepped in. "Six years ago, your mom brought Mandy home—she was just a kitten—and you found her wrapped in a towel inside a shoebox. She had just her pink nose sticking out."

Her name was Mandy.

Hannah put one hand on top of the box and rubbed it back and forth. "She loved to hide."

"Yes, she did," his dad said, as if he had known the cat personally.

"What was her favourite hiding spot?" Daniel asked.

"My bed. She could flatten herself under the covers so she hardly made a ripple. She loved bags too. If I put a paper bag on my floor, she'd crawl inside. She was so cute when she did that."

Max's family had a huge black-and-white cat that didn't like anybody. In all the times Daniel had been to Max's house, he'd only seen the cat once as it was streaking across the living room and diving under the couch.

"What colour was she?" Daniel asked.

"Black mostly," Hannah said. "She was really pretty."

Daniel wanted to be able to picture the cat when he sat under the apple tree. If Hannah couldn't be here, he'd visit for her.

"She had long black fur and three white paws and a patch of white on her forehead and green eyes, same as Sammy's."

Before they'd come into the yard, Daniel had rehearsed what he'd do if Hannah started to cry: stand close and keep his mouth shut, pass her the wad of Kleenex he'd stuffed in his pocket. He'd seen Hannah cry twice already—once when his dad carried her up from the cellar and once when she broke that glass of water. He didn't want it to happen again.

"I'm ready," Hannah said, breaking their silence, her voice not the least bit scratchy. She was dry-eyed as she got to her knees and lowered the box to the ground.

Alarmed to find his cheeks wet, Daniel needed something to hang on to. He did not expect to be the one to cry. As Hannah reached down into the hole and cupped spoonfuls of earth over her cat, he just stood there, clinging to the shovel as if it were the only thing keeping him from blowing away.

———

Betty arrived a few minutes early, wearing a felt hat with tassels and a Santa Claus ornament stuck on with a safety pin.

"Ho, ho, ho," she belted out as soon as Eric let her in. Thorn went lumbering down the hall, pretend growling, stupid and sleepy from his guard duties in front of Hannah's closed door.

Betty squeezed Eric hard. Thorn tried to get between them but settled on sniffing the backs of her pant legs.

Ellie came up behind the pair, reluctantly ready to shake Betty's hand when the woman untangled from her husband, but Betty whipped around and squeezed Ellie too, her large breasts jamming against her like water-filled balloons.

"Thought any more about what we talked about?" Betty whispered in Ellie's ear, not letting her go. "You know you've done a good thing here, you and Eric."

Ellie fought back tears, wanting to push her away, but she held on tight and they just stood like that, pressed together, for the longest time.

"Hi, Mrs. Holt," Daniel said. He'd come up from the basement two stairs at a time, but when he saw his mom getting bear hugged, he stopped short of the entryway and kept a safe distance.

Betty released Ellie and laughed, looking over at Daniel. "You've grown an inch since Friday! And you promised to call me Betty."

Daniel blushed deeply, smiling.

"Santa good to you? No lumps of coal?"

"No lumps this year."

"Didn't think so." Betty peered into the room and yelled loudly. "Hi, Sammy, Walter!" Sammy ignored her. He sat close to the tree, rearranging his soldiers on another branch. "You boys look snug as bugs on a rug. Merry Christmas!"

"Sammy's come down with the sniffles," Ellie said. "Too much excitement these past few days."

Walter hadn't looked up from his puzzle. "You can turn around and let yourself out," he yelled. "Already got a nurse."

Daniel snorted. "She's a social worker, not a nurse, Grandpa."

"Hah! Don't need a social worker."

"Dad, it's Betty Holt," Eric said. "Ida Holt's daughter-in-law."

Ellie willed Hannah to stay in her room and out of the open. Ellie wanted to be out of the open too, behind her closed door, under a pile of covers where she couldn't see the girl be taken away.

Walter scratched his balls, his arm moving up and down vigorously under his table. "She here to fix the furnace?"

Eric sucked in his breath and stepped sideways, shielding Betty from more. "Walter thinks the furnace is on the fritz."

Betty laughed openly. "Winter is on the fritz if you ask me. That was some storm. And you could shingle the fog out there today. But I'm handy with a wrench if you've got a problem in the basement."

Ellie wanted to get them out of the entryway, away from the door, away from the sight of Betty's SUV, still running in the driveway. "Can you come in for a minute, Betty?"

"Thanks, Ellie, but no. Hannah and I should get going. I told the Baxters we'd be there before one. They're waiting lunch on us."

"Mom already made Hannah's lunch," Daniel said, sounding defensive. "Sandwiches and cookies."

"You did?" Betty looked past Ellie to the empty countertop. "Well, that's just so thoughtful."

"It's to eat in the car," Daniel added, not willing to let it go.

"It's not a big deal, Danny." Ellie moved away from Betty, who looked as if she might grab her again. Hannah still hadn't come out of her room, despite Betty's deafening voice and Walter yelling about this and that.

Ellie looked to Eric for support, but he stood there stiffly, his feet planted far apart, as if he could feel the foundation of the old farmhouse shift beneath him. He'd been seriously off-kilter ever since they'd buried Hannah's cat. Earlier that morning, Ellie had found him sitting on the edge of their bed, hands on his knees, staring at the wall.

"A hobby farm," he'd said. "That's where we're sending her. What kind of quacks raise ostriches in this climate?"

Ellie steeled herself to go fetch Hannah when the girl's door opened. She wore her new Christmas sweater and pulled the battered suitcase behind her. Her eyes were too clear, looking right through them.

Thorn left Betty's side and pranced over to Hannah, nudging her thigh until she bent and scratched under his chin. Sammy hopped to his feet too, lured by the rumble of the suitcase wheels, soldiers in both fists.

"Can I pull?" Sammy asked.

Hannah smiled at Sammy, handing him the suitcase handle. "Put your soldiers on top and they can go for a ride."

Walter called out, "Done the sky."

"That's the hardest part," Hannah called back.

Sammy wrangled with the suitcase, pushing and pulling until the soldiers tumbled down and got caught in the wheels, the suitcase falling sideways, banging to the floor. Daniel marched over, retrieved Sammy's soldiers from under the wheels, and set the suitcase right again.

"Pull slowly, Sammy," Daniel ordered. "Then they won't fall off." He turned to Hannah, fingering the angel under his t-shirt.

"My bird is in its box, in the zippered pocket," she said, as if he'd asked the question. "I'm going to get a chain for it. Someday."

"Here's my cell phone number," he said, passing her a folded piece of paper. "In case you're allowed to call."

Hannah took the paper and led the procession toward the cold entryway, toward the decision makers in charge of her, her eyes moving from one adult to the other.

Ellie couldn't bear to look at her tearless face. If she would only show it, the wretchedness of this moment, Ellie's instincts might kick in. They might think to place an arm on a shoulder or squeeze a hand.

But Hannah seemed all business now, matter-of-fact. "I'm ready to go."

No one said anything, so Betty jumped in. "All right then. No sense in long goodbyes. With luck, the car might even be warmed up. I swear some days I could drive to California and see my breath the whole way."

Hannah turned and took one last look about the room. "Thank you," she said, a small tremble in her voice. "Thank you."

"You've still got my card?" Eric asked.

Hannah patted her jeans pocket.

"You should take the sandwiches." Daniel rushed to the fridge, pulled out the large paper bag, and brought it over to the group. "There are cookies too."

"We'll have a picnic on the way," Betty said, taking the bag. "Back-to-back lunches are good for the body. And Hannah and I can just nibble if we want to when we get to the Baxters." Again, no one else said a word, so Betty filled the silence. "Never hurts to surprise the digestive tract, mix it up a bit, keep it on its toes."

Hannah pulled her new jacket out of the closet. Eric held it up for her as she reached in the sleeves, first one arm and then the other. Ellie passed her the bubbly knitted scarf with the bright colours, one of Myrtle's cheerier creations. Hannah wrapped it twice around her neck and tied the ends together.

Eric slipped on his jacket too, not bothering with zippers and gloves.

He turned to Sammy. "Okay, slugger. Let's have it."

Sammy had his small arms wrapped around the suitcase, now standing upright, soldiers resting on top. He refused to budge, fingers squeezed white tight along the edges of the scruffy canvas.

"Come on now, Sammy, we need to get Hannah's things out to the car," Eric said.

Hannah got down on her knees, level with Sammy's face, not too close. She held the soldiers in her fingers and marched them across the top of the suitcase and through the air. Sammy clung to the sides of the suitcase.

"You need to take these guys back to the tree. There could be a battle. These are your best guards."

Sammy repeated her request word for word. He finally let go and flapped his arms, then reached out and took the soldiers from her. She smiled at him and stood, reaching for the handle. But he didn't move away, just stayed right there and wailed.

Daniel looked down at the floor and rocked back and forth on his sock feet.

Ellie had become paralyzed, unable to move the parts below her neck, wanting to comfort her boy, both her boys, all her boys.

Walter came clunking across the floor then, pounding his cane with each step. "You going on a holiday?" he yelled to Hannah. "Again?" raising his voice a notch to drown out Sammy's sobs.

Eric turned around, blocking Walter from getting too near.

Hannah said to Betty, "I think we should go. We should go right now."

"I think you're right," Betty said, starting toward the door.

"I'll take your suitcase to the car," Eric said.

Hannah said, "No, please don't. Please don't come with us."

Ellie watched Hannah pull the suitcase past their ragged group. Then Hannah turned and glanced back at her. Their eyes locked for a second, a look of pleading. A look of possibility. Ellie could feel its spark burn a hole through the centre of her chest.

———

A whoosh of frigid air slammed into Hannah's face, Sammy's sobs getting fainter as she bumped down the stairs. The suitcase was too heavy and the wheels spun in the unevenly packed snow, so Betty came up beside her, Ellie's giant lunch bag in one hand, and the two of them half dragged, half carried the suitcase to the back of the car. Together, they heaved it up into the trunk and wiped off the snowy bits before Betty slammed the door hard.

Betty told her to hop in the front seat and hurry quick, faster than a fart in a skillet, because it was so bloody cold they'd be sure to freeze their lady parts, so Hannah slipped in and closed her door and waited for Betty to get her out of there. She kept her head down, concentrating on the shape of her fingers, not wanting a last glimpse of the family she was leaving.

Betty arranged herself, her seat pushed forward to accommodate her short legs.

Please, please, please don't talk to me, Hannah thought. Betty must have heard her wish because she didn't say a word as she backed the car down the driveway.

But then Betty slammed hard on the brakes before the curve near the end of the driveway, causing the car to zig back and forth, hurling Hannah against her shoulder strap. Hannah swung her head around to look out the back window toward the main road, thinking they'd crashed into a moose or a deer, but she could see nothing in the sea of fog to cause such a sudden stop.

"I'll be damned," Betty said, staring straight ahead, lips turning up into a smile.

Hannah looked out front too, toward the house. There was Ellie, running out of the mist, coatless, slipping to her knees on the icy path, picking herself up again, barrelling now, getting closer, Eric behind, trying to catch up, her coat in his arms.

"Wait! Wait," Ellie yelled, flailing her hands to get them to stop, though they were clearly stopped. There was nowhere to go.

Acknowledgements

I am deeply grateful to Stephanie Sinclair, my lovely agent, for her belief in me and this book and for making me feel like I'm the centre of her universe. The entire team at ECW Press has been stellar, and I so appreciate their unwavering dedication to producing beautiful books. A special thanks to my wonderful ECW editor, Jen Knoch, who is the best of the best and has worked so hard to help me find the right words.

I owe much to the warm and welcoming writing community in this province. The Writers' Guild of Alberta in particular has given me so many rich and lasting friendships. Many of this book's pages were written at Strawberry Creek Writing Retreats, an unplugged and sacred space tucked into the misty woods near Edmonton. I'm in debt as well to the Banff Wired Writing Program and Marina Endicott, who miraculously shepherded me through my first "god awful" draft with patience and wisdom. Heartfelt thanks to Leslie Greentree, Astrid Blodgett, and Audrey Whitson for offering suggestions and providing the right kind of encouragement. Thanks to Patricia Anderson for her keen editorial eye.

I gratefully acknowledge the Alberta Foundation for the Arts and the Canada Council for the Arts for their financial support.

Big love to my family, especially my dearest girls, Breanna and Megan, and my great love, James Leslie. You are my home and the light in my world.

Book Club

DISCUSSION QUESTIONS

Are you reading this selection in your book club or planning to? Here are some questions about *No Good Asking* to help spark your discussion.

1. How does winter's shadow fall over the novel in terms of the storyline and atmosphere?

2. Ellie wants to move to Neesley so the family can have a fresh start, but what new challenges does the move create? What problems can't they escape?

3. Who is your favourite character and what draws you to them? Is there a character you dislike, and do they have redeeming qualities?

4. Hannah has been through such hardship and yet she still seems resilient. What influences throughout her childhood have helped shape her thoughts and actions?

5. Before Hannah arrives, how does each member of the family view Sammy? How does Hannah change these views?

6. How does Ellie see herself, and how does it differ from how others see her? What is your impression of Ellie? Do you become more or less sympathetic toward her as the story unfolds?

7. As a relationship develops between Daniel and Hannah, how do they each benefit?

8. How are Eric's and Ellie's parenting styles different? Why might they be that way?

9. Eric describes Christmas as the deepest of blue for Ellie. Why does she have such a difficult time coping during Christmas?

10. How would you describe the marriage and power dynamic between Eric and Ellie? How does Hannah's presence affect their relationship?

11. When Ellie stared at the tattered raven, "she couldn't understand the mechanics, how the bird stayed upright, its skinny claws attached to the wire." What other birds did you notice in the book and how are they meaningful?

12. How does the small-town setting and the isolation of the Nyland road affect the story? How would the story have played out differently in an urban setting?

13. Consider the title: how do you see it reflected in the book?

14. *No Good Asking* contains many small gestures with big emotional resonance. Was there a moment you found particularly poignant?

15. Are you satisfied with the ending? What do you think will happen next for these characters?

FRAN KIMMEL is the author of *The Shore Girl*, which was named a CBC Top-40 Book and won the Alberta Readers' Choice Award in 2013. Fran's short stories have appeared in literary journals from coast to coast and have twice been selected for The Journey Prize Stories anthology. Born and raised in Calgary, Fran now writes and teaches in Lacombe, AB.